SEDUCTION BY A SOLAR SMILE

SEDUCTION BY A SOLAR SMILE

a novel

Constance Larsen

CHARLES SKILTON

Made and printed in
Great Britain by
Whitstable Litho Ltd.,
Whitstable, Kent
and published by
CHARLES SKILTON LTD
29 Forth Street
Edinburgh

ISBN 0248 986836

DEDICATION

This book is dedicated to my parents in the year of their fiftieth wedding anniversary. Love is indeed the "gold of life." And to C. L. and C. W. – wherever they may be.

el trece de marzo
de 1996

A Teresa –
Este libro fue producto
de una epoca en Madrid
que me alimentó enormemente.
Fue en españa donde
descubrí el arte de
averiguar "el paisaje interior"
de los seres humanos en un
ambiente lleno de riqueza
Espero que te guste Seductor
un abrazo
Constance

Seduction by a Solar Smile

DEAR ALEXANDER. I don't know where to begin. Begin what? And who are you who doesn't recognize the simplicity of a beginning? Earlier I might have dittoed your retort. But in the space of more than a year since I last saw you I find that what I called the beginning of our connection was only a continuation of something that began long ago. And what I called the end of a relationship with you never really terminated in a conventional sense. So where am I? All of the baggage of our emotional tie sits in my mind, unpacked. Consequently, I have no choice other than to retreat to a monastic existence where I can sort out what belonged to you, what belonged to me and what belonged to us communally. Perhaps hindsight will help us transcend ourselves to become more than what we were. This has happened before to me. Why shouldn't it happen again!

You may note certain discrepancies in my recall of our historical past. You may disagree with my perceptions of you. But what you can't fault me for is my intention to expose both of us as part-time frauds, two beings whose currency of language was sometimes counterfeit. Neither of us sufficiently shared with the other our interior language – our insecurities, our doubts, our feelings of worthlessness. In this we are representative of a whole race of beings because there is hardly any "cat" who doesn't belong to the collective norm of fear, obsession, anger and all feelings we outwardly chastise as inappropriate to our notions of propriety, dignity and chicness.

I am determined, Alexander, to strip away the curtain of falsity and if necessary let you see the gutter of my soul. I'm fed up with hiding behind my silences. Silence too is fraudulent. In remaining mute you do not run the risk of exposure.

Of course you must know who is speaking to you. It's Wine, your former girl friend, your friendly, intoxicating Siamese cat, the

1

one with such a lusty fragrance for life though this part of me you never knew. I'm the cat seeking perpetual rebirth within the nine lives accorded to those of my species. . . . Well, at least I'm not a Spanish cat. They only live and die seven times which maybe is an advantage – less wear and tear on the psyche. Since you last saw me my soul has added a few more wrinkles but these lines within are not matched by any external laugh lines or frown marks, a shame to be sure. The wrinkles left by age and experience create a facial character like a musical composition imitating counter-points of sorrow and joy.

Nor has may cat hair shown any signs of greying. It still has its natural red softness, still straight as ever. Maybe my body is a bit more plump these days. Thinking does this to you. It makes you temporarily withdraw from an active life until all things are set in balance or put in order. But once I finish reliving with you all of the following chatter, I plan to go out and have a hell of a good time in the few lifetimes left to me.

Alexander, there are some people, humans they're called, eaves-dropping on my soliloquy. They don't believe you and I are cats. They think I'm making up an animal fable. I don't want to argue with them. I just want to cite a fact which might show them that you and I have something in common with them and it's this: in life you may die so many times and after each death a resurrection occurs, a recovering from adversity and out of each of these tragedies, defeats, disappointments, misfortunes and losses comes further understanding about ourselves and the world we live in. Indeed, maybe you humans and we cats are all confused about our identity. Perhaps we are all descendants from that mythical bird known as the phoenix, the one who rises up alive again from its own ashes after its death. In this case you can't call yourselves humans with any greater assurance than I can call myself a cat. But since this is only speculation, we are back to where we started – humans eavesdropping on the words of a cat called Wine.

Let's all forget our differences. Maybe I'm a cat or maybe I'm an eccentric human in disguise who feels forced to camouflage the characters and places I'm going to talk about. You, the human voyeurs, won't be called upon to answer any questions. All I ask is that you maintain a respectable silence while I monologue to you, to Alexander and to myself. I promise one thing. This story does not belong only to Alexander and me. It belongs to all of you who have known the happiness and tribulations of love.

An acquaintance I once knew before his death named Henry Miller—oops, I've let the cat out of the bag so to speak regarding my identity. Forget his name. He couldn't have known me. I'm only a cat—, anyhow, he used to say: "Love is everything. Without it we're lost."

I think we're *often* lost!

* * * * *

Alexander, do you remember our first meeting? (Obviously I've chosen what is at least a visible, logical beginning). No, you couldn't be expected to have it as strongly imprinted on your mind as it is on mine. You didn't hear my inner dialogue screaming away for hours on end that day. Probably all you recall is a huddled up creature inside a rusty old garbage can.

The garbage can. My favourite retreat! My sanctuary where I used to hide myself from curious eyes when I fell into the grip of one of my typical attacks of depression. That day I was so fatigued by my own gluttony, too much romping with life, so overstuffed with life that only an emotional stomach pump could abate the pressure on my soul. I wanted to vomit up all the knowledge and experience I had stashed away because they served no purpose other than to illuminate chaos. There were no universal laws other than life and death and even these were questionable. There was no softening blanket of a cosmic purpose to life into which I could sink. Thinking that all life was interpreted differently by every one of us rang a cold, clanking sound of further isolation.

Was there anyone who might perceive life through the same shaft of vision as I did?

All I could say to myself was: I have lived, and I have been free, drowning in freedom, a freedom painted in the colours of joy, ecstacy, hell, indifference, confusion, stupidity, lucidity, hunger, fear and other hues of feeling long forgotten.

How my former masters and mistresses knowing nothing of my soul used to tinge their voices green with envy, observing me in moments of repose saying, "Ah you lucky cat, doing nothing more than sitting on your haunches, watching the world go by."

Their words would fill me with a prickly fear. Could they trick me into entering their thoughtless world? No! No! No! Their complacency was my enemy. The green light in my cat's exploratory ego propelled me to once again imitate those I most admired – birds. Contrary to most cats I was unable to feast upon them. What I devoured was their way of taking flight, of moving from point to point. When doors blocked my liberation I devised a crafty plan. I would strip away my veneer of quietness and erupt with volcanic

3

force, clawing my way through all palpable objects – rugs, curtains, furniture – and to seal the security of my removal from a household, I would administer a gentle scratch to a child, painful for both of us. I was then quickly booted out, labelled a wild beast!

Me? Wild?

No!

My life was ruled by question marks which needed to be shot down by experience. No sooner was one question answered than another question would begin flapping its wings, signalling another take-off. It would have been so soothing just to stay in one spot. Often there was no-one to care for me, no warm house, no affectionate caress. Then I would forage in the streets during adoption intervals where I gradually honed my cunning survival skills until they were sharp enough to make me queen of the survivors. The rule in our world was basic and simple – do what you must in order to survive. If a flimsy piece of rat meat could satiate a shrunken belly you ate it even if you were sickened by the rancid stench. And if a rival challenged you to that morsel of meat you fought viciously, drawing blood from this opponent if necessary.

Yet the harshness of survival had its interruptions. Sometimes while streaking through nightly gardens looking to fill a tiny space in my belly, I would be smitten by a drooping flower so wilted that the slightest brush of air could have scattered its petals upon the ground for burial. I would then try to tread lightly past the flower, wanting the final hint of loveliness to subsist a few more golden moments. I was the conservator of beauty until my empty stomach growled back ferociously and then consideration of the ethics of behaviour was relegated to the fringes of hunger – quite unlike one of my former masters.

He was a doctor who insisted all men ought to inherit the right to free medical care. He wore the cologne of an arm-chair philosopher who upon rising from the throne of his lofty thoughts sent out fur-lined bills to every patient alike, the fur warming his cold greed. His offspring danced to the same lyrical tune of hypocrisy, marching once a week, demonstrating for equal human rights. They brought home smug smiles, chastising those who made no public appearance on behalf of ethics and then ordered the maid – in moderated tones – to serve them champagne. How easy to right the world's wrongs with maids and starched nurses perusing your purse, attending your every need!

I couldn't challenge them, not even if my larynx had emitted more than a meow. Hypocrisy has a language all its own. Besides, I

4

was only a wild animal, an ingrate, an untitled nothing, pretty, without pedigree papers.

All this and more started peeling off my soul in that theatre of a garbage can. I hadn't erased the joyful occasions which had landscaped my life – the many lovers and friends who had transformed the harshness of existence into orgies of joy. But sadly such memories of enchantment provoked no more feeling than dry fish bones dug up in an archaeological dig.

So much living . . . so much living . . . would the nomad in me ever find an oasis? Would I ever stop asking questions? Would I ever know enough? Why couldn't I have been like other cats, content to sit and breed? But truthfully motherhood frightened me. It was such an enormous responsibility, such a state of permanence. Once a mother, always a mother! Nor does the shutting of a coffin sever the umbilical cord. It merely pinches it. I could still envision she who had bore me, she who had been transported to another dimension of twilight. Her feline features had blurred in my photographic memory of her but the crystals of her being still shone through me. And I would always be her kitty for all my nine lives just as she had remained the perpetual kitty of her own mother.

Don't get the idea Alexander that I never contemplated abdicating my freedom in exchange for an offspring. I did. With my professor of love, my first important lover who was not a kitty but a full-grown cat. He was a cat of domesticity, splitting his time between his female cat mate, with whom he had shared many seasons, their kitties and myself. From him I learned about the joys of fatherhood and indirectly motherhood. Yet, his stalking and lusting after me underscored a certain inherent contradiction between freedom and parenting. Papas could escape the needs of their offspring, have a night off. How did mamas manage if they had my adventurous temperament? Taking a single night off from the kitties might be too brief a time considering that from the earliest days when I could stand on my own paws, unaided by anything or anybody, I was a kitty who upon catching the whiff of any strange, new scent would follow it anywhere, however long it took until my curiosity had been satiated. It didn't matter if the novel odour revealed only a dirty old sock or the tiny cock of a male kitty. It was the act of nuzzling my nose into everything which was so vital to my existence. Many was the time I got swatted for poking my nose where it didn't belong. Such punishment proved to be no deterrent toward altering my character.

5

Fortunately my professor of love not only accepted my inquisitive urges, he unselfishly encouraged them. How lucky I was to have savoured the sweetness of a first love within an atmosphere of tolerance. His acceptance of my nature endeared him forever to me and was responsible for my never falling into the mud of cynicism about love, no small accomplishment when I consider the pain that love later brought me.

When my masters of that epoch decided to undertake a long voyage to foreign lands they deemed to take me with them, constructing a special cat box decorated in the muted pastel colours I adored. I had long anticipated this journey with zeal until my passion for my lover diluted the excitement. Ambivalence haunted me then, tempting me to run away from my masters' house to some deserted basement hideout so our loving sexual forays should not be interrupted because of long distance.

My professor wisely spoke to me: "To impede the dream of another is to exchange love for bitterness. We resent those who roadblock the path to dreams. Seek your dreams. Sprout your wings. Love does not disappear for those who are seekers. By fulfilling yourself you become more capable of loving others."

How right he was as I later learned! But how was I going to ease the emotional pain of separation from him? On our last night of love-making I ardently desired a drop of love's liquid to rendezvous with my procreative egg. I cried out to him, "I want your kitty, I want your kitty. With your kitty in me there can be no separation, ever!" And he too succumbed to the same wish. "Maybe someday we will have a little one." His words illustrated to me the male soul to be constructed of a similar material found in females – the urge to create life with a loved one.

From then on motherhood debuted as another temptress to scotch my freedom. I decided to reserve it for a much later time in life, if at all. Better to chance a difficult birth, a risk run by older cats, than to deliver a kitty purely from the womb of youth. A mother well-fed on freedom suckles well her progeny without resentment, without naming her offspring an intruder. Yes, someday I might settle down, I used to tell myself. But when? When the idea of permanence seemed less odious? Always this rebellion against immutability!

Today, sitting in the same garbage can, musing over the same thoughts running through my mind when you first found me, I notice that I was depressed then because I had the intuition that permanence was a mythological creation. Fallacious. Erroneously suggesting all things to be fixed, immobile, fossilized. If there was

6

one law to be learned it was that all living creatures, indeed all of nature fluctuate, change, alter, evolve. I might curtain my vision with the illusion of permanence because it is emotionally more comfortable, avoiding the question of whether something is going to stay the same or change in the course of time.

Didn't I first glimpse this knowledge upon reuniting with my professor of love after months of separation from him, after knowing the heat of other bodies because I was determined to take advantage of each living moment, a teaching he had espoused! My passion for him then only glowed as a firefly in the night. How I mourned for our communal past because he too seemed less intense toward me. My conclusion was I must seek again an unchangeable love. I didn't understand then that love, like life, is a flowing feast of emotion and we – being the variable creatures that we are – can never sustain it at the same pitch of intensity. This doesn't mean that love is lost if passion does not explode within us. Love wears different faces on different days. Love even sometimes takes a holiday but it doesn't disappear easily. The contact between my professor and myself didn't end. It went on in an altered form of friendship. And then it was halted for several cat lives. Recently we had a reunion and to my astonishment the passion between us ignited with such heat that I thought we would scald ourselves to death!

If the transitory quality of life was cause for pessimism last year it now is no longer the full-time enemy it was. It has added a new dimension, a sense of poetry. Certainly my experience with my professor of love confirms that alterations or change may indeed spike out to a higher level of joy, exemplifying the growth, rather than the death, of an emotional bond between beings.

And you, Alexander, must be heartily thanked for playing an inadvertent role as a catalyst, provoking some changes in my perception of the world. Now, instead of trying to define life as this or that I gracefully bow to the reality that life is a plurality – lives are, not life is –, a matter of shifting definitions naming our moods as we move from one existence to another. I feel more capable of surrendering myself to this flow of life, this magnificent gift we are privileged to receive, however long we have it.

Pessimism may still reign supreme at times because it likes to wage war with the poetry of life as a squabbling child might do. It always will. I accept this most of the time. But I fight harder than I used to against the taskmaster of despair because my past reminds me that no matter how much I slosh about in the pits of hell there is always a possible kernel of joy sprouting up from the landscape of life. Then too, there are the joyous seedlings not planted by others but created by myself in either abundance or scarcity, depending on the labour I am willing to exert to cultivate them.

To recall our story, Alexander, means you have to listen to a voice you don't recognize. You won't only hear the soft, timorous purr of my past voice. You will also hear me roar! You will hear other voices belonging to many different Wines, voices which were clamouring to be liberated while we were together, voices which were jailed in by a horde of self-doubt, voices which remained subdued in deference to your needs.

I want to reel back to the garbage can, recalling the dismal sight of Wine the Cat who could be seen as an aging actress getting more and more depressed and discouraged as she reviewed the movies of her past lives. Fortunately, the terribly empty feeling inside of me was intercepted by the appearance of a kernel of joy – by you, Alexander.

* * * * *

A sudden clanging of the garbage can lid made my tail twitch. Staring down at me in my embryonic safety was a smile of solar energy, a smile powerfully charged enough to illuminate the entire world. Immediately the rays of the smile sent a balmy warmth through my depression.

Had I seen that smile before?

"What a sorry state you're in," he said. Agilely, bearing the protruding stomach of a well-fed, middle-aged cat about my age, his fur a mangy grey, he crept down to my burial spot, and embraced me.

"Cry if you must," he urged, "and don't lament the pity you feel for yourself. Self-pity is not a crime. The tears from self-pity help wash away inner pain, a pain that many creatures mistakenly diagnose as self-indulgence. Remember, pity is the embrace we give ourselves in the absence of someone to comfort us."

His consolation lifted me from the guilt of self-pity.

I oceaned us both in a deluge of pent-up tears.

Finally we surfaced midst waves of smiles.

Then on the dusty surface of the can he printed a word: L O V E .

Here was a universal truth whose need glittered with clarity. Forget the philosophic machinations which boil in your head, I said to myself. You have been without love for a long time. You are hiding your need for it, you are starving for it because you have known love and you cannot live without it.

Who was this saviour resuscitating me?

"Who I am is not important. Today you must not share the spotlight with anyone. You need to be held, to be caressed."

Alexander, every time I recollect that scene I am filled with a spontaneous combustion of warmth toward my fellow beings. That scene is my eternal memory of you. Just a few choice words and one simple gesture so unselfishly given by one stranger to another, demonstrating what love ought to be about, what it can be about. What prevents more living creatures from reaching out to others? Fear? Inadequacy? Embarrassment over the display of emotion? I try to copy your example whenever I sense a hidden tear in someone.

No further words passed between us. None were necessary. The infusion of warmth from his smile and his concern made me relish being cradled by him for an hour. Recharged and revitalized, I left him sitting in my safety zone, padding the streets once more, at peace with myself and thereby with the world.

At an earlier stage of life I might have sought to know him. Now I did not. I couldn't risk having my saviour tainted by any trace of disillusionment which in turn would have exhumed ancient devils of my past who had once called themselves caring cats. No, I only wished to be left with the calm feeling he had inspired.

I enthroned Alexander on a pedestal that day, assuming his image would fade. But it didn't. Weeks later his smile kept flaunting itself with greater and greater intensity. A restlessness assaulted me. I wanted his presence. So day after day I returned to the garbage can, sniffing for hints of him, a futile mission it seemed . . .

One rainy night when indoor warmth could hardly have been induced to be renounced, my cat hair defied gravity, each strand acting in unison with the others, all behaving like thousands of compass needles swerving continuously back to a fixed point, no matter which way I turned. A vibrating tension made my back arch, straining every nerve ending until each resembled the floating tentacle of an octopus. My heart pounded a double time stacatto beat. I was *possessed*, possessed by something impalpable, an unknown frenzied force.

My sixth sense was receiving an indecipherable message, the broadcasting source unknown. A pulling sensation then magnetized me out into the perspiring night and I began moving like a creature in a race toward a finish line shrouded in mist. The ground resembled a grid of hot wires which made my body perpetually twitch. The sensation was not uncomfortable for it felt like spasms of erotic pleasure. Not surprisingly, the possession in charge of me took on overtones of sensuality. I was becoming a cat in heat, perhaps sniffing around for a partner!

My route through the dark streets continued unhaltingly in the same direction.

But what was my destination?

Suddenly I knew I had found it. My fine cat hair slumbered down to rest.

Across the street from me was the alley leading to my garbage can! I could see it phosphorescing like the North Star.

I hurried to it and leaped onto the top of my sanctuary, casting aside the metal lid. It clang upon the ground, sounding the end of confusion. I had located the one who had been mesmerizing me.

My broadcasting station smiled up a look of expectancy. There he was again, Alexander The Caring Cat, wearing his solar smile.

He reeked of a female odour, a fresh musky one which puzzled me.

"So it was you who pulled me here," he said, adding, "I was with one of my sleeping partners when I felt an unrelenting urge to leave her. I felt I had to meet a certain female but I didn't know who. I left the other one baffled and hurt. I couldn't help myself. I was . . . *possessed*!"

Who was possessing who?

His explanation conjured up the magic spice which made our rendezvous seem an inescapable destiny. Perhaps that first meeting with him had seeded a foetal attraction which had grown into a full-blown obsession demanding a consummation, a wedding between fantasy and reality, a need to know him more than just as a saviour.

Sexual desire now silenced the language of words. It was time for the language of body magic.

I squinted my eyes into more exaggerated semi-lunar slits . . . slowly . . . slinking down toward him . . . my haunches swaying from side to side in a shamelessly suggestive manner . . . . The dust in the garbage can reclothed itself into sparkling sequins . . . We began a ravenous charting of bodies, each tonguing the velvet texture of the other's fur. This was the initiation ceremony of beginning love, the tin can metamorphosing into a royal boudoir where a princess bestows her regal kisses on to a prince of dreams, a prince no longer shadowy but made of palpable flesh.

All the ordinary outlines of the earth began to waver. The earth was put to bed for the night.

Alexander and I joyously discarded our physical separateness . . . setting aside the "he" part and the "me" part so we could become

10

a "we" . . . swimming in a space . . . where there is no gravity . . . no time . . . no light . . . no darkness . . . no cold . . . entering a universe of hushed silence to backdrop our sensual journey of sizzling sparks . . . and after each fusion of togetherness there remained one ember of desire which brought about encore after encore after each spent moment . . .

It was a sexual consummation seemingly wrought by some unknown mystical power which had brought us together rather than a display of showy, sexual technique, a state of being under a spell in the same way as those who are bewitched into a loss of self by an onslaught of religious fervour.

Alexander, never have I given with such total abandonment all of the feelings which poured out of me into you that night. And if you want to criticize my description of our love making as too richly embellished with adjectives or too baroque, well go ahead. Any experience which glitters with such a specialness demands a language different from the one of our more mundane life.

When we returned to the peace of the earth he confessed.

"You are only the third female out of hundreds into whom I have been able to explode. I can almost never let go at the last moment. So I provide pleasure to females and receive my pleasure from theirs."

Your confession confirmed the fabric of a gentle and extremely sensitive cat. It was this quality I responded to when you first held me.

His smile wore a special sheen as he spoke. "Wine, you have a loveliness, a softness about you. I like you."

He fell into a kitten's sleep of innocence and later awoke with a start, asking in a pleading tone, "Do you still like me?"

"Of course," I replied in an astonished voice.

Affirmation glazed him back into a dream of safety.

What tragic bondage you have known, I thought. How hard you must have fought to bury yourself in ecstasy only to find yourself buried in the insecure world of another who turned loving into a vicious war, determined there should be a victor and a vanquished.

How close I felt to you that night, Alexander, as I lay by your side, slightly cramped, disregarding my normal urge to find more comfortable quarters in my mistress's house. I dared not leave you, for it would have broken our bond of reciprocal gift givers.

* * * * *

The following night our meeting was not left to psychic destiny. It was pre-arranged. But the short space of apartness had raised the

11

shades of his fear that I didn't want him. Its strength was so strong it moved into me, making my voice less secure. Did he want me? The fear was shoved back and forth, muttered in the disguise of remoteness, nervousness, strangeness, newness. We were draping one another with ghosts of the past who had left us stranded as dusty, emotional skeletons.

He had a name for this constrained fissure between us. He called it the unveiling of illusion.

I was not quick enough to pinpoint his definition. What he referred to as illusion was this: if you see my weaknesses, my needs, my harshness interlaced with the foundation of my strength, will you still *want* me? Will you still *accept* me?

There wasn't time to separate the threads of confusion. He announced an imminent journey of importance, a visit to see his only offspring, mothered by one he had added to his list of disgusting traitors, a list of names of those who instead of accepting him as he was, saw him as an object for conversion to be a creature he couldn't be. Another list he had compiled in his head also bore her name as one who sought to take and take from him without considering he might need something too.

The impending separation pained me. It meant I had to cloister my feelings, pull them back inside of me because Alexander wouldn't be physically present. Or was it my insecurity that he might not return which deemed it wise to freeze my feelings? Past practice with separation had made me an expert in the revolving door of love and its ever potential loss.

I wanted to cry out, – Alexander, it's too soon to be apart. Let us spread ourselves together for a few more days. I must de-mythify you, see you in your more day-to-day character, your multiplicities of beings. Your compassion of that first day vibrates the memory of another whose compassion once bridged my development from a selfish kitty to a more mature one, a kitty more responsive to the needs of others.

He was the only cat with whom I had ever spent every hour of every day and night. I was his cat mate, his *soul mate*. He was my *best friend*. I left him one day, not thinking it was a permanent separation in order to seize some breathing space alone where I could contemplate where my identity began and his left off. You see, he possessed the power to absorb me until my existence was nearly pulverized into dust. Such a power must be met by another power of equal force, otherwise it devours everything in its path. I did not have the strength or the wisdom to know how to rebel openly against his suffocating magnetism or the courage to speak honestly of my dilemma. And my guilt further increased over all thoughts and feelings not befitting the goddess he had envisioned me to be. It was wonderful to be worshipped, to be treated so tenderly, so adoringly. I could have stayed frozen forever in the role of a deity but another Wine saw to it that I tumbled off my throne, taking a temporary vow of emotional poverty so I would go in search of myself, a search which seemed more often than not a quest for fool's gold.

What I really wanted to say to you as you were preparing to leave, Alexander, was please let me have the chance to confirm it is you I am responding to and not the ghost of my past.

At least you softened my separation anxiety when you implored me to wait for you. "I'll be back," you promised. Words of weighty proportion for a worldly cat. Alexander treating me as if I were his *first love*.

I waited for him. Not quite long enough. A month passed. My faith wavered. I gave my body to another, all the while recalling my emotional oath to Alexander. An engorged moon helped me conjure up my solar smile, the fantasy imbuing this nameless flesh I embraced with Alexander's spirit. It was the spirit and not the flesh which roused me to orgasm.

The next day Alexander returned. He came directly to the garbage can and made only one inquiry. "Did you sleep with anyone while I was gone?"

I admitted my physical unfaithfulness. He blinked pain in his eyes, gashing me at the crucial pitch of understanding. I had neglected to comprehend his parting words to be a subterranean wish and test: would I please not tamper with the first act of our love by introducing another actor no matter how insignificant a role the other played: would I accord him his wish because it was Alexander asking! Would I give him a famous first: guard the wish, preserving the purity of an illusion, a new world time record for holding the breath of this illusion.

During his absence he had refused all potential understudies for me.

But he had made me promise to be honest with him before he left.

Should I have lied?

I had come to believe that the act of two copulating bodies is simple, unlike the harmonizing of souls which is so difficult and rare. So too, it is easy to utter truthful words but living with the psychic shivers, the upheaval they produce is another matter.

My honesty had laid a chilly touch to Alexander's heart.

Phase one of the unveiling of illusion you might have called it.

The conflict about truth-telling evoked a playback of my past, the cat life succeeding the one which had belonged to my professor of love. His successor, an emotionally warm cat too, was a cat with an ebony colour fur. I remember his hue because others scoffed at him, saying black was neither beautiful nor fashionable. What did I care! Such a tremendous fuss about the colour of fur. Maybe I was colour blind but those who dubbed me a traitor to our species were life-blind, vicarious livers whose only mission in life was to sit on their haunches, gossiping and judging others on a scale of hypocrisy.

One balmy spring evening this cat failed to meet me at an appointed time.

"I was miles out in the country, too far away to get back here," he explained. There was a stretched pause. Then came the pulverizing punch. "No, that's not true. I'm lying."

He had gone to visit the exquisite Siamese he had once mated with, "a siren without soul", and while they had slept together it was nothing more than an accident of habit. His explanation did not console the seed of mistrust which took root in me. Pain splintered every nerve end. Most damaging was the snapshot in my mind of an unknown apparition. A vision or a truth once seen never loses its lines of clarity. It is eternal, standing straight in our centres of agony, bedding down with us at inopportune times.

My failure to punish him for his transgression upon our love made him search out defiant acts, hoping that chastisement would come from me, effacing his guilt. He felt he had betrayed me. I felt betrayed. Finally the summation of his provocative acts brought me to death. My spirit died. I had acted the impossible role of infinite understanding. I had deluded myself, lied to myself! My supposed understanding of the naturalness of sleeping with a former mate had been purely a masquerade for jealousy and hurt, emotions demeaning to the chic cat I had portrayed myself to be. By the very nature of my livingness, these and all other emotions formed the tapestry of my being. To deny them meant to deny the beating of my heart.

If there is any truth to tell let it first be to myself. Truth for truth's sake between two beings is another matter and needs to be weighed for its relevance. If it does no more than unnecessarily slash the fabric of another's soul, then I wonder why its value is so revered!

Dear Alexander, were you wearing my "cast off" chicness after I told you the truth? Was I your unwitting assistant in the further unveiling of illusion? Wasn't the truth only part of other truths, a need to install another body in your place, simulating your presence because I missed you, using another body to fortress the insecurity brought on by separation from you, an insecurity bred by fear of opening up my heart again!

Only through loving and losing love do you understand the power of love to twist your existence out of shape, to inspire you with fear.

A cynic has a decided advantage as opposed to those of us who cannot become brittle or indifferent toward love. A cynic does not let love enter the front door of his soul. He lives in the stale atmosphere of his own oneness, uncontaminated by the presence of another.

Your wince of pain, Alexander, did not emanate from a citadel of cynicism. It was the pain of one capable of knowing both the creative and destructive faces of love . . . .

Hmmm. Alexander. I may have just expressed some verbal garbage.

Is the destructive side of love really love, or something that passes for love but really isn't?

* * * * *

It was the night after Alexander's return.

A meowing symphony of sound cascaded throughout back yards of houses where humans had shuttered themselves in for the night. Behind one of these white-washed dwellings was the site of The Milk Bar, a gathering place for strays and habitués of the neighbourhood. Enormous saucers of milk, both skim and regular, and water were lined up in a long row, set out each night by a hand that cared. The donor preferred to remain anonymous, content with the medley of purrs.

The crowd was a parade of preening cats with slicked down fur exposing the golden glow of youth. Cats on the prowl for companions. Cats seeking to pare away the sharp edge of loneliness.

The rays of the moon on this sultry night and the bouquet of cat scents created a seductive atmosphere, bodies brushing against bodies with feather-like lightness, cat hair tingling slightly with anticipated inner excitement – what unknown surprise would the night hold and for whom?

15

Alexander had said to meet him here. I located him by the prevailing sound of his dominant, deep voice. He was ringed by a group of male cats, turning his head from side to side, as a king addresses his knights. I was meeting Alexander The Public Figure, an Alexander whose flyaway fur was also slicked down.

The group circling him was engaged in a heated discussion of milk prices, boring talk to my ears, too pragmatic. Nearby, several females were quietly discussing the merits of cat boxes lined with silk as opposed to those covered with rayon. That didn't interest me either. Maybe it wasn't my inability to engage in every day chit-chat so much as my preference for intimacy, that face-to-face sharing with one other being at a time which made me such a loner, the cat who always seemed to stand at the margin of the herd. The more beings together, the more diluted the emotional intensity of interaction. Or so I thought. And the talk was all so practical. I couldn't believe that on such a balmy night the groups could hold such a mesmerizing effect upon all who were partaking. Surely there were some who wished to stoke up the imaginative brain cells, who wanted to sing and dance, freeing themselves for a little while from the drudgery of routine.

I stood at the sideline purring a greeting, alerting Alexander to my presence. He motioned me to come closer, his glittering smile making me sparkle inside. His tongue played the trick of sensual arousal, gliding teasingly over my erogenous zones. Another un-veiling. Alexander The Public Figure was publicly demonstrating his feelings for a female. Our relationship was definitely not going to be relegated behind a screen of secrecy.

He introduced me to his companions, who interrupted their discussion long enough to make a guided tour of my body. I could hear their minds' assessment – not bad for an older cat! Their talk resumed. I observed Alexander The Witty Conversationalist and Alexander The Observer. While his mouth rang out with airtight logic about the laws of economics of supply and demand, his eyes shifted everywhere, eyes of a pilot surveying diminutive landmarks. No one noticed this facet of him. His eyes were a mixture of a laughing devil and a mischievous kitty, bold eyes which hunted you down, eyes which made others squirm as they burrowed through the external facades of conviviality. Alexander used his eyes like a child's rattle.

He ceased speaking.

One female cat near us flinched uncomfortably from the sting of his stare.

"What do you want from me?" she asked him

"BE YOURSELF," I shouted.

"Perfect answer," replied Alexander.

The poor female remained mystified. I had caught the scent of his game – who was bold enough to return his stare, who was confident enough not to twinge under the glare of an interrogator's gaze? Alexander knew I knew what he was doing. He had lured me into trailing his stare, to see if I could track down a hint of his intricate mind, our communicative vibrations like two camera shutters clicking simultaneously.

Alexander's voice dropped to the octave of hoarseness. I padded behind him toward a saucer of milk, watching him voraciously lap up an enormous quantity. Evidently the paunch in his stomach was the sediment of rich cream consumed over many years.

Dipping my tongue into a nearby saucer of water, I explained, "Milk makes me giddy, even skim milk. I like a lick or two of the creamy richness now and then. But if I'm feeling good, I ride upon a crest of my own joy not to be found in pasteurised liquids. If I feel low, milk liquifies my natural barriers to depression and then a flood of demons enters. Milk unhinges my equilibrium."

"I can't live without it," Alexander admitted. "It makes this garbage heap of a world tolerable. It makes those arse-licking-fools I talk to less obnoxious, those stupid cats with their flea-sized brains who wouldn't know how to rescue themselves from drowning in a cupful of milk. You see, they know I have access to the largest supply of milk in these parts and that's why they hang around me. They're waiting for a handout, just like the one you see here, waiting for me to say 'Come round to the house, kitties, help yourselves to what I've got.' You think they want to sniff around on their own? Never! They want someone else to do their surviving for them. If they could get away with it they'd even steal my food and milk my soul dry."

A glassy look came into his eyes, softening the scorn covering them.

"I suppose you'd call me an addict, a milk addict, wouldn't you?" He waited for the typical programmed reply.

"Alexander, when you found me I was drowning in depression. You are drowning in another substance. *Drowning is drowning.*"

Teardrops chased one another down his face.

I wrapped my paws around him. "You helped me one day give *me* back to myself. I would like to give *you* back to yourself. You are such a loveable cat, a cat with a beauty part which you try to lock away."

He remained in my embrace, unshamed to share the kingdom of

his unknown sorrow to which only strong, feeling males belong. Were his tears born from the same endless repetition of wins and losses as mine?

His tears subsided. His public image arose.

"I must *control* myself," he commanded himself. His body straightened to his command. He gulped down another swig of milk. A light-hearted Alexander resumed, chasing away the shadow in his voice. He appeared to make a mental space leap, hurling himself light years away from me. Then he returned.

"What land did you just visit?" I asked.

"It's not for you to know. You have neither the intelligence nor the controls necessary for interplanetary voyages." He grinned a period to his statement. Arching his back proudly, he edged his way back to reopen court with the motley crowd.

Baiting me? Testing the bedrock of my security?

He was the second cat in a score of months to misinterpret my quietness as a lack of mental acuity. In an earlier life I might have duelled with him, hissing out a challenge. Those days were gone, the tenacious warrior in me subdued. Besides, Alexander's contempt costumed his gentle heart. It was this gentleness of his which drew out my own brand of softness. Yet for some reason my warmth seemed to create a disturbing polarity of feelings within him, drawing out tears which he then had to counter by verbal thrusts drawn from his repertoire of scornful entertainment.

I suddenly tired of passive vigilance. It was time to go in search of joy. I found it with a singing choir of cats screeching their hearts out. We were interrupted by some sultry strains of a saxophone infiltrating the night, the melody floating out toward us from a hidden radio, someone's solitary companion. I commenced to capture the notes, creating an island of dance where I began to imitate the gyrations of a slinking serpent . . . undulating figure eight after figure eight . . . circling every tree trunk . . . and the others began to follow me into their lands of hidden images . . . and we began to gain altitude . . . climbing . . . ascending the trees . . . higher and higher . . . attaining a height of giddiness . . . an ascension of ebullience . . . round and round . . . spiralling in accelerated motion . . . until breathlessness descended me back to the moistness of earth . . .

I lay my body to rest on the wet ground, swimming in peace.

Alexander remained rooted to his milk prices, oblivious to my joy.

A lovely Persian kitty made her way over to the group of frozen pragmatists. Her supple body brushed against Alexander's, its pre-

18

sumptuousness suggesting she had nestled with him in a posture of intimacy more than once.

He excused himself and talked sombrely with her.

A hushed tension permeated the crowd. All eyes bulleted in my direction. All awaited my reaction to this triangle of emotion.

I sang! To ease their awkwardness. Hissing and spitting were not what I felt inside. She was too young to compete in the arena of experience. A cat like Alexander, while having an eye for beauty, also had an eye for soul. I depended upon the latter as my showcase of beauty.

My only complaint was I did not wish to be upon the stage of someone else's past. Scents of former lovers always linger behind, intermingling with new odours. Who in moments of doubt about a loved one can separate the staleness of the past from the present freshness without confusion. Our minds bear so many imprints of the past that every tiny detail of smell, sound and vision is capable of evoking dead phantoms, restoring them to life.

Was she part of the past or the present?

Their consultation ended. She walked away, slowly, sadly.

"She used to be my girl friend," Alexander explained to my curious eyes. "She's still in love with me."

"She has good taste."

He fixed a mooching, glassy gaze upon me.

"She is very lovely," I added, smiling.

He broke out into clairvoyant laughter. I hadn't spiked myself upon another of his tests. I didn't need to lacerate another female from a pool of jealousy. Experience with self-love had slowly lowered its water-mark, rendering the few remaining drops impotent to do harm.

Then he did a sudden swivel in his mood. Pain streaked his eyes as if someone had peeled off the outer layer of his skin without anaesthesia.

"What's the matter, Alexander?"

"YOU MAKE ME FEEL!"

"That's the pain, isn't it? You DON'T WANT TO WANT AGAIN."

His eyes closed affirmatively. Somewhere in his past there must have been a troublesome skeleton in the closet of love.

His drunkenness was no more effective than a sip of water.

He raced back for more milk, his balming exit from pain. He sought to capture solid ground, feeling himself falling into a depressed state. He danced his ambivalent dance for a few more minutes with the group, then returned to me, a returning to his sensorial self.

19

"Let's go home," he said in a voice of companionable familiarity.

"Where is home?"

"I'll show you."

Home was a palatial estate, a living monument to the history of art and architecture with its Renaissance façade and interior mixture of rococo and baroque grandeur and gaudiness, a visual feast so lavish I had to occasionally close my eyes, overwhelmed by this barrage of eye-popping stimulation.

Thick carpets sprawled over the marble floors, warming their iciness. (Without such a covering a cat's paws could freeze). The walls dripped with tapestries portraying women clothed in diaphanous gowns who were strolling in lush gardens where fountains sprayed diamond drops of water. I looked for signs of animal life in these scenes but found none, certainly no cats. I felt a little discriminated against, especially because I had been taught that women had a special fondness for my species. There were also paintings populated by handsome youths with satiny flesh being serenaded by musicians plucking stringed instruments. The youths looked more female than male. The lunettes in the ceiling were decorated with cherubs and angels flying in a celestial world, children of God in a cosmic playground. Then there were the porcelain figures encrusted with jewels whose poses of lethargy and debauchery suggested the owner to be a connoisseur of decadence but an undetected one because his taste in art bore the rubber stamp approval of cultivation. Nevertheless, seeing all this and then visualizing the seediness of the garbage can in my mind made me wonder if I shouldn't attempt a few improvements in the decor, maybe dust out the inside of my beloved sanctuary.

I gazed once more upon this fairy tale scene, illuminated by crystal chandeliers and electrified candelabras and gasped, "Who lives here, Alexander?"

"A rich old widow. Her deceased husband was the world's largest distributor of furs, exporting and importing. He converted his profits into the lavish trinkets you see," explained Alexander in a nonchalant voice.

"Trinkets, you call them!"

"I was born here, into a world of garishness. I have also lived in the world of hunger."

He led the way into a gleaming white kitchen, the size of a ballroom, where on one wall wine racks of milk bottles were stacked like book cases. Nearby, on the floor was a small blue and black Persian rug, richly contrasting with two gold saucers – no doubt fourteen carat – which sat on the rug, the saucers cupping the white substance of intoxication – cream. Alexander made no move to have a sip.

"You are a well cared-for cat. You must have charmed the mistress of this palace to receive such royal treatment."

"I was always her favourite. That used to gall the male who sired me, my father. He would crawl on to her lap expecting certain favours such as a scratch behind the ears. The moment I appeared she would set him down on the rug and flaunt herself in front of me, waiting for me to rub up against her stockinged leg. This outraged my father. The moment she left us alone, he would cuff me with his paw and gouge my back until blood dripped down yelling 'You no good cat, how dare you tread upon my property – she's mine' – and he would continue to claw me apart. My hisses and screeches brought my mother, a Calico cat, to my side to do battle on my behalf. But she was too small and too frail to separate us. She would plead with terror in her eyes to please stop this brutality. This only provoked him more. He transferred his sadistic rage fed by the smell of my blood and made her his next victim. In spite of my smallness then – I was only a kitten – I limped to her rescue, tumbling all three of us into an inferno of bloody battle. Three other kitties from the same litter I was born into, all younger than I, would inevitably arrive, standing horrified on the sidelines, help-less and confused. My father lived for the day when one of his clawings would make me plead and beg him to stop his attacks. He was determined not only to tame me but to break my spirit, to render me a spineless, controllable kitty. He never succeeded! I finally grew big enough so I could tackle him and return his mad fury. One day I emerged victorious after the most vicious fight we had ever had. The trophy awarded me was exile. I was banished from this palatial home to an alien world. You see, my father had feigned a near mortally-ill pose to the master of this establishment who was his twin in sadism. I received a rib smashing blow from this respectable pillar of the financial world to whom all bowed a slavish reverence. He and my father shared the same cleverness for locking up their cruelty behind closed doors, emerging un-blemished in the public spotlight of decency. It was my master who made huge, charitable contributions to support anti-cruelty campaigns for animals. Many an animal shelter was erected on the base of his money. That he should thrust me out into the street was of no consequence to him, nor to my father."

The scorn in Alexander's voice spoke of a festering wound from which he had never recovered. His story singed me, summoning up the desire to bear arms against the executioner of this atrocity committed against a kitty, a defenceless creature. I felt a mourning for his loss which really couldn't be called a loss because it didn't have the starting point of a beginning – there had never been a father to lose, only a competitor masquerading as a father, a father who like so many, never outgrew his own kittyhood to become a mature cat.

The glassiness in Alexander's eyes now seemed to come from tear-ducts of memories.

"Why am I telling you all this? I've never recounted this part of my life to anyone before."

Ah, Alexander, you were not the first to entrust me with the private drama of your life. From my youthful days I was viewed as a safety net into which others could fall. Mine wasn't a mothering instinct, I don't think, for I was too insecure and too selfish a kitty. Because of this I dared not pass judgement on others. They misread my veil of insecurity and called it strength. Not wanting to disappoint them I offered a soft shoulder upon which they could rest their battered souls and in the absence of criticism out surged all manner of secrets – this one was a homosexual, that one had a fetish about smelling the same piece of yarn, this one lusted after his mother, that one killed goldfish on the sly, this one hated all cat-kind. The list went on and on. The size of their pain and shame often fitted my own, eliciting my velvet empathy. They did not know we are all born from the same mother of emotion.

"Go on, Alexander, keep talking."

"After I was expelled from this place I moved into the streets, naive and green at first, but I soon learned the laws of the jungle, the laws of survival. I was Mr Hustler. There wasn't anything I didn't do."

"You mean like eating rancid rat meat and attacking anyone who challenged you to that morsel of food?"

"So, you've been there too?"

"Yes."

He paused. Then his voice ballooned up with shame. "I would never tell you of the disgusting deeds I've committed."

"Do you think there is anything that could shock me?"

He shrugged his shoulders. By the frown on his face I deduced he was reaching into his cesspool of shame, sucking out what he called a disgusting deed.

"I was responsible for the death of two kitties. It happened years back when I was a cat of the streets. It was late at night. I was very tired. These two kitties were new to town, not familiar with where to raid the best saucers of milk. Our lapping hours were finished and I was going to show them the way back to their neighbourhood via a short cut – a clothes line strung out three storeys high between two buildings, a more dangerous way than the longer ground route we could have taken. I wasn't very intoxicated but the others were unsteady on their paws. We began to manoeuver the crossing. I could feel the rope swaying as I edged toward the other side. Suddenly the rope moved wildly like a swing. The kitty behind me lost his balance and fell screaming toward the ground. The other one panicked, couldn't maintain his balance on the swaying rope and he too, followed in the wake of the other. A large truck, going much too fast down the street to stop, ran over them. Do you know what the howl of death sounds like?"

"No," I said.

"It's an echo which has an echo which has an echo. A perpetual wail you hear in your sleep, an echo accusing you of murder because I was too selfish to think about anything other than my own need to get quickly home that night. I undertook a responsibility and then reneged on it . . ."

At such moments you want to be able to offer comfort and solace when the naked agony of another being is so exposed. But what can you do? Pat someone on the head and say, there, there, little kitty, everything is all right. Don't worry about a thing. That works well with the young. But when the meaning of responsibility becomes more than just a word there are no facile words or gestures to ameliorate the guilt steeped in one who thinks he fell down on the job of protecting others. Such a feeling marks the first major step from kittyhood to adulthood. And that first taste of regret has such a lingering, bitter aftertaste which never seems to go away. But there is a lesson to be learned, Alexander, and you proved much later that the point was driven home to you. You become much more careful when other people place their faith and their lives in your hands. I can only add one thing which I eventually scribbled out to you. *A mature cat learns to forgive his immature past.*

But Alexander, what if those kitties had not died, had only sustained minor injuries? Would the incident then have been relegated to your unconscious cemetery of memories? And what about spiritual death? If you had caused this in another living creature would you have suffered the same guilt? Assassination is assassination whether you destroy the body or the mind.

Let's shift to a different tract for a moment. Can you be sure, Alexander, you had a free choice that night between the short cut and the other road? Did we freely elect to be possessed the night we were magnetized to the garbage can? Can you wholly assure me that it is we and only we who pick and choose our actions, as if choice were a mere product to be picked out from a host of choices sitting on a supermarket shelf? Could there be some fatality to which we have no conscious access? What do we really know about this universe we live in other than that we know very little. How vain and presumptuous we seem at times, ascribing to ourselves a grand feeling of importance to the speck of space we each occupy. I say vain and presumptuous because the task of knowing a little about ourselves is not easily undertaken. And so if I say that we do not know if and where the limits of our control over our personal world end, you will not butt in and say, "Look out, she's getting God in her soul." Maybe I am. But I have undergone a whole series of experiences which don't lend themselves to an easy, flip answer. For this reason I keep asking myself a question: is there some other dimension of life, some unnamed impalpable force which some call destiny and others dub God?

The first time I was forced to ask this question over the extent of our control in life came about owing to a dream I had had long before I met you. I had been romping about in a forest and then during a brief siesta I saw an old woman who I didn't know hang herself. The following day I returned home to whatever family I was living with at the time. I overheard my mistress talking to her husband about the old lady next door who had committed suicide by hanging herself! I was startled by this and then dismissed my dream as a fluke. I was too pragmatic a cat of the earth to believe in a world I couldn't touch, lick, smell, see or hear. Except more dreams or visions or whatever you want to call them happened in like manner every so often.

Then fatality costumed itself in a different guise, this time during a waking state. I was prowling around the Colisseum in Rome, the world's greatest gathering place for cats. It was then the "in place" for jet-set pets and there you could become acquainted with the most refined, sophisticated cats you'd ever want to encounter. Out of a throng of faces I suddenly spied a cat who captivated my attention. I was overcome by a gutsy feeling I was going to know him intimately. After a few seconds the spellbound feeling left me. I thought myself foolish and forgot the incident. Days later in another part of Rome, new to me, I struck up a conversation with another stranger. While we were talking he became distracted and called out to some cat friend at the other end of the street to come and join us. Because my vision isn't very good – I'm somewhat near-sighted you know – I couldn't make out who this cat was until he was almost next to me. My heart nearly stopped from shock. It was the cat from the Colisseum! Now I'm no expert in matters of arithmetic but the probability of meeting this cat was too small to ascribe it purely to mathematical chance, though it's possible. So my prophecy was right! Within ten minutes my "divined" friend proposed we take a stroll. There I was, a Cheshire grin on my face, walking with him along the path of his predestination? my predestination? We stayed together for some months and then I left him because he bored me. Were we serving some tiny, fateful mission in one another's life? Was this fateful experience the chance for us to ply our "earthly" skills to the moulding of our actions, an exercise solely of free will within the context of some larger power? Was the experience nothing more than my bedding down with this cat because my poetic divinations became true?

Questions. Questions. Questions. I warned you at the beginning that I am a cat with an insatiable curiosity.

I will now recount another strata of experience, another variation of the confusing partnership of fatality and individual control.

One day, again, long before I had met you, Alexander, I walked in a park. It was sunshine warm. On the shore of a small pond stood a giant willow tree, weeping tapered tears of leaves. A slightly murmuring wind struck up a solo song. I stood . . . listening . . . watching the willow . . . becoming transfixed by it . . . as though it were a beckoning siren or a magician manipulating an irresistible spell over me. Slowly, very slowly, my spirit began to sway from side to side along an undulating path toward this lovely statue, sculpted by nature, and soon I felt my spirit enter this tree, my body beginning to elongate upward, becoming one with the tree until I no longer felt any boundaries between myself and the willow. I was imitating the willow, moving as the willow. *I became the willow.* My brain ceased thinking. My body lost its physical sensations. *I did not exist!* Later when consciousness of my "self" returned, I marvelled at this alteration, this blissful state of non-being. Had I been a privileged guest at death's banquet, granted a preview of what death would be like?

Maybe you'll say that's nothing more than meditation. Wrong, Alexander! I wasn't meditating on anything. All I was doing was minding my own business and *pow*, once again I felt as though I were a "medium" for something I didn't understand and still don't. I don't look for these experiences. I don't work at them. They just

25

happen, just as we "happened" to meet under rather mystical(?) circumstances.

This entire diatribe came about when I was reflecting on your guilt. I don't want to downplay the importance of culpability in your life, Alexander. Sometimes I wish it were guilt which nagged at me rather than these questions about different dimensions of life. With guilt you can approximate its origin, at least in theory . . . How miniscule an issue guilt is when you compare it with the vastness and mysteriousness of the universe. Yet how powerful guilt is when it sweeps through us. Maybe we give guilt too much importance, using it like an opiate to soothe the judgements made about us by our fellow beings.

I suddenly feel myself back in the land of clumsy mortals when I talk about guilt. What split existences we can live! We are such lack-lustre creatures, while at the same time we carry within us a spirit of divinity that either we evolve into by opening up deeper layers of consciousness, or some power confers upon us. Where is the source of this divinity? I'm basically back to the same question and still no answer, as if I've made one entire revolution on a wheel. Now I'm not sure what the starting point was in this digression. Maybe there are no questions and no answers, no beginning and no end to anything. Maybe life just *is*, and it is impossible to define anything.

Don't think, Alexander, I was a stranger to the world of crime and guilt. I could have matched you crime for crime except I have consigned my guilt to the back-room of my consciousness, accepting it as a natural price paid for living.

I once stood accused of demanding the abandonment of kitties. I, a kitty myself, commanded the ghost of my past to make a choice – his offspring by another cat or me. I was too hungry for love to share him. And I accused him of suffocation! He carried out my bidding until one fine day his fury lacerated my selfishness, which, more aptly stated, was a vacant space in me, a hole of emotion needing to be filled. I began to stretch my heart beyond the two of us, demanding, in reverse fashion, he resume contact with his two kitties. My vampire lust for proof of his love had been degenerated to a minute proportion by his sustained, tender nourishment of my spirit. He had tutored me well in the art of giving love. The receipt of his gift was a liberation, a freedom from my self-immersion where I did not always need to be the star of every encounter with other beings . . .

Do you realize, Alexander, that the exposure of your crime was another kind of gift to me? A gift of trust. Perhaps you knew by that fine instinct of yours I would not chastise you for your crime. Were you aware you didn't touch a drop of your intoxicating cream? For a short while you took a chance on sobriety, the feeling part of you which let itself connect with me from time to time.

Your talk kept flowing out almost non-stop.

"My life in the streets and my poverty finally ended. Worry for the well-being of my mother and my siblings finally propelled me back to this palace. My master's demise facilitated my re-entry into the household. My mistress welcomed me back like a long-lost child. And my father semi-retired from bullying after reading the cunning which lined my face from my bouts with survival. Our unsteady truce was filled with mistrust of one another. (The paranoia you pick up from vicious attackers never swerves into repose). I sensed he was still looking to catch me during an unguarded moment so I had to be alert for the tiniest hint of aggression. It became necessary to control my every movement."

Alexander's control skirted before me in the image of a weeping Alexander in The Milk Bar stiffening up his body as if the clowning crowd had been an enemy on the verge of attack. What a contrast between this tender Alexander and the wary cat!

"Where is your family now, Alexander?"

"They live in another of the master's, or I should say, mistress's, houses. I visit them once in a while."

The story of his family provided a key to his capacity to care, to give, underscoring that the Alexander who had first held me was no emotional fraud. That he had sought to protect she who had suckled him was proof that she, his mother, must have poured into him all of the finer emotions of love to offset the tilting of his growth. Her warmth had fed him the power to dodge an emotional collapse when others without such support might have caved in.

"Why did your mother remain with your father? Why didn't she leave him?" I asked.

Alexander The Mature Cat supplied the answer in a voice without rancour.

"Because she loved him, in spite of his cruelty. She loved another face of him which he revealed only to her. Perhaps she saw in him the image of another! I know when none of the kittens in the family was around that their life together was peaceful. Then she had only him to mother. And that suited him!"

And perhaps it suited your mother, Alexander. Maybe her need to nurse others was so compelling that she accepted the slaps of cruelty. Maybe she thought cruelty was in the natural order of love. Many cats believe this. Maybe she received a spartan caress once a month from your father – that face of him he revealed only to her – and this act of affection balanced out his clawings in her accounting book of love.

How some beings balance emotions is not only miraculous but it rivals all mathematical laws of measurement. Sometimes you see couples where the negative feelings between them far outweigh the positive ones. Then you ask each member what it is that holds them together, and the range of answers seems to be grouped around a few basic needs – security, protection and habit. And if you point out to these couples living in misery that having nine lives as a cat means they can re-do their lives, start over again, they look at you blankly or with fear in their eyes. The fear reflects their fear of change, fear of the unknown, fear that they will lose something which they can never recoup. Since so many lives are grounded in this fear I presume there are few cats who live the entire span of their nine lives.

I'll tell you one thing, Alexander. I don't blame them for being afraid. The risks are high when you willingly or by necessity enter the arena of a new experience or a new life. Based on my past, I feel like I have walked through a fair number of emotional infernos. The worst one was when my soul disappeared, when I lost myself and I was reduced to copying the existence of ashes scattered on the ground, good for fertilizing a few weeds. I can't advocate this to everyone as character building. Many the spine of a cat has been crushed by the weight of taking a chance. Yet, many the spine of a cat has also been crushed by the failure to take a chance!

Usually there is one source that seems to bulldoze the existence of many cats into the ruins I've just mentioned. It goes by the name of love, though I suspect this is only an alias for everything which is not love, because I never heard of any cat being annihilated by mature love. Consequently I assume that the word "love" has come to be the most abused sound in any language, a word requiring pyramids of books to house all of its diverse and at times perverse definitions. Keeping in mind that everyone invents his own definition. I suppose Alexander that your mother called love "suckling" and your father called it "being suckled." Fortunately their individual notions of love meshed so that their relationship fell into an acceptable balance, each giving and getting what they imagined love to be.

But there was a sentence you said about your mother which later became more significant. You said, "Perhaps she saw in him the image of another!" There you hit upon something, one of those more obscure subtleties often found on the under-belly of love, when one being becomes a substitute love for another . . . I then asked myself as we talked in your kitchen: if you could grasp a possible hidden bond between those who had sired you, where was the source of your one step forward, one step backwards – your ambivalence toward me?

* * * * *

A cathedral gong announced the hour was late.

The dredging task of scooping up his past, propelled Alexander toward one of the gold saucers where he gulped down cream in order to coat his pain. And he gulped and gulped.

"Let's go to bed, I'm sleepy. I've had a lot to drink."

We bedded down in Alexander's cat box, an enormous treasure chest lined with fur. Paper currencies of every denomination had been sewn together to make a patchwork blanket. You could see that Alexander was a well-travelled cat.

He began to stare vacantly at the ceiling. Nonsense syllables, like an abstract design intelligible only to him, popped out of his mouth, as if he had chosen to voice aloud every third word of a sentence. My third eye saw him being hoisted back to the land of his private riddles. His absent spirit lowered me into my cata-combs of solitude, at a depth of glacial emotions where I sought to protect myself from his comings and goings.

"Let's make love," moaned Alexander.

I heard him say, cocoon me, make me forget some undisclosed memory.

I tried to rouse myself from cheerlessness. The love making matched a wedding ceremony attended by a disinterested bride and groom. Alexander heaved his heavy body into one of a hundred cats without a face which delayed the climax in me he was waiting for. His violent urgency hurt me inside and I wanted to complain "stop punishing me." But I was the actress on the stage of his sensitivity, expected to bring the act to an electrifying conclusion. I looked wildly for a cue so I wouldn't forget my body movements. Suddenly I relived the opening night magic of our initial enchantment and simulated my movements to that orgy of joy whose flashback produced my clasping spasm, convincing Alexander he was an adequate lover.

He remained turgid and tense, unable to hide behind the same subterfuge of relief I had consummated for myself. I licked and licked his barometer of interior comfort. It never fell during the night but stood stiff and hard.

I felt dejected. He had forgotten the intoxicating Wine who lay by his side.

* * * * *

Daylight's brashness slashed into the embalming blanket of night.

I awakened with a glacial mood which had thickened in my sleep where I had journeyed back to obscure re-runs of cats who had once been cruel to me. My tongue had the sour taste of fear which shrivelled me up into a furry foetus unable to cuddle up to Alexander. I was translating my past into the present, reading possible treason into Alexander's character. Nor did his cold, tough mood dispell this when awakening. Without the slightest tenderness he rolled over on top of me and ruthlessly detonated his sperm into a "me" who voluntarily handed him a receptacle, like an attendant guarding his valuables.

A contented Alexander then reclined midst his boudoir like a pasha, his recuperated esteem booming out. "What are you going to do today? I have things to accomplish."

I invented important tasks in a hollow voice.

"What's the matter with you?" he fliply asked.

"I feel strange inside."

"Well, get a hold of yourself!" he commanded.

Anger sliced through the frozen zone around my heart. DON'T TELL ME TO GET HOLD OF MYSELF. JUST HOLD ME. GIVE ME A TENDER WORD . . . LIKE MY POWERFUL GHOST USED TO DO. I DIDN'T HAVE TO BEG HIM FOR ANYTHING. HE ANTICIPATED MY EVERY NEED, ALWAYS GIVING, GIVING, GIVING. HE DIDN'T METE OUT HIS AFFECTION IN PARTIAL DOSES, ALEXANDER. HE WENT WHOLE HOG. But not a word of this slipped out. My mouth could only form a silent circle. Muteness. I had reverted back to that dreadful kittyhood disease – fear to expose my need for warmth because it might be scoffed at, rejected. Here is where Wine The Fraud hid behind silence. I hated you Alexander in that moment for navigating my return flight to the world of fear. Or did I do that to myself? I could have unveiled my silence, if I had been disposed to take a chance! But there was another consideration which said that a provocative hiss would have made you scamper away deeply bruised if I had chastised you, an ungracious gift of flinging mud into your face after you had exposed some of your unedited life with me the previous evening.

I was beholden to the image of Alexander The Consoling Cat.

I suddenly saw the image of Alexander's mother chained to his father.

I saw myself chained to my own paranoid sensitivity.

I saw myself still chained to my powerful ghost. Or, was I chained to the image of love he represented?

His memory was now presiding with me in Alexander's cat box. *He*, into whom I had confided my secrets, my fears, my dreams, my love. Had he really been such a suffocating influence? Shouldn't I have known that no-one lives without contradictory feelings towards those we care about? And wasn't Alexander somewhat like *him*, a multiplicity of selves – tender, caring, cold and heartless?

I had later tried to return to my ghost after locating fragments of my "self." But it was too late. He had mated with another. It seemed a cruel irony that my reward for self-discovery was "loss." Once again my spirit turned to ash. My "self" disappeared. Or was it that I still didn't have a "self" to lose . . .?

If Alexander was in a hurry to leave his cat box he made no effort to do so. I watched him emerge into his world of self-immersion. Alexander The Circus Performer was elevating his hind paw, a prolonged holding action meant to challenge gravity.

"I used to do this as a kitten, to see how long I could remain in this position. This is how I trained my will, my control over fear."

"What are you so afraid of?"

"Death! I am deathly afraid of death . . . I am a coward who walks along the edges of high buildings, knowing that if I'm not steady on my paws I will kiss death!"

His swivel back to honesty and humility raised my mood to empathy.

"You aren't describing a coward, Alexander, because cowards don't confirm their fear. You are confronting fear in your own style rather than following the temptation to avoid it. Maybe it was this need to test your valour which prompted you that night to take the high-wire short cut with those kitties who died, to do the very thing you didn't want to do – flirt with your mortality . . ."

How well I understood your need to spit in the face of fear. I've been doing this throughout my lives.

Were you ever afraid of the dark, Alexander? I was and still am when nightmares decorate my sleep. You awaken, wanting to have a light on to burn off whatever imaginary demons visit you, especially when it is the demon of death which glows so brilliantly in the darkness. But sometimes you become exhausted from fear so you decide to undergo the withdrawal symptoms of terror by remaining in the dark the next time nightmares strike. You sweat and shake and your heart palpitates and you keep reassuring yourself that nothing is going to hurt you and for a few minutes you illuminate the darkness with your enlightened imagination. And if the fear returns you repeat the same rites until a light switches on in your mind. Dear Alexander, facing fear, conquering fear is a way of life.

And what about the other form of death, not the physical one but emotional death – the power of others to torture your soul!

Long ago your father gave you your first lesson in the martial art of emotional destruction. You fought this, raising your paw, swearing allegiance that you would defend yourself from him and all other worldly harm. Nothing would touch your heart. The cost you pay for this oath is a mustering up of so much energy that you are squeezed dry, you can't let go sexually with most cats. No wonder your warmth was like an occasional sweet, meted out when there was no red alert to put you on guard . . . .

It became tedious watching you carry on with your acrobatic act. It hurt me to feel you drop a curtain of silence between us again. Did my comment about those dead kittens seal you up in isolation?

I hopped out of the cat box, washed out by understanding, bombarded too by over-exposure to the ghost swarming around in my head. The luxurious ambiance was beginning to pall on me. It contrasted so greatly with the simplicity of surroundings I preferred. Mostly I needed to get away from you. I was resenting the constriction of my emotional state.

"I must leave, Alexander."

He watched me depart, detachment written on his face.

"I'm going on a trip again," he boomed.

"So am I. Merry Christmas in advance." My flat tone shattered his sound barrier.

"Will I see you when I return?" The humility in his voice kicked away his mask of detachment.

I pretended I didn't hear him.

The sultry sun took me into its arms, giving me the warm companion I hadn't located with Alexander. I was relieved to be alone. His presence had spaded a flurry of grave-digging into my past, where my powerful ghost had arisen, shimmering a memory of affection, luring me back in time because the present seemed emotionally vapid.

The warm, semi-tropical sun began to thaw my glacial mood.

I left the land of riches for Alexander to play in, or cry in, or do whatever he wanted. There in his mighty palace dwelled a kitty, not a full grown cat, a frightened creature whose preoccupation with power and control eclipsed the loveable cat I knew him to be. The cat who had caused an earthquake of sexual responsiveness in me was stifling in a world of control. Alexander's fear of death appeared to be more like a fear to live, a fear to love, a fear to plunge his whole being into another. To love is to put yourself wholly in the flow of life.

I had many fears too, Alexander. I was especially afraid of not living, knowing that the more you live, the less fear you have. And, the less fur!

* * * * *

The interim separation brought me to a quiet peace place. My mistress flew to a northern land, taking me to a house I had never seen, a house of history where human life had spilled out for three hundred years amidst a posh green countryside, swelled by subtle hills. The simplicity of the stark, wooden house, unembellished by artificiality, and the change of scenery embalmed Alexander into a tiny container in my memory. This new land, of picture-postcard beauty, was situated in a cold climate, contrasting vividly with the searing, heated place where I normally dwelled, chilling my sensuality to sleep.

My mistress being of a generous bent, permitted me free rein to explore the environs. Each day I padded through a grey fog enshrouding the landscape, a countryside breathing mystery suitable for lyrical backdrops where no hint of treachery is detected. There was an unshaven silence, dreamy in its unrealness. Nothing moved in this windless region. There was no visible life, no animals, no humans. A cry for help would have echoed into infinity. This realization made me edgy. I felt cast adrift upon the solitude of a moonscape, coasting through diaphanous pathways of unrelenting fog . . . until . . . one day a barking dog cracked the silence! Splintering my eardrums, raising the hackles of my anxiety, fear clutching at me, pinioning me to a statue's pose.

Alexander's words came to me: GET HOLD OF YOURSELF.

Wine, you who have challenged so much, afraid of a dog?

I batted my eyelashes with fear as the beast prepared to charge. He was a raggedy old mutt, howling and snorting his way around me, increasing his agitated howl each time he caught sight of my broadening smile. I told myself, beam your effrontery to him, send off your life beams, your survival beams!

33

He circled me a dozen times. My hissing life force kept him at bay. He never touched me. Finally, tamed by my bravura, he lumbered off, dragging his shaggy tail between his legs.

I felt weak from fear, every nerve end quivering. I thought how lovely it would be to return to the house of security. I thought how cowardly it would be to renounce my exploratory quest. So I proceeded farther and farther from safety, all the while, planning a frontal attack because I had to retrace the same country lane of danger.

Finally it was time to turn back, though fear tempted me to walk straight ahead to infinity. The confrontation could not be avoided, only forestalled. Better to face it sooner than later.

I drew out my claws, ploughing the ground, watching the dirt fly up at a desparate tempo. I was practising for a frontal attack. I breathed in the air of pride and determination and renewed my fury so the beast would not think he was dealing with a wishy-washy scaredy-cat. I was angry that this useless animal had slashed my peace.

I was ready now with my own charge of assault, ready to fling myself upon the dog the moment he came into view. I was approaching where he lived. It flashed before me that he might not appear after all of this preparation. Wouldn't that be ironic!

Irony won the war.

The mangy dog did not surface. He must have received my vibrations and deciding my spirit to be stronger than his, he accorded me the status of a victor. A weary victor! Fear is so fatiguing.

My courage collapsed as soon as I entered the safe haven of my house. Alexander's presence exploded inside of me. I felt a yearning for him and a willingness to accept him as an immature kitty who habitually resided with Alexander the mature cat. I had fallen off my pedestal of superiority, brought down to earth by a howling dog. I renewed my admiration for Alexander's struggle to confront his fear. I forgave the pragmatists who populated The Milk Bar. We were all caught up in the same web of simply trying to live, however we could.

I began wondering where you were, Alexander. What were you doing? I didn't imagine you bedded down with another cat, a change in me from earlier lives. If you had slept with someone else it would have been to expel a moment of loneliness. I couldn't envision you readily duplicating the love-making as we had known it that first night. The other dissatisfying sexual moments I preferred to forget because they belonged to the more normal hit-

and-run sex that no one escapes from. What sent shivers through my body every time I encored that magical night in my memory was its blending of eroticism and spirituality, a combination that makes for a strong emotional bond between two beings. In fact, it was this same bond that I had had with my professor of love . . . and my ghost. No wonder I couldn't forget them!

Like you, Alexander, they too had been impotent with me, though in the more traditional sense of being unable to get an erection at times. They, like you, were not machine creatures whose cocks spurted off at the press of a button. I read their impotency as indicative of their intricate, emotional status, a sensitivity to outside forces and tensions. Only feeling males, and there are quite a few, suffer from this malady just as females do in whom frigidity is the twin sensation to male impotency.

Don't you believe, Alexander, that while you males and we females are physically designed differently that once we probe into our emotions it becomes clear that the differences between us are illusory, more myth than fact? If there is a war between the sexes might it not be one of displacement, that each sex is seeing in the other qualities which it refuses to acknowledge in itself. Males and females, in spite of the distinct window dressings they wear, both display every emotion you can think of – anger, fear, joy, tenderness, the need to see to the well-being of the young. If there are variations in character they are not because of sex. The differences are individual ones.

* * * * *

The Christmas holiday season had stained my soul with a widespread melancholy. It was always at this time I profoundly felt my status as an orphan, alone, without those who had sired me, without offspring to lick clean. While my mistress obtained joy in illuminating the Christmas tree and toasting in the New Year with a few friends, I thought how impossible it was to celebrate holidays simply because they were inscribed on a calendar. My emotional celebrations were always based on a hastily improvised calendar, corresponding to emotional elation over an unexpected happy event.

Any day which births a smile in your heart is the real meaning of rejoicing.

Returning to the land of sunshine meant looking for my solar smile.

I scampered to The Milk Bar for several nights in a row.

Alexander was not to be found. Nor were many of the usual habitués present. The New Year merry-making had cast them into a lethargy of hangovers. Even the anonymous donor must have fallen victim to the festivities, he or she setting out only a pittance of the usual ration of milk.

There was one cat, Mack, one of the regular patrons, who shared my holiday sentiments. He was lying in front of an idle saucer, playing with the milk, his paw flicking drops of liquid to the ground like a young girl tearing off leaf after leaf from clover, incanting: he loves me, he loves me not.

Singing was Mack's metier, his source of relief from the daily drudgery of living. He was one of the joy seekers I had met my first time at The Milk Bar. Singing, as I was about to find out, was also a buffer against troublesome preoccupations.

"Wine, are you afraid of dying alone in your old age, when you're in your ninth life?"

"I may not live that long, Mack. Who doesn't die alone, whatever the age? We die alone because we live alone, no one inhabits our skin. If someone is with us when death comes it's a comfort, to be sure. But dying is a solo act."

"Do you think much about death?" persisted Mack.

"Do I ever! It's my most unfavorite hobby! It occupies more and more time the older I get. It has already killed my sense of immortality. Now the only thing it can annihilate is myself. I first met this monster in my kittyhood, when my mother died. I remember while I was mourning for her how I used to lie awake at night imagining death as a big black hole and I would try to draw it in my mind, an impossible task, like trying to draw space. Night after night I struggled to measure this death, this infinity, battling to grasp a world forever unfolding without my *eternal* presence, terrorized by the impossible task of denting timelessness with a speck of comprehension. I used to feel too frightened to sleep, fearing I would succumb to perpetual dreamlessness. During the day I would have the sensation of gliding over the ground like a somnambulist – nothing in the everyday world dented me. I felt completely detached from my body and it was this disassociated part which watched others go on with the business of living. And I would silently shriek to all who came into view: do you know you're all going to die, do you really know this? What are you doing about this? No one gave me a clue that death also walked with him or her too. I felt so alone. No longer part of anything. Slowly the impact of death simmered down and a day dawned when I moved back into my body, rejoining my fellow cats. Death stayed on as a silent partner to life and I sometimes conversed with it because I didn't want to deceive myself by its shadowy existence.

"But are you still afraid of death?" Mack's middle-aged cat's voice adopted the high whine of a curious kitty.

"Some days, yes. Other days, no – an improvement over earlier years when the answer was always 'yes'. I must live longer. I must *live*. Then perhaps I will answer your question with a resounding 'no.' I would like to be able to confront death with serenity, with the grace of a ballerina dancing into its arms as though I were oozing into another dimension. Yet, I don't want to deceive myself by calling death a name other than its baptismal one."

I did not want to recount my experience with the willow tree to Mack. It was too personal and too impossible to convey. At best I might have likened it to a state of dreamlessness. But I smelled a strong odour of fear behind Mack's question and sought to track down his dangling anxieties.

"Mack, why are you so preoccupied with death?"

"It must be the holiday season. It was around this time of year when my mother threatened to kill herself while poised on a bridge, ready to jump into the river. I was only a small kitty then. Only my screaming meows dissuaded her from carrying out the act. After that, she became a very confusing cat. She twisted life and death around for me. She called living 'dying' and dying 'living.' She made death sound both horrible and fascinating. As young as I was, I scented that if she mated with death I would lose her and so I begged her to promise she wouldn't kill herself. But she gave no guarantee and whenever she was out of sight I would be terrified that I would never see her again. Eventually she was removed from the house where we lived because of her erratic behaviour. But she left me with so many unanswered questions."

"She left you with an overwhelming legacy, prematurely knighting you a philosopher, you a tiny kitty who was supposed to have the wisdom of defining what is living and what is dying, a gigantic presumption that you were somehow capable of swallowing the whole cosmos with one comprehensive gulp . . . ."

Why couldn't she have owned the courage to fight for life, to look for specks of joy instead of disseminating pessimism to the winds like so many of her ilk, infecting others with this same disease. But maybe she was windblown first by another cat who felled the atmosphere with this malady, this demonic killer of the life force. How glib and slick to say living is dying and dying is living. Why not say day is night and night is day. Nothing more than a scrambling of words, words, words. It takes guts to rouse yourself from this sort of philosophical charade. Yet not everyone appears equal to the task of surmounting despair. Some cats seem to be born with more courage than others. To sit in judgement on Mack's mother is really not fair. Maybe she never savoured any sweet dessert in all of her lives, never knew that rising-up of joy from the horizon of her drab existence. There are cats who live in only a grey zone of life.

Mack was moving into the quagmire of memory. I had to pull him out.

"Mack, let's sin. Let's erase this holiday depression and *live*."

He looked at me with a smirk on his face. "You sure are direct."

"What do you mean?"

"You just said, 'let's sin'."

Belly laughs blew out of me. I didn't hear the word "sin" escape my lips. A genuine slip of the tongue? In between my laughter I tried to rectify my lying mistake. "Sing, Mack! Sing! Let's *sing*!"

We sang and sang and finally sang our way into a consoling embrace, hiding ourselves behind a nearby tree . . . each of us touching one another's solitude with tenderness and with gentleness . . . the feather-like touching causing erotic tingles . . . surging through my body . . . how long it had been since I had been caressed by Alexander . . . and a zingling thrill of carnal desire raced through every locale in my body . . . and I wanted Mack to stimulate me everywhere at once . . . and his stroking began to harmonize with his licking . . . his darting tongue running up and down my body, teasing it to want to feel the clamping spasms which would release the raw, pent-up sexual desire which was now so hypersensitive . . . and the smells of sex began to waft over us and my secreting juices made me well lubricated . . . I urgently wanted his rock-hard cock to enter my cunt . . . I wanted to be fucked and fucked well . . . I pulled him inside of me and sucked on his cock with my cunt . . . But he suddenly broke the mood!

An ecstatic pleasure darted out from his eyes. He pulled out of me . . . and began massaging his cock at a furious pace . . . and he begged me to play with myself . . . female masturbation gave him such a kick . . . and his sexual preference iced my desire . . . I dabbed my moist lips a couple of times . . . caught off guard by this unexpected switch . . . and he went into a frenzy of movement, squirting his juices all over himself.

Why had he ostracized the entrance to my womb?

He nestled in my paws like a new-born kitty, looking to be nursed by a me portraying a sexual missionary, and how could I feel anger at such a young cat who harboured no viciousness? My desire had vanished with the ease that is only possible when the one you love is not your lover.

"Do you ever have unusual dreams?" asked Mack.

"Yes, lots of times." He was alluding to something related to the incompletion of our sexual act which he had had to abort. He was making a detour, nervous about exposing himself and so I brought out of my warehouse of dreams the most bizzare one I could recall, sure that most cats would have been appalled by its contents, or more honestly said by the revelation of it.

"Tell me about one of them, *please*."

"There was a lovely woman in this dream, lovely in the sense that her soul swam through life with a constant gentleness. Her face bore the scars of burns. This all too-human being was in bed with a monkey. She was trying to copulate with it without success, while the monkey was eating a banana. She had been driven to this desperate measure after not having found any human with whom she could either emotionally or sexually connect. I felt so sorry for her plight that I crawled into her bed, swatted the monkey aside and began licking her clitoris. At least a furry cat of feeling might be more satisfying to her than an indifferent monkey."

"Wow, that's a weirdy. How do you interpret that? A pure case of sodomy? Lesbianism between two females?"

"Neither of these."

"How do you know? Maybe there is some secret, lurking desire in you to have sex with another female."

"That's just an idea a lot of cats have, that all dreams have sex as their leitmotif. Besides, I once experimented sexually with another female and I found the experience rather bland, neither disgusting nor exciting. Anything which leaves me so indifferent does not correspond with anything that is essentially me. Anyhow, I remember upon awakening how washed out I felt by a terrible sorrow. I knew that woman's aloneness, her loneliness. You've known it, Mack. Everyone has known it. It's that nagging anguish from feeling that no one gives a damn whether you're alive or dead, that not even a mirror will give a hint of your visibility. You might even put your forehead up against a cold wall, as I've done sometimes, just to prove you are alive, albeit, alive in your aloneness."

A green light of freedom brought forth his confession.

"I have a lot of sexual dreams," Mack said. "Usually I'm making love to my mother. That sounds sick, doesn't it? Do you think I physically desire her?"

"Mack, most things are not sick if seen in the light of understanding. Too often we superimpose onto others our personal experiences and whatever deviates from what we know, we call sick. The tragedy of this word – sick – is that it brands us as freaks, makes us feel we haven't the right to belong to the camaraderie of other beings and so we slink around the margin of life as though we were fugitives, camouflaging a crime, carefully exposing only those facets of our mythology we think others want to see. Don't you think that making love to your mother in your dreams is expressing a desire for closeness, a desire prematurely severed before you were ready to be weaned from her? You had to protect her from herself. You had to mother her instead of her mothering you. Making love can be like an adult's version of cuddling up to a mother in kittyhood, a seeking of warmth, a seeking of emotional nourishment."

I welcomed Mack to my circle of adopting offspring, suspecting I had evoked an incestuous conflict within him because he had been *taught* mistakenly to associate closeness with a female as perverted lust and any sexual act he engaged in thus became like the forbidden fruit – a condemned act not to be consummated.

Was it my emotionality, my warmth, which hinted maternity to him?

Maternity once again parading herself so nakedly in front of me . . .

I can't put off any longer denying a piece of news I wasn't going to relate because it seemed superfluous to our story, Alexander. Until now. My mistress had me "fixed" right after our last meeting. She must have thought I was too much of a cat in heat! The event wasn't exceptionally traumatic but it was upsetting and I was very angry at her for such a careless action. She had usurped my freedom, cancelling out my choice to breed or not. Sure, I was past my prime for bearing kittens but that didn't seem a good enough reason for killing my chance to become a mother. *But I was already a mother*. I had been practising motherhood for quite a while, with Mack for example. Seen in this perception, I know that my mistress eradicated only the physical facet of my procreation. No incision had cut away the tissues of mothering, of caring, of giving, of encouraging others to find their particular path in life. True motherhood is not limited to the expulsion of a foetus from one's body. Motherhood is an attitude toward others of the same fibre as fatherhood, the expression of being responsible for the lives of others such as you felt, Alexander, when you blamed yourself for the slaughter of those two kitties. . .

Mack pried me with one last question, seeing in me the image of a mother he had never had.

"Is it wrong to look in a pool of water and love yourself? Is that narcissistic?"

"Only if you stay at the surface and don't dive into the bottom of your soul. When you make this slow submersion you will find yourself entangled in the sweet tendrils of self-love and upon splashing back to the surface of your reflection you will bring with you an awareness of foolishness, wisdom, humour and sorrow. You will know about your potential to be a creature in a constant state of evolution. And it is this baptism into self-love which makes you tolerant of yourself and facilitates your making the world more tolerable for others. I remember, Mack, one special morning when I peered into a gritty mirror. There was my same, familiar face, the one I had seen a million times, except on this occasion I saw my soul instead of the facial blemishes I had so often scorned. There it was, my beauty part, the part which had always waited in the wings of my existence, patiently waiting to be discovered. I fell in love with my soul . . ."

I thought about you, Alexander, in that moment. Why couldn't you have poured a few drops of self-love into those milk saucers which nourished everything but your soul? Your beauty part might have been located with the same piercing stare you haughtily directed at that female in The Milk Bar. Why couldn't you have pointed that stare inward? Or did I miss that ray of your vision?

* * * * *

Several moonlit nights later Alexander's broadcasting beams lunged at me like rough waves, steering me to The Milk Bar. The instant I glimpsed him a blaze of shivers coursed through me, my cat hair straining with electricity from his sensual charge. His smile enflamed the embers of desire and I brushed my body against his every chance I had, content to anticipate a slow, leisurely episode of love-making later in the night. The presence of the pragmatists was not a pestilence but merely an appendage of Alexander who on this night rejected all forays into his prison of non-feeling. Had separation made him hungry for me?

We sojourned to our special place and there in the garbage can we re-enacted our opening night magic, a magic less intensified but embossed with a hint of peace born out of a truce within each of us where ghosts did not tantalize us with maddening lust.

Daylight sashayed in from the horizon, highlighting the speckled grey spots on Alexander's fur. Watching the peaceful warrior asleep, I fantasized and hoped for more quiet mornings like this, lying by his side, where talk is unnecessary and even sexual arousal is tempered because you are content just to be in the atmosphere of the one you care about and something about the emotional auras of the two makes it feel so right, as if it were writ on a page of destiny.

Alexander was infected with the same peace, crowning me his companion for the day, the first time he had had a female by his side in many years.

It was a day of intimacy, a sharing of each and every little detail arising on the surface of life, commencing with the banishment of sleep from both our eyes, performing the morning ritual of licking away dirt and emitting little grunts and groans usually done only within the privacy of oneself; then padding down streets and bumping into one another because the relaxed pace of moving side by side required no fixed rhythm, and occasionally smiling when the interior glow flowed from one into the other without verbal provocation; and a host of stimuli from the surroundings registered in a similar fashion and the comments made were simply to confirm shared perceptions.

Our destination was The International Fur Fair, a yearly attraction where fur pelts dazzled the eyes of buyers and sellers from around the world. Housing this extravaganza, this carnival of wealth was The Crystal Exhibition Hall, a gigantic glass dome, patterned after the world's largest diamond, an homage to the good life to which all humans aspired. The dome shimmered shafts of refracted sunlight with a blinding brilliance. A red, velvet carpet prepared the transition from the grimy street to the entrance of this enormous vault of valuable skins. With each cushiony prance up the ramp there was time to meditate upon the wonder of wealth, poverty becoming anesthetized, step by step.

I had slithered upon luxurious velvet in my past but I could now easily renounce it because I preferred the rugged terrain of bumpy rocks and smooth, desert sand. I was a cat of the earth and the hearth, not needing a glamorous setting to distract me from the drama and comedy between living creatures. Besides, whether it was the backdrop of Versailles or a garbage can, I always carted around the same soul which either glittered or wilted, depending upon the interior comfort of my psyche. Through the years I had yearned more and more for a simple life-style. The important things which counted were having a few friendly cats for good friends, sufficient food, good health and someone to love. The order of importance of these varied, dictated by the need and availability of what I could and could not have, of what I could find. What else was there in life except clutter and ornamentation!

Upon entering The Crystal Palace I let out a gasp of astonishment, similar to my reaction to what Alexander had dubbed his humble abode. There before us stood rack after rack of fur pelts, crammed together; pelts hanging like strung-out spaghetti; pelts invoking the name of every animal you could think of – foxes, squirrels, deer, tigers, antelopes, mink, black seals, raccoons, rabbits – an international bank of wealth far exceeding the combined circulation of dollars, deutsche marks, pounds, lira, yen and Swiss francs. Who could measure the value of these animals whose hearts had once beat like our own!

"Alexander, are we safe here? Shouldn't we discreetly move around while we look at this grandiose spectacle. If we're not careful we might be stripped of our skins, for I don't see any cat skins among the profusion of pelts."

A confident Alexander roared with laughter, a dangerous situation, for we might have been mistaken for two tigers.

"Don't worry," he said. "The world still perceives you as a pet. Redefining your status would be too much of a challenge for most humans."

"But if humans get desparate, they're capable of anything, just like us. Don't forget, styles do change with humans. One day you're a nobody and the next day you're treated as a unique discovery – instant transformation from a faceless crowd on to the neon lights of elevated fame. I still think we must guard our fur well, keep on making ourselves indispensable as warm, cuddly pets, instead of this sometimes stand-offishness we cats are prone to so that if the moth balls in the closets of humans don't combat moths eating their way through furry luxury, we will not be sacrificed upon the altar of artificial decoration in order to compensate for a depleted supply of fur."

"I'm indestructible," grinned a cunning, looking Alexander.

"I believe you. But I'm not. Let's go and sit inside that camping tent over there."

As we approached it I noticed a cow-hide sign tacked on to a hugh potted palm tree, gracing one side of the tent. It said: FOR THE MAN WHO HAS EVERYTHING – A SUEDE TENT. Here was proof that there was more than one way, beside fur coats, to utilize a skinned animal, or more than one way to skin a cat, I thought with a shudder, to coin a human expression.

We hopped into the tent and lay down on our bellies, peering through a slit of space offered at ground level because the tent was not flush with the floor. This limited our vision to a parade of passing feet.

"Qué impresionante! Wie schön! C'est merveille! Meraviglioso! I say, this is all terribly impressive!"

A concerto of exclamations of awe sauntered forth from a pot-pourri of international tongues whose procession of marching shoes passed by us for inspection. Square-cut men's shoes, round-toed men's shoes, high-heeled ladies' shoes, low-heeled ladies' shoes, shoes showing peek-a-boo toes, and austere shoes conceal-ing all flesh. The non-precision clomp clomp noise stomped a counterpoint beat that any military general would have rioted against.

Alexander and I began playing a guessing game, juggling national stereotypes, good for a light laugh.

"The oxfords belong to the English, sturdy looking."

"The tapered stiletto heels belong to the Spanish and Italian sex pots."

"The well-polished leather sandals with white-socked feet march-ing in four-four time must belong to the Germans."

"The gleaming white tennis shoes waddling awkwardly, beating an irregular metronome sound, belong to the Americans. Their stomping only harmonizes when they are rooting for their favour-ite sports team."

Alexander The Professor began postulating his theories on the narrowness and liberality of national egos.

"Who says you can't tell a nation by its shoes? To step into the shoes of a country is to step inside its mentality. Do the shoes pinch? If so, there isn't much breathing space for deviants. If the shoes let your feet swim in them then that's a good sign – not much rigidity to hem in your individual style of life. If the shoe exposes the foot, then prudes beware, – you're in a nation of sensualists. And if the shoe rejects a naked foot, covering it from heel to toe, then you've just joined a monastic order where sensuality is of a skimpy nature. Notice I said sensuality, not sex. Sex is for every-one, sensuality is not."

"Bravo, professor. Have you any other elucidating theories?"

"Yes. Language too, like shoes, corroborates the distinct men-talities of countries. I will illustrate what I mean. The word 'the' is probably the most inaudible word to most human ears. In English, 'the' forms a couple with either 'one of a kind' or with 'several of a kind.' And, it doesn't matter where you place 'the' in a sentence – whether it is a cohort with a subject noun, an indirect noun or a direct object noun, it never changes its form. Just as a rose is a rose is a rose, so too, 'the' is 'the' is 'the'. You can interpret this as an ability of those who speak this language as being blessed with a good organizational facility. They don't waste time over superfluous matters. Now the German language has an obsession with 'the.' It is the only modern language I have heard in all of my travels where 'the' has sixteen forms! Not only does it have a specific form with each gender – masculine nouns, feminine nouns and neuter nouns – but you also have to slot in 'the' according to the singularity or plurality of the gender! And to frustrate all but the most persistent learner, 'the' alters its form with nouns depending on whether the noun is acting as the subject, the indirect object, the direct object or the possessive case."

"Alexander, what are direct and indirect objects?"

He reflected for a few moments. Then a sly glint darted out from his eyes.

"As you know, the subject of a sentence is like the principal actor or actress of a movie. The direct object is usually a thing, or various things, that the star wants to share or give to someone. And that someone who gets something from the star is the indirect object. For example: ALEXANDER GAVE WINE A KISS."

He translated the sentence into a smooch on my cheek for emphasis.

"I get it! Alexander is the subject, kiss is the direct object and . . . Wine is the indirect object. Hmmm. I'm not sure I like being an indirect object and playing second fiddle to a kiss even if it is one of my favourite things. Maybe we'll switch that sentence around and let you feel how it is to be in my skin."

And with that I kissed him. And just to keep me in my place he kissed me back. Such comportment was in danger of summoning up a different direct object to be received by me. We chose to wait. Our teaching session continued.

"Alexander, I'll wager those Germans applaud English grammar. Any group of people so preoccupied with one tiny word like 'the' probably places more value on things rather than on humans. For sure they aren't sensualists. Compulsive people seldom are."

"But they are precise! It is their paying such meticulous attention to detail which makes their currency so valuable. They know how to produce!"

"Produce what? An assembly line of 'thes'? And what about these genders you mentioned? Does that mean that there is one 'the' for men, another 'the' for women and another 'the' for things?"

"Something like that."

"At least they have a sense of logic."

"Not quite. While they are precise they are not always logical. Not all 'things' are neuter nouns. Some 'things' are also masculine or feminine and there is no rule to determine which is what. I can think of one controversial item which would make you sputter with anger. You say 'Das Mädchen' for 'the girl' in German. It is a *neuter* noun."

"You mean they don't have the decency to consider a young girl as feminine? She's only an 'it' as though she were a 'fixed' cat?"

"Yes. And they don't subject boys to the same humiliating role. 'Der Jũnge,' the boy, is born with a masculine 'the.'

"Alexander, those Germans are sexual bigots. What does a young girl have to do in order to get a feminine 'the'? – wait until she is ready for menstration? – like parallelling the same ritualistic significance as male circumcision at birth? I know one thing. Some humans would set up an instant boycott if they were informed about such sexual discrimination. Why don't the Germans just make everyone a neuter and erase some of the friction between the sexes!"

"For some, that might create more haggling. But your idea would achieve a state of equality in the best of democratic traditions . . ."

Of course I took none of our conversation seriously. Everything I said was in a pseudo tone of seriousness. Then Alexander cast aside his own fake professorial tone and laid a verbal trap, another test of my psychic acuity.

"There is one idiom, without an official name," he said, "where the vocabulary of love-making words is astonishingly vast. The verb 'to love' has nine synonyms. Imagine, nine different ways to say 'I love you!'

"Or, nine different *lives* to say 'I love you!' Is there a word for 'soul-mate' in this language?"

The game backfired, even though I had zeroed in on the language of cats. A shudder scudded through his being, a spasm of fleeting depression contorted his face. I could hear a microphone blaring away in his head, saying control yourself, control yourself. Control? Against what? What unknown celebrity occupies the apex of this triangle to which we are chained? If I could unravel this mystery I would blacklist this phantom forever so that we would become the soul-mates that I am trying to pollinate.

"You don't need a word for 'soul-mate'," answered Alexander, condescendingly. "Any language so rich in words of love must be based on an awareness of 'soul-mate'."

That was the first concrete clue you gave me, Alexander, confirming that you too had once shared your soul with another.

No, the words didn't give you away. It was your tinctured tone of condescension, your unspoken words of what does it matter if soul-mate exists or not in a language. It is an experience, not a word and I would have concurred whole-heartedly. But I forbade myself to tread further into this mystery. The day was to be a relaxed one without detours into our more densely populated emotional realms. Wine The Actress took over Alexander's teaching role.

"Alexander, after you remove people's shoes, denude them of their clothes and reduce them to silence, don't you find that stripped of these encumbrances, you eliminate the props which separate and divide nations and individuals. The naked human no longer wears the colours of his country or his tribe. People only wear their inner emotions, a rainbow of emotions which makes each man, woman and child kin to every other man, woman and child."

"And to punctuate your final comment, we are more alike than not, humans and animals. Isn't that what you mean?"

His eyes had regained their twinkle and his voice became gracious, debonair. His smile shone with the solar intensity, manifested earlier in the day. Oh, Alexander, how often your various dispositions resembled those of a Yo-Yo, that wooden disc with which children like to play. You would pitch out one mood – gentleness – then reel it in and then you would sling out another mood – scorn – and reel in that one. Maybe we weren't all that different. Maybe I concealed my moods more professionally than you.

"Come on, Alexander. Let's leave this tent. Guide me through this land of legally sanctioned slaughter."

Alexander, the auctioneer, raffled off the sights as we padded along slinky, carpeted corridors. The solar light streamed in immodestly, capturing every blemish of dirt and powder on the glass partitions which separated one display area from another. Guards in royal blue pants and shirts casually surveyed the clientèle entering each display area, searching out spies from unscrupulous competitors who would lower the price of fur coats and pelts in order to jack up the day's sales.

We halted midway down the shopping arcade. An electric drone, monotonous in its unrelenting sound, rang out from a sophisticated, calculating machine, summating numbers faster than you could create them. Commanding the machine, or vice versa, was a technician whose head pivoted on the same axis, turning to the right, then riveting back to face the machine. He was reading the sales slips which he then translated into the machine and an endless ticker-tape undulated down to the floor, coiling about itself, snake-like as if the key punching technician were a Moroccan flute player serenading his pet serpent. The act had no intermission.

"There seems to be an endless supply of money these days, Alexander, in spite of all the economic predictions to the contrary. Maybe money is growing on trees."

"Wrong, it's fur grown!"

Suddenly I could hear pop corn spiralling around in Alexander's brain.

"You know, money, like shoes, is another way of flaunting national differences and these run more than skin deep. Take the English and the Americans. They cry they're broke the moment they have to dent their savings accounts. The Germans and the Japanese don't make a fuss. Their money is like minted gold, ever increasing in value without the slightest effort on their part. Of course they work harder than most. The Italians prefer a more fatalistic approach, ignoring their lack of money today, thinking that tomorrow they'll look for discarded lira in a sewer. The Spanish, instead of complaining about poverty, hide their paucity of money behind a façade of false pride, and yet manage to come up with pesetas like a magician pulling rabbits out of an empty hat. The Arabs have such an embarrassing amount of wealth that they even line the walls of their tents in lime green hues called petro dollars."

"Similar to your cat box?"

"Sort of . . . This showcase we are now observing was inspired and owned by my late master. No one will threaten us if we explore it. Let's go in."

We wound our way through a crowded path of hospitable legs, offered by humans standing in stances of enjoyment, of contem-plation, of restlessness, of weariness. Vertical sky-scraper legs, juxtaposed next to fleshy, knock-kneed girders threatened to squish our innards to rigor mortis if the feet holding them up decided to lock together in parallel formation.

"Wonder what the view is like up there?" shouted Alexander, cocking an eyebrow on his leering visage. He was under a tent of starched linen, held up by a pair of shapely, female legs, freshly shaven. "She's got on sheer black, bikini panties. Her furry black hair is dangling out on all sides, escaping containment. I'd like to bury my face in her pussy." He stuck out his tongue and licked an imaginary puss.

"Alexander, you're a dirty old cat! Hey, from my vantage point,

48

I'm under someone who's got on pleated trousers."

"What do you see, Wine?"

"Indented pleats in the crotch."

"He must be one of those castrated males, who never developed his balls."

"You mean one of those males who plagiarizes the role of a man? No guts?"

"Right. Get a load of this! Here's a female who has her pussy locked up behind a snowy, white cotton habit which starts at her waist and runs down to her thighs, pressuring the flesh beneath into two bloated inner tubes."

"You must be referring to her girdle. My, my, my! Alexander, I'm underneath someone whose trousers girdle him. A few crotch seams are screaming from the strain of stretching. The cloth must be supporting an elephant's sexual apparatus. It looks like a convex bag ready to drop its load."

"Someone with a cock bigger than mine?" mused Alexander.

"Yes, but so what? You're only a cat. Anyone who has to strut his stuff so blatantly is nothing but a cock, a big bore. A big cock is fine, Alexander, provided you know how to do more than use it as a probing instrument. What really arouses me is an expansive soul . . ."

It was time for Alexander to meet Wine The Raunchy Cat, a long term unobtrusive resident in Wine's house of ethereal mist and occasional mirth. My poetic language was being supplanted by the language of the street.

"Alexander, we must make love on a bear-skin rug today, dust a few pelts with sperm!"

"All right, but later on, when the crowd thins out. I don't want any human stepping on the little bit of cock I've got."

We tunnelled through the last of the mass of human legs, free again to breathe. We were now in front of the audience, staring at a wall, completely decked out with panther fur, a sirening temptation to lure you to its furry surface where you could claw your way up and down and tingle from the touch of such a satiny texture, the sensation similar to two bellies of flesh, slowly massaging one another.

A fashion show was about to begin. Human mannequins, of the pencil variety, with painted up harlequin faces looking more like relatives of store window dummies, were rotating in stationary circles on a low ramp, one after the other modelling fur coats and fur jackets. It was suggestive of a high-class peep show – hands gracefully slipping open one side of the coat so you could glimpse the furry, inner-coat lining and be rewarded an unexpected surprise of a swelling breast pushing through skin-tight red sweaters, with nipples seeming to cry out, "Suck me, suck me."

"Alexander, I think they're selling more than furs."

"Sex always sucks out money, even from the stingiest pocket-book."

A tinny voice rang out. "Alexander." From the side-lines, an ermine clad woman, belonging to the fragile warble, scooped up Alexander with her arms and stroked his fur. Her face copied the geography of a moonscape. He turned on a purr he had never used toward me. It was the purr of mockery. The woman responded to the purr of flattery and insisted upon hugging him until he dug his claws into her neck, while licking her face.

"You naughty cat," she coyly said, putting him gently back down on the floor.

He grinned sarcastically and said to me, "She's the best client around, an old friend of my mistress. She wears furs when she bathes, furs to bed, furs upon rising and furs to talk to God. She also cries into fur hankies. She's looking for a fur to fuck. Her own furry fur is like a burned-out forest. She'd like some life planted inside of her. She's looking for a gardener desperate for a job. Even a cat will charge her up."

"Poor thing. It's awful to be ugly and lonely."

Alexander didn't hear me. He scampered off toward a nearby bar on one side of the ramp which was done up in fox fur. I could hear ice crystals chiming a pinging tune while they were being dropped into cut-glass goblets. Behind the bar were fur-lined shelves of sealskin sheltering plump bottles, gawky bottles, skinny bottles and squat bottles, all shimmering an artist's palette of colours; rum-red liquids, cobalt-blue liquors, golden-yellow Scotches, and rose-wine intoxicants. A well-rehearsed barman responded to every client's taste, playing with the bottles like a piano player who never strikes the wrong chord. The mixtures he concocted up were the witches brew of salesmanship, guaranteed to elicit signatures on blank checks, assuring the lineage of animal slaughter to be forever unbroken.

Upon seeing Alexander, the barman pulled out a bottle of cream and emptied it into a purple platter. He came out from behind the bar and placed the intoxicant in front of Alexander. After a few pats of friendship on Alexander's head, the barman retired to his post, leaving the important honcho to lap up the cream of his heart's content. Alexander slurped from thirst rather than from pain. He rejected a goodly portion of his potent potion and motioned me over to his side.

50

"Now the real show begins," he said, "the twentieth century version of the feeding of lion skins to the Christians."

Flash bulbs began to pop and pop, telescoping exaggerated looks of sultriness and importance on the models' faces. Fashion photographers were the Gods who promised immortality to those whose faces framed themselves within the camera's viewfinder. The models played mistresses to the photographers, pliantly following every order to pose "this way and now that way and lift your hand and hold it and look as though the fur were your lover whom you ardently want to caress"; each model would stroke the fur as if it were the unattended prick of the photographer and the stroking suggestively continued, provoking explosions of flash bulb orgasms.

The clicking of the cameras abated for an intermission while the models moved among clusters of prospective customers. It was time for business, time for the subliminal soft-sell to give way to hard-core persuasion. Salesmen came out from the dressing-room wings, all dappered up in blue silk suits and rose-coloured ties with nary a trace of a wrinkle, and their hair bore the same lacquered, sweet scent as that of the models peddling their wares. It was a discriminating crowd of men and women used to fine quality and they demanded to be shown every style, every permutation and combination that man could envision in the design of fur coats.

An hour later, creases of irritation began to mar the make-up of the models as they continued to trudge back and forth between the showroom and the fitting-rooms where they exchanged one fabulous creation for another. Finally the expression on the faces of the mannequins began to degenerate to an animal's ferocity, owing to this fatiguing drudgery, and you suspected that they wanted to bite the hide that had fed them.

One client in particular, doffed in a rabbit dress, insisted she be shown no less than fifty different coats. After reviewing the entire collection she became distraught. "Oh dear, I can't make up my mind whether I will buy another fur coat or not." Upon hearing that I would have bitten her too, had I been a model! She was offered a couch where she might lie down by a gracious salesman whose widely distended smile portrayed him as a mule with a buck-tooth grin on the verge of using a mule's language, wanting to bray a hee-haw, hee-haw at this poor woman who was near to fainting from the strain of undertaking this unctuous decision. The salesman's silence now hung in the air. He was breathlessly awaiting a word, one word which would lead to more words whereby the woman would pronounce the sacred marital vow between seller and buyer. "Oh speak to me", vibrated the message from the salesman's brain, the emission intensifying until the woman caught his unmistakable brain waves. Finally, she sealed the contact in a priestly tone. "I will buy a rabbit coat." Thus spake the client! She had obviously decided to mate her dress with a coat in the typical fashion of a match-maker.

"My goodness, Alexander, much ado about nothing. I'm glad I'm a cat donning the same coat day in and day out."

Alexander began to pontificate again.

"It is the 'nothing', the sublime superficiality which lubricates the wheels of civilization, churning out work for people, oiling their brains so they don't atrophy. There is an irony in the empty tasks and decisions to which most people devote their lives. In the arena of life they always insist upon boxing with light-weight challenges, such as you have just observed, in order to side-step the more heavy-weight issues of existence. That woman will go home and feel that she accomplished something today merely because she *laboured* over what to do. Think of the guilt she would have felt if her decision had been made effortlessly, or if she had made no decision because there was nothing worth-while to ponder. Civilization would crash to a halt if too many people microscoped what they normally regarded as important because they would see that their energies are geared mostly toward embellishing what is inconsequential. If that woman were as agog over a tree as she was over a fur coat and others bought her sentiments, the beauty of the world would unfurl such a splendour as has never been seen. But this nothingness, this mindlessness is what detonates the destruction that man heaps upon man and upon the earth and this inattentiveness to what is and isn't important is seeding a heredity of unconsciousness that in the end will turn the world into a gigantic sewer unless humans become aware!"

Alexander The Idealistic Preacher ended his sermon.

"Very inspiring, Alexander. It's too bad you aren't a human. You might give all those charismatic witch-doctors who preach to humans some stiff competition. However, you'd have to add one more topic to your repertoire."

"What's that?"

I outlined the letters on the rug: L O V E . "Humans must love one another. But first, every human must learn to love himself . . . . And now that this show is over, let's wander around and see what else is going on."

Before leaving the site of his deceased master's empire, both of us slurped up some of the remaining cream in Alexander's platter, a disgrace to our reputation as being dainty, genteel cats. Suddenly, I could feel a buzz of giddiness take hold of me, a giddiness created by all of the scenes we had seen so far. Everything was beginning to appear like a human comedy, an amusing, yet terrifying, surrealistic dream.

"A toast to our rainbow of selves, housed under one roof!" I exclaimed.

Alexander looked at me quizzically.

"A toast to my yellow, orange and red moods, my happy, sensual, fun *selves*. Today the purple, blue and black moods of disgust, depression and despair have flown away. One half of my population of selves is present and the other selves have been sent on an enforced furlough. Lead on Alexander, lead on." I giggled like a drunken cat.

I tagged behind Alexander as we walked down the corridor thinking that only a Siamese cat would obediently trot behind the male of her species. Or maybe I was more like a pup on her master's leash. He could have led me to purgatory that day for all I cared. Every minute was of such divine pleasure that had I died right then and there it would have been just fine. You could have then engraved on my tombstone: SHE DIED WITH A SMILE ON.

"Look at that!" shouted Alexander.

Along one glass partition stood a shoddy bench, worn out, exposing only its grainy wood, a bench not covered with fur!

"That must be a relic from the great depression of the thirties. Someone is going to lose his job for letting such a piece of poverty be seen midst all this sumptuous wealth."

"Maybe it was intentional. It looks like a sort of pit stop, a refuelling place where people can take off their shoes and relax from the rigours of fur buying," chuckled Alexander. "Take a look at the other side of the aisle, Wine."

A man was standing unobtrusively with a camera, clandestinely held in his hand. When a group of people sat down on the bench he held up his camera. But something was strange. Instead of aiming the camera directly at the people he pointed it at a ninety degree angle, or a quarter of a pie away from them.

"Why would he want to take pictures of a glass partition, Alexander?"

"Don't be fooled by what you see. He's got a gadget on top of the camera which is like a revolving periscope. He's after candid shots, wanting to strip away the veneer people wear when faced with an instrument of indelible imagery. He wants a true photo, untouched by artifice."

53

You could hear a series of clicks by this unbribable eye which was busy composing a rogue's gallery of the seated people seen amiss and messed up; a lady slumped on the bench with her legs spread apart as though she had just dismounted from a horse; a man furtively scratching his balls; an off-duty model picking her nose, watched by a teen-age boy whose eyes popped open, aghast that this epitome of beauty might do such a human thing; a couple giving one another private squeezes, the woman keeping a poker face, watching to see if anyone spotted her hand in between her consort's legs. The camera continued to faithfully record these naked moments and while I'm in favour of truth and nakedness, I asked myself what the camera was capturing other than exterior façades, a few universal habits. I will invent a special camera which x-rays the interior of the human soul, a camera whose click records a human heartbeat and I will insert into it a special spool of film which exposes the circulatory system of human emotions. And then I will mount an exhibition of all of these photos, extolling the beauty of humans, photos which rival those taken by this amateur photographer who only ridicules humans, portraying their ugliness. Any amateur photographer can expose deformity, squalour and unsightliness. It is only the true professional who knows how to capture the challenge of beauty.

"Alexander, he's playing a dirty trick."

"Well, he's got to have some fun, too."

And so I unplugged the cord from my philosopher's brain and flicked back on the button to my mirthful self – all work and no play makes for a very sober Wine.

A group of five well-dressed men divined this photographic ruse. They sprinted toward the photographer, hastily straightening their ties, drawing broad smiles on their faces, puffing themselves out as though they were peacocks, spreadying their plumage. The group stood motionlessly, unruffled by the delay of the photographer's having to insert a fresh roll of film.

"He could be using the slowest film and they wouldn't budge. It's the only time you'll see them in a state of repose where they aren't wildly gesticulating their arms."

"Who are they?" I asked.

"A group of Spaniards."

"So, you've also conducted studies on the national habits of picture posing!"

"Yes, I have. And Spain is the only country I know where the seduction of a camera will interrupt all other activities, including love-making, and that's saying a lot for a Latin temperament."

The camera's click smeared away their smiles.

"Vanity, thy name is no longer woman, thy name is a Spaniard . . ." I was tickled by a giggle from the cream percolating in my brain which was weighing less and less with every click of humour.

"WILL ANYONE KNOWING THE WHEREABOUTS OF THE OWNER OF A CAR WHOSE LICENCE NUMBER IS: C . . . A . . . T . . . ONE TWO THREE . . . FOUR FIVE SIX . . . SEVEN EIGHT NINE . . . PLEASE COME TO THE INFORMATION DESK . WE MUST *REMOVE* . . . and a slushiness garbled the rest of the waltz-time message sallying forth from the loud speaker. There was a hint of malice in the authoritative voice speaking on behalf of a human God in charge of the parking lot.

The coincidence was too much! Apparently some human had advertised his ardour for cats by mounting our species' name on his licence plate, using those numbers in their proper order to taunt the one quality which made us the envy of all pets – our remarkable longevity. The message was so perfectly timed that its zaniness nearly blew Alexander and me into laughing smithereens.

I flowed into my role as the histrionic actress I could be.

"Alexander, they know we are here," I said in a throaty, operatic voice that might have been the envy of the most famous soap-opera actress. "We've been found out! They'll be looking for us. Where shall we hide?"

"Stay with your act. I mean stay where you're at. Damn it, I'm slurring my words. Just play possum. Don't move. The hunters won't spot us if we're inert."

We froze into poses of two animals who might have been stuffed by a taxidermist, two kitties behaving like vaudeville comedians having a contest . . . who could hold his breath the longest . . . and I could feel my body puffing out . . . responding to a swelling, bubble-gum laugh . . . expanding and expanding until my insides began to quiver from the pressure of internal merriment, threatening to explode from a bursting belly laugh which would splatter alll of my innards hither and yon when I exhaled the next breath of buoyant hilariousness . . . . I was an intoxicated Wine . . . riding high on waves of joy authored by that wonderful day . . . seeing humour in everything; the biblical reverence of the money takers; the donkey salesmen who had yet to greet their twins – the asses; the fur-wearing folk who couldn't decide which fur to fuck; the poor, overworked models whose voices wanted to roar like animals in pain, wounded by the heavy load of fur they wore . . . and my imagination was beginning to leap out of control . . . I was now superimposing my own devilish message on the voice of God piped in from the parking lot, meowing to Alexander "S. O. S . . . . SAVE

55

OUR SOULS . . . It isn't an unattended car which bothers the horde of serious folk, fondling their furry purchases but a CAT . . . an escaped CAT streaking through The Fur Fair and won't the folks become paralyzed in their tracks with anger at the gall of this animal attending a function to which she hasn't been officially invited . . . She should have stayed at home, minding the kitties, waiting to be ritualistically summoned to the fair by a human gunshot, the calling card which admits all bearers free of charge to civilized celebrations such as this one . . . ."

Chortling snorts and guffaws of laughter came gushing forth with a torrential force from Alexander and myself . . . and no one else was privy to this booming noise we broadcasted over our special, private frequency . . . we collapsed from our fossilized poses, rolling from side to side in puddles of laughter . . . yes, two woozy cats drunk on laughter, inebriated by the silliness, the absurdness upon which the world of humanity spins, gyrating on the tip of senseless seriousness.

Finally, the last tear drop of bursting giggles dried.

"Ah, Alexander, we must pump some sort of joy back into the world where something other than fur excites human beings."

"Forget it, Wine. You'd be wasting your time. Come here and let me pump something else into you."

"Oh, you want to give me your direct object?"

Alexander kept his promise. He located a bear-skin rug where we made love.

No one arrested us for indecent public exposure, one more advantage to being a cat!

The Fur Fair slowly shuttered down the scenes of action, the furs no longer catalyzing the aphrodisiac potion of joy in the departing humans. The heartless pelts and the fur coats dangling from the thousands of metal racks were whisked away with the swiftness of an ambulance bearing bodies in agony to a first-aid station.

Alexander and I exited from The Crystal Palace at a slackened pace down the sumptuous rampway. The night air had a slight nip to it, cooling down the emotional afterglow of that wonderful day. A languid, descending fog of heaviness commenced to seep through our atmospheres of being, pushing each of us toward our separate planets of existence, the solution of our corresponding together-ness evaporating drop by drop. We were like lovers shucking off the golden glow of hidden intrigue, that time of imminent separation when one or both returns to other parts of one's life and night then becomes the darkness it always is. At least, I told myself, the memory of joy would lie tucked away within blinking distance.

Alexander arrived sooner than I at the portal of his house of depression while I procrastinated at an intersection of the moods of my mind. Should I resent the inescapable, let-down blues which always encores after a marvellous sense of elation, or should I listen to a voice in the grandstand of my mind reiterating that joy can be only an intermission in life, a refreshing pause to fortify the inevitable confrontation with the daily chores of life? How to fight copying Alexander's depression?

I began to scan the pages of my memory book. Somewhere there was written an experiment where I had sought to prove that euphoria could remain as a faithful companion if I did not try to mix it with the dross of existence. I had come back with my masters of the time from a wonderful trip. They had even given me permission to use the special aeroplane cat box so lovingly decorated in my favorite colours. I had decided to carry on with the helter-skelter arrangement of no fixed schedule which had been the key to our travelling. My eating and sleeping hours remained anarchistic, meals occurring at any hour of the day. Nighttime sleeping gave way to nocturnal cruising through the streets and sunshine hours ceased to be recorded by my eyes. I refused to lick myself clean, content to look like a vagabond traveller. If there was a pile of waste in my cat box I simply shoved it into a corner. I would do nothing smacking of routine. My only occupation was the sybaritic devotion to visual re-runs of my travelling adventures. This lasted for about a week. Then a malaise of discomfort attacked me. My delight in this hedonistic existence departed. I began to feel as if I no longer had any framework to my life, all was reduced to disorder. I suddenly wanted to return to my housekeeping chores. What pleasure this ritual gave me and what pleasure it was to resume a regular schedule of eating and sleeping! This dissipated my feeling of chaos, forcing me to reappraise the reputation of routine as the banality of life. Routine was now accepted as indispensable, an anchor tethering me to a sense of order to which I could always refer. It gave leverage to the conflicts which so often cursed and disrupted my existence. Indeed, this dullness of life supplied the necessary time when I could reflect upon the sediment settling down after romping with an unusual, exuberant experience.

So I sought to repeat to myself, as Alexander and I padded through the streets after the Fair, that after every joy there must be a humdrum time. Joy, like everything else, must be put away . . . in mothballs if you like.

Alexander instigated a barrage of angry words, his personal weapon for fighting his way out of his depressed shelter.

"You have just witnessed the inhuman legacy humans are creating for their children. What pride they display in their talent for killing defenceless creatures! Humans treating the world as if it were merely a slaughterhouse, maiming and murdering to soothe their petty vanities. And what an obscenity to charge admission for the privilege of viewing those dead creatures we saw today."

"Alexander, I can't react with the same vigorous hatred, the same sense of involvement you feel toward humans. I can't grasp or conceive of some gigantic lump of human masses. Humanity is too broad an idea for me. All I can envision is the one-to-one contact I have had with various members of the human race – my masters and mistresses. For everyone who might have born the genesis of destruction, another bore the seed of creation, the will to see nature and its creatures grow and flourish. To go on the warpath against humanity is to forget that our lives touch only a minute sampling of humanity, a sampling so varied that I see no purpose to condemn everyone under the same label of destruction. Evil deeds flash throughout the history of man with a glaring brightness. But what never seems to capture attention is the kindness manifested by humans. Think of the milk donor who night after night cares enough to take the trouble to give us liquid refreshment. Some may abuse his kindness but that's not his fault. Think of your mistress who treats you like a prince, an Alexander The Great. We forget this breed of humaneness because kindness, being so soothing and so anesthetising, doesn't have the same jolting, spectacular quality as violence."

Alexander lashed out at me.

"When the human hunters come to gun you down you will revile them for failing to design a legacy which protects life."

"But you said earlier we aren't in danger of bullets. All right, I see by the look on your face that you don't appreciate my moment of humour. Of course I'll fight the human hunters. But guns are only one form of destruction. What about the day-to-day responsibility of protecting life, not only physically but emotionally? How many cats and humans have perished for lack of stroking, lack of warmth, lack of love? Too many, Alexander, far too many. We cannot protect the whole of our species from physical murder but we can do something equally as important. We can extend to each and every cat whose life touches us the kind of legacy which promotes, enhances and fertilizes his emotional growth. You said at the fair, humans must be aware. We must *all* be aware, aware that

58

our actions ripple through a multitude of cats, and humans. The quality of how you interact with one creature sets the tone for how that creature will interact with another. This is how we create our "last will and testament" not only to our blood line benefactors but to all catkind. If each of us took time to disseminate joy, laughter and compassion to each cat we knew, we would be doing our small, but important part in making this a more tolerable world for some. We wouldn't achieve any grand utopia but at least we wouldn't be the instigators of destruction."

"That's all rather esoteric, highfalutin', idealistic. The only issue which has any real importance is survival, teaching the skills to stay alive. That's my legacy to my offspring . . ."

How you have exasperated me, Alexander! First, wrenching away from our splashing fountain of earlier humour, shutting off the jocular flow by your seriousness. As always your depressed mood trailed into me along the highway of our unspoken vibrations. Instead of being contaiged by your blue mood I should have leaped upon you and given your cock a couple of licks, restoring it to its earlier robust enthusiasm. But it would have been too late. Whatever happened in your soul also swayed the tone of your sensuality. And then you criticized me for the same idealism and the same value of responsibility belonging to you as though my speech mimicked the tender part you kept trying to squash out in yourself. Idealism and survival don't cancel one another out. Survival simply tries to guarantee a base for the realization of idealism. My mistake was in committing the same unpardonable sin of opening myself up, exposing something I believed in, which smacked of just enough compassion to seduce you against your will to draw closer to Wine the Gentle Cat. The less you knew of me, the easier it was to keep me at bay from your heart . . . As I search my memory book now, I don't seem to locate a single entry where you ever asked me one direct question about myself. This is a telling clue to support my hypothesis . . . Yet, it's also possible that Wine The Listener was a rare discovery for you in a world not accustomed to cultivating the art of listening. And this Wine gave you the full glare of a spotlight where your presence radiated itself to a rapt audience of one. This Wine you welcomed . . .

"Washington! WASHINGTON! You lazy bum. Get your arse out on the street and hustle for some food. You being the oldest gotta learn it's high time you take some responsibility. I can't go caring for six kittens all day long, cleaning them and finding them food without some help. Get along now and don't come back 'til you got something for us. You'd think you're some sort of kitty with a fancy pedigree the way you loaf about, putting on airs when folks walk by. You think they're gonna give you a hand out? Wise up. Nobody gives you nothing in this world. You gotta fight for what you want."

"Aw, Maw. Stop nagging me. I found a rabbit foot today . . . That's a good luck sign. Someone is gonna give us a pile of food."

"I don't care if you found a four-leaf clover. That's only good for cows who chew their cud. We ain't cows. We're cats."

"Maw, what kind of cat are you if you don't believe in lucky omens?"

"A hungry cat. Now let's stop all this foolish talk. Get out on that street and hustle. And one more thing. Make sure you don't step in front of no humans. No one wants a black cat crossing his path . . ."

It was too dark to see you, Washington, whoever you are. But if you're listening I want to give you a big hug. That dialogue with your mother applied just the right touch to shove Alexander toward his more optimistic rainbow of selves, his brighter colours.

"That mother has the right idea," said Alexander. "She's trying to tutor her kitty in a school of values which teaches respect for hard work. Now that's the kind of legacy I'm preparing for my offspring. Even though I'm a rich cat my kitty is going to learn what it means to forage in the streets, eeking out a survival existence just as I had to do when I was younger. I'm not going to let him turn into a lazy bum like that Washington."

Alexander The Father, a personality scarcely known, had introduced himself. The sternness in his voice suggested the echo of another voice, one I surmised as having belonged to his father, the intonation unconsciously well-imitated after countless listening sessions. Then the voice dubbing halted. Another Alexander, independent of his father's influence, took over. The taut muscles in his face were being transposed into his solar smile by the image of his offspring. Now the voice of Alexander The Proud Papa debuted.

"You should see my kitty, Wine . . . he's like a tiger. He already knows how to scale walls – I taught him this before his claws were fully developed – and he's learning to distinguish different scents emitted by humans, knowing which ones might harm him. He's the only kitty around his neighbourhood who isn't afraid of water. As a matter of fact he took to the water like a duck. He fell into the swimming pool of the house where he lives with his mother and instead of putting up a big fuss, shrieking and hissing in that way that most cowardly kitties do, he started to paddle around. I was nearby at the time and a little nervous he might drown so I got into the water with him and gave him a few swimming lessons. He sure is a bright kitty. He can already count to nine and when I ask him the meaning of nine lives he says 'It means I've got nine times to fuck up.' Of course he doesn't grasp the full significance of this yet but he will, the first time he gets emotionally stung by life. But he'll survive. He's a fighter just like me. He even looks like me when I was his age."

Alexander The Father was a decidedly different character from the other Alexanders. The role suited him. This precinct of his existence was not marked by thorny ambivalences imbedded in the rest of his soul. Here he walked confidently and securely.

"Alexander, why didn't you have more kitties?"

"Because his mother didn't want any more. She didn't really want Claude, he was an accident, but now she has a use for him. She knows she can get whatever she wants from me. All she has to do is say 'Claude misses me' and she's got me back in the house with her until she decides to go off on another sexual mission – see how many cocks she can squeeze dry . . . that's her whole purpose in life . . . it's why I refuse to live with her for more than a few days every so often . . . I only do it to be near Claude . . . even my own father would like to have a poke at her . . . I've watched her many times stir the cauldron of sex, parading herself in front of my father's lewd eyes . . . ."

Once again, memory made Alexander's smile set beyond the horizon of visibility, all because I had opened Pandora's box by a simple question. The evil which flew out of it was further proof that Alexander had mated with another relative of his father's cruelty, one more battlefield where a straying mate reinforced the worthlessness of attachments between living beings. Did Alexander have any allies in his past retinue of caring cats besides his mother? Talk about the legacy of humans slaughtering animals! Alexander's father and his cat mate were the indisputable heads of a branch office of genocide in the cat world! No wonder Alexander had to will his offspring a legacy in survival for it enabled him to keep his own survival skills finely honed. When your cat mate and the one who sired you conspire in the backroom of lust it is a form of cannibalism – a shredding machine for one's soul. Once again Alexander had taken me swimming in the cesspool of his family secrets. But not for long!

The taping of his words faded to an inaudible level. The only noise I could register was a repeating, thunderbolting boom, a name playing over and over in quadrophonic sound in my head. . . Claude . . . Claude . . . Claude . . . The one name I had denied saying as if by refusing to pronounce it I could control the impact of my powerful ghost from parading across the panorama of my

61

existence. What a nasty trick of fate! Alexander's offspring had been christened with the same name as my once beloved Claude. Was destiny teasing me again? Was there some special mystical bond yet to be discovered in the trinity of Alexander, Claude and Wine?

Oh Claude, it has been so long since my mind blared out your name. When I utter it I feel I am speaking a synonym for intimacy and your name flashes with neon brightness across the foreheads of every male cat a reminder of what I have lost, of what I relentlessly seek to regain. I was not mourning the lost of joy between Alexander and myself as we tramped away from The Fur Fair that night. No. It was something deeper, sadder. I was fighting the recognition that the interlude of intimacy with Alexander was at best an intermission between two cats who were orbiting in separate worlds . . . Intimacy as we knew it, Claude, is such an exclusive world of twoness, togetherness, so much so that it excludes all others – there's no desire to be with anyone except your beloved one. Yet the day comes when some tiny need magnetizes you away from this communal sharing as it must, for there is no single condition in life which can furnish all the nourishment we require. And then when we satiate this need we seek once again to return to this exclusive world of intimacy and when we do not have it we go into mourning.

Oh Claude, why did I forfeit the sharing of both the marvellous and the mundane with you? Why did the clock of my development have to point to a different hour than yours? If I were to see you on the street, could I synchronize now what I couldn't mesh with you then? A purely rhetorical question. You have another life now, with another cat. I hope she treats you well. You deserve the best. You deserve a mature cat, someone who knows how to give. When you found me you found such an immature kitty, a kitty who was recovering from one more defeat in life – the loss of the black cat. Your love rescued me from despair and filled up the four chambers of my empty heart so that I could rejoin life. Thus began the saga of your giving. How much you gave me in so many ways! You opened up my sense of awareness to the thoughts and feelings in other cats because with you as my anchor, I no longer had to think solely of myself. You helped me see the value in the doing of a thing, rather than concerning myself with the end result, for nothing has an end you used to say. And when I needed a laugh you were there to provide it! How you pampered and spoiled me with your inexhaustible patience! You read my every mood so clearly. If my palate demanded a bit of tuna fish you would scurry through every garbage can no matter how long it took just to please my appetite. When I was sick and too weak to move you would be the one to lick me clean.

You were my sun toward whom I leaned for the oxygen of my life!

You were my eyes, my ears. Your thoughts became the seedlings of mine. I not only lived beside you, *I lived inside of you*. Truthfully it seldom occurred to me to exit from the security of your soul. I was too enraptured, too hypnotized by your brilliance, your experience, your rich tapestry of emotions.

You were my schoolroom of life, my teacher. I was the passive pupil sponging up your teachings. And hadn't this always been the pattern of my life? Pick other brains! Gulp down with gluttony, rather than in a dainty fashion, all knowledge and experience beyond my body boundaries. Eat the world up. Do it so quickly that I didn't notice the tiny pangs of indigestion when something did not sit well inside my brain or heart, when only instinct sang a song of dissonance. I was gobbling up life with no concern for the digestive process. And you, Claude, were abetting me by your nursing and your suckling. You bloated me up with your endless giving until I couldn't receive any more. You were a natural born giver. Giving was your greatest pleasure. Your past experience as a loving father to the offspring you had had before we met transferred itself to me as if in the loss of your kitties I became the new substitute. And that suited both of us!

But evolution pushed me out of your womb. An uncontrollable compulsion to move on, alone, along the road of a nameless quest. As your adopted offspring I had to leave home sooner or later. As your protégé and student I had to annul our connection. I was no longer comfortable with the inequality, the imbalance which tilted our relationship where my light-weight force was no match for your dominance.

Imbalance in life, in nature, is an unacceptable attack on our homeostasis, on our balance, and so it must be righted, be put back into equilibrium. I had to cast my own shadow instead of living in yours. Perhaps you too were reacting to this disharmony for there were times when you raged at me, your blind anger unable to pinpoint the words which pressed so heavily on both of us, words which said *grow up*. I made some progress in this aspect – the time I told you to resume contact with your kitties. But that was only a beginning step. The time had come for me to author my own anthology of life without your prompting. This wasn't a conscious conspiracy against you. The richness of your teachings had pollinated all of the natural elements in me, elements demanding room for growth, an inner dictatorial demand which I had to obey. All offspring of mother nature – plants, trees, flowers – sprouting from tiny seedlings, seek to grow, to expand, to ripen, to bloom. All living creatures are also offspring of mother nature and must accept the dictates of her legacy to flourish. Maybe you can tame animals but you can't domesticate their evolution nor that of any living being.

So, dear Claude. It was not freedom but an inextricable bond to mother nature which wrenched me away from you. Unfortunately nature's legacy and yours collided. Evolution of a being is basically a solo path, contradicting the "twoness" of intimacy. Perhaps the "we part" of a couple only successfully evolves when the "you part" and the "me part " are clearly delineated, when each can exist alone anywhere, anytime, when the thing called "self" has enough form and shape, enough solidity so that the presence of another being is not a threat to one's security. By going our separate ways, we never had a chance to test this out.

Dear Claude, to have been the beneficiary of your intimacy is such a bitter-sweet legacy. What a void the absence of intimacy brings! Its narcotic power sends me scurrying after any source giving out the slightest hint of it. Whenever I meet another creature willing to expose a minute portion of his personal world, I am an easy target for seduction – sexual seduction and the emotional seduction upon which friendship is formed. And no matter how many abortive attempts result in this search for intimacy, such as the one with Mack, I am still an intimacy addict looking for a fix.

I cannot renounce intimacy. It is the gold of life. It is the gold that you Claude, and I unearthed. It is the gold in Alexander's life with his offspring. It is the golden legacy for which all beings arduously hunt. This, perhaps is the common bond threading the trinity between Alexander, Claude and Wine.

Maybe love is misnamed and ought to be called intimacy.

Now that you have heard the playback of my inner dialogue which blocked out whatever else you said about your Claude, what do you think, Alexander? Does the worshipping tone of voice I employed make it sound like I was mated to a cat God? If Claude erected a pedestal for me, I reciprocated. I built one for him which towered over mine. And from this lowly height I gazed up at him in wide-eyed wonder. This ought to give you a true reading of how insignificant I thought myself to be. Surprised? Maybe those humans listening to me are a little perplexed. Surely the cat slinging out the insights she does couldn't have developed from a base of nothing. What about the B.C. period of her life, the epochs "Before Claude," the Wine who was loved by her professor of love and the black cat. What about Wine's early kittyhood, her friends and those who brought her into the world? Surely Wine The Adventuress and Wine The Curious Kitty were clearly in evidence at a very early age. These Wines brought her considerable attention from everyone who knew her, everyone except herself. All these cats whose importance and influence were supposed to have been felt by Wine were like mirrors, unable to offer a clear reflection of what Wine was like. It wasn't until Claude that Wine got an inkling that relationship with another being is the mirror in which you begin to discover yourself.

It was the intimacy with Claude which awakened my dormant possibilities without naming them. This I had to do myself. And after living inside of Claude I had to relocate myself back inside my own skin. The next stage was to get out of my skin in order to perceive myself in truth and in depth. For this reason I have to get on with the business of telling our story, Alexander. I think I am becoming more than what I was when I began this serpentine monologue. . . .

Alexander and I automatically wound our way to The Milk Bar as if the gesture of being in a public place would rekindle the daylight radiance of The Fur Fair. But the rush-hour commotion of a huge crowd of cats proved to be more than I could tolerate. The noise level produced by the boisterous throng was being bolstered to a new high owing to extra rations of milk set out by the generous patron. It seemed like a contest was in the making – who could shriek the loudest – and the orchestra of pitches composed a series of dissonance akin to warring fingernails on a blackboard. My sensory apparatus verged on the threshold of pain. My head felt like a vice was pressing on it. The carnival atmosphere of The Fur Fair had already supplied enough stimuli and to subject myself to any more at this moment was beyond my endurance. My only desire was for silent repose where I could leisurely sift through what memories I would retain from this special day.

When Alexander rushed to the milk bowls he broadcasted he was turning me out for the night. I welcomed his detour from our togetherness. His need to move away from me and mine to retire coincided. No wonder I felt no sense of personal injury.

"Alexander, I'm going to the garbage can. If you want to return there later, I'll leave the lid off so you can come in quietly."

"Don't be a party pooper, Wine," complained a faceless cat from Alexander's retinue of friends. "The evening is just beginning."

"Enjoy yourself," I said.

A block away from The Milk Bar I began to breathe in the sweet aroma of silence. Such a special moment! The earth hanging in balance, framed by stillness. That same feeling of peace after a friendly invasion by invited guests who finally depart, leaving in their wake a lovely quietness. Silence, my nocturnal friend, my downy bed upon which all the glitter and rust left behind by the cabaret show of life comes to rest. Silence, my needed tranquillizer, soothing the mind which was never designed ceaselessly to record the activities of life without regular periods of surcease. To be denied silence was to open the door to madness where stimuli would rage out of control, pounding away on the inner lining of my skull. Silence, the rejuvenator of psychic energies, more restful than sleep: for dreams often attacked me with more ferocity than the howling winds of a stormy night. And this night proved to be no exception.

The gateway to sleep greeted me the instant I was comfortably ensconced in the garbage can. A showy dream on a variation of fur took me on a long excursion. A fleecy white cloud was winging me through an emerald sky with the evenness of a glider in motion. From somewhere came a hushed, repetitious sound of a lamb . . . "Bah . . . bah . . . bah . . ." I looked to see if anyone was sharing my voyage upon this sheep-skin cloud but I couldn't detect the presence of anyone, so I stretched out my body upon the furry warmth. I couldn't resist the temptation to sample the rippling texture of my downy chariot and as I tenderly stroked it a human voice was heard. "Baa, baa white sheep have you any wool?" No human could be sighted belonging to the voice. A few moments later my cloud coasted down to earth, landing with a velvet lightness. I caught a glimpse of a lady with long red hair playing a purple guitar. She was regally seated in the centre of an enormous couch, upholstered in peach-dyed mink, a profusion of scattered, multi-coloured pillows composed of cat skins hugging her on both sides. Hers was the human voice I had heard and she kept crooning the same song in a rich, lilting voice and then she ended her nursery rhyme and began copying the contented purring of a cat in the aftermath of sexual repose. From a nearby grove of trees, a number of kittens and older cats haltingly peered out from behind a broad expanse of chunky olive trunks where they had been hiding, their eyes like arboreal satellites. Twisting, gnarled tree limbs were stretching torturingly in every direction, suggesting something sinister was about to happen. The spectators became more and more brazen, venturing closer and closer to the lady with the purple guitar. The olive trees, too, responded to her seductive voice, initiating a tantalizing strip-tease, casting off their bark with the slow motion of a young virgin shyly dropping her dress to her feet. The undergarments of bark exposed black, silky, seal skin. A contagion of nudism pervaded the air. The crowd of cats, now thoroughly hypnotized by the haunting lullaby of purrs, began to claw away at their skins with a perverse exuberance until they nakedly stood with only their bare bones phosphorescing a silvery glossiness, their bones clicking like castanets.

Suddenly this human temptress eyed me with a quizzical stare, her eyes questioning why I was still dressed in my natural skin. Rather than answer her, I darted away from this grotesque drama, crying "S.O.S.... S.O.S.... SAVE OUR SKINS... SAVE OUR SKINS..." I kept running and running, looking frantically for a shelter, a place to hide and just as my breath began to give out I located a cave where I hoped no-one would find me. It looked like a giant beehive. From inside, shafts of steel moonlight slivered in. The light unmasked an enormous wine rack housing a multitude of wine bottles, each bearing a different label of the varying vintages of my character: Wine The Dreamer, Wine The Thinker, Wine The Fool, Wine The Joker, Wine The Coward, Wine The Warrior. And there were more bottles too! I decided to have a big sip of wine from one bottle which had no label. Surely some of the intoxicant would tame my anxiety about being hunted down. After my mouth pulled out the cork, a voice jumped out of the bottle saying "Come... Go... Come... Go..." It was Alexander's voice. A moment later a drop of red wine fell to the ground and instantly materialized into a gigantic teardrop which spoke with my voice saying, "Please Alexander, make up your mind, do you want me or not?"...

Abruptly the curtain slipped down over the dream, unhinged by a loud, rasping noise. Had the red-haired lady located me, discarding her guitar for a tin drum? I partially awakened, disoriented and confused. Where was I?

Alexander had stumbled upon the metal lid of the garbage can. He was cursing to himself as he made his way up the side and then slid down next to where I was curled up. Remnants of the sleeping world hung heavily before my sleeping eyes. Was this the Alexander of my nightmare or Alexander The Caring Cat ploughing his way through the hazy mist of my veiled eyelids? Had the lady with the purple guitar performed another magical trick, posturing herself in the guise of my solar smile, or was this a flesh and blood Alexander?

The vividness of the dream shoved me into Alexander's waiting paws and I embraced him with an arduous fervour. The strength of my feelings must have deeply affected him for he soldered his body to mine as though someone were trying to wrench me away. To be held by him was to affirm that the reality of the dream world was no match for the challenge of a waking reality in which Alexander's body cocooned me from harm. The touching of his paunch supplied an ample testing ground for my preferred reality where with each stroke of his body, the lady with the purple guitar was banished further and further into a dreamless exile.

Unaware of the source of my passion, Alexander lit a fuse.

"With treatment like this, I'll move in with you Wine, full time."

All traces of sleep were now fully discharged.

A proposal of intimacy! Alexander offering the most precious gift he could present, declaring himself ready to slay his negative ambivalence. Finally! A declaration of affirmative action made by Alexander The Space Explorer who had travelled to many a distant star and finally he was touching down on my planet of existence which had waited for his landing.

But his touchdown sent out a red alert, sirening a warning! Panic swept through me with a gale force. My heart started to throb the beat of fear. No longer was I threatened by the shadowy figure of the lady with the purple guitar. Alexander's overture draped a new menace whose essence was at first confusing. How shocking to discover myself recoiling from his offer as though I had touched a hot, electrical wire which made all of my fur stand up on end!

Wine The Cat was now feeling Alexander's emotional ambivalence, the same conflict between shared intimacy with another being or remaining alone.

Had I deceived myself about intimacy? Did I really desire it? Was I *ready* for it again? This last question blew about me very lightly, its significance rooting itself much later when I realized that readiness is too visceral an experience to be analyzed. You know you are ready for something when you can devote yourself to it in a totally effortless manner, when your action is given a green light by your vibrations or instincts without the punctuation of a question mark. But what obstacle blocked the readiness of Alexander and me to join ourselves in a state of intimacy? This was a question I couldn't ignore.

A fragment of my dream skirted back to me, blown up to a

clearly perceptible size, crystallizing the conflict. Once again I could see the bottle of wine from which Alexander's contradictory message had escaped – come, go, come, go. In reviewing the historical pendulum of his emotional swings toward and away from me it was obvious that the climax of my dream had highlighted what I didn't want to admit to myself, for truth telling sessions hurt when they unmask illusions. It is as though we are sculptors of myths and the characters *we* so skilfully build up begin to crumble because there is no material other than illusion into which we can cast them.

The exposure of illusion revealed an essential cornerstone to intimacy. I did not *trust* Alexander. His emotional erraticism had drawn an invisible membrane of self-protection around me during our various encounters. The membrane might have gone unnoticed if the offer of intimacy hadn't brushed against it.

Yes, I wanted intimacy. Yes, I wanted to share. But I couldn't delude myself any longer about the quality of Alexander's sharing. At best it could only be fickle, unpredictable, given and snatched away from moment to moment. Maybe I was beholden to Alexander The Caring Cat who had rescued me one day from my despairing self by his gift of solar warmth. But this act ought to be viewed as a charitable contribution. Surely any reinbursement on my part stopped at the point where I was obliged to deliver my trust if it wasn't truly felt. I did not have to jump into the fire of an emotional hell because of a faulty accounting system in which I equated kindness with intimacy. Alexander had the capacity to be compassionate. But he had also confirmed his unreadiness for sustained sharing with me. My sixth sense had known this with its typical cunning from the outset of our relationship. But as always it was several steps ahead of my conscious awareness and only now in sending out a warning did it assume its role as the prompter in my life, waiting for the moment when truth was ready to be faithfully rendered.

But we do not yield to truth as rapidly as it presents itself to us. While one eye focused on Alexander with mistrust, the other eye still needed to view him with hope, a hope that with time Alexander might be able to choreograph a dance of intimacy with me which excluded his perennial one step forward, one step backward. In the meantime his offer of intimacy was discarded, fixed with no greater meaning than an amusing pastime on a rainy afternoon when two kitties play house, each pretending a part he will someday grow into. Then I promptly forgot the offer.

It's impressive the ease with which I effaced Alexander's words after that night. Only in the retelling of events does the amnesia lift pertaining to my mistrust of him. And why was it so necessary to clamp down on further considerations of this? Why did I blank it out? Why did I remember so many little details and forget a fragment which was to be a clear-cut watermark plotting the future road of our togetherness?

Why this ever present shyness when I'm confronted with mistrust?

It's not that I don't live without caution or calculation in assessing other beings. But this sizing-up is usually a routine response on behalf of self-preservation. Nor can I equate caution with mistrust because the latter is such a negative road toward all creatures, a cynical assumption that all beings are evil and out to destroy you. In this sense, mistrust contains a lethal quality which corrodes compassion, love and concern for others. Without these finer fibres lining our hearts we are fossilized in life, converted to the diabolical religion of cynicism. And it is the cynic who so often relegates intimacy to the unattainable world of illusion, the cynic who draws all creatures as motivated solely by the most base of motives, the cynic who proclaims that living creatures in the pursuit of their own well-being never rise high enough above their own needs to see to the needs of others. Certainly this is sometimes true. All living beings have to perform the essential tasks which guarantee their survival. The mistake made by the cynic in ascribing all creatures as purely selfish misses the point that survival is more than the physical protection of one's life. There are also the unseen struggles to come to grips with numerous crises which plague all of us sporadically. Under such circumstances it is not selfishness motivating us to forget the needs of others but the need, the urgency, to get ourselves back into psychic balance. If we do not see a mass of all-giving saints it is because of the precariousness of this balance from which we often totter.

To channel one's vision through the eyes of a cynic is to be paralyzed in life, passively saluting the rising and setting of the sun with gloom, expending no energy or enthusiasm for the gifts life gives us. I suppose cynicism is a lazy cat's answer to an easy existence – no emotional strings are ever vibrated. But if you seek to defy the lethargy of cynicism then you must greet each morning with a freshness, without dwelling on the disappointments of yesterday; you must guard your wonder and joy so jadedness does not disease you. And most challenging of all, you must sustain the hope, the belief, that failure in a relationship with one being does not mean failure with all beings. Perhaps failure is not applicable to describing the demise of relationships. Maybe the word is *unreadiness*.

I was often tempted to charge all male cats as being charlatans the moment one of them disappointed me. Indeed, those cats with whom I had encounters after Claude drew out of me a scent of mistrust, for they were all inferior in quality to him. They toyed with my emotions, more accidentally than purposely, because within the drama of each affair they sought their vengeance on for cruelty to animals which had befallen them in previous relationships. It was as if I had to atone for the emotional crimes of neglect and carelessness wrought by those cats who had preceded me in their hearts. At such a rate of disappointment I knew I was going to exhaust my nine cat lives at a premature age, without time for my hair to turn grey. Each failed relationship – and I only use the word as I thought of it then – became cause for questioning my capacity for intimacy. Notice I say *my* capacity, not *theirs*. By scanning inward I devised a way to buffer myself against resenting the stack of misdemeanours enacted by these cats, though there were times when with the first rays of morning sunlight despair over their unkindness would overcome me. Then my morning would collapse. Then my life would collapse. Such was how Alexander had found me, hope draining away.

Such was how Claude had known me too.

Dear Claude! I am beguiled by the memory of your ambushing all renegades from life whose religion was cynicism and mistrust. I envision you as a Zeus-like force, a robust doer of action, not a being who lamented what you couldn't possess. You knew that to live with regret and hate was to live in a contaminated atmosphere.

Wait a minute! Who was I just describing? Claude? Or myself? Have I forgotten Claude's paranoid mistrust of other cats, his suspicions that all males were constantly plotting to seduce me? Am I forgetting a Claude who could behave like a mad devil, bound up in some mysterious form of moroseness when he would toy for hours with the idea of suicide? Am I forgetting a Claude the stealer of my emotional virginity, who wrenched away my rose-coloured glasses of naivete and trust, lecturing on the necessity of recognizing the world for what it was – a cold, hard place where you had to study every move in the chess game of cat behaviour?

Whose brand of warmth was the softening agent for this streak of distrust in Claude's multi-layered cast of characters? Mine, of course! Who was the ringleader always plotting the death of cynicism and mistrust? ME!

Did I exclaim not long ago that I didn't know where the boundaries of my being began and Claude's left off? Was there really this blurredness, this haziness of overlapping identities, or was it the eternal, wrinkled problem of thinking myself to be less than what I really was?

Another drop has just been poured into my cup of self-love.

Keep on the track, Wine. Your panning for golden truths is paying off. One more layer is being stripped away, exposing the real colour of reality. Bravo!

One less link has just been unclasped from the chain binding me to Claude. Claude is no longer a full-time God. Does this move me closer or farther from him?

But if I'm going to sell reality then there still remains another truth. Time has not tarnished Claude's gift of intimacy. If anything, it is more valuable and more real now than when I had it.

Excuse me, Alexander for this long interruption. It seems I have just demoted Claude to a lower position on my worshipping tower. He is now only a part-time God though he still remains on the payroll of my heart.

Alexander didn't wait long for an answer to his offer of intimacy. He dropped off to sleep in a milky bliss. The subject never debuted again. If this was one more of his devious tests he never let on.

Another preoccupation arose. Did words uttered by a heavy milk drinker mean anything? If, as was commonly supposed, cats only spoke their honest sentiments while under the influence of intoxicants, what happened during their no-drinking hours? Were all their words to be used as discarded rubbish? Yet, Alexander manifested none of the effects of heavy drinking. He seemed to live in a world of lucidity twenty-four hours a day. To his knowledge, no intoxicant had ever been invented to erase pain, only to soften its serrated edges. But a milk addict is still a milk addict I told myself, lying in the darkness next to him. What I couldn't accept on a daily basis was the over-dependence he had on powers other than his own. Nor could I criticize him. Milk was for him what Claude had been for me.

If Alexander had come to occupy one of the four chambers in my heart, was he ever going to move into the second one or would he vacate my heart completely? Who was going to initiate which move?

* * * * *

The following morning after The Fur Fair an alien presence drew me out of my sleep. Two cherubic children were staring down at us, two little human boys the age of mischief. I rapidly shuttered my eyes to the position of narrow slits, while unobtrusively spying upon these intruders. Alexander was still immune to the hinting rays of sunlight, his sleeping face twitching intermittently as he snorted out asthmatic wheezes, the sound like a hideous prelude to death.

"Which one do you like?" said one of the children.

"I don't know. I think the one with the red hair. I've never seen a cat with that colour before," replied the other.

"Yes, I like that one too. It's prettier than the grey, mangy cat," said the first child in an apprenticeship's voice for judging future beauty contests.

How dare you call me an "it" I thought. My dignity is bruised. Of course I'm prettier than Alexander. I'm a female!

"What sex do you think they are?"

"I bet they're both female, both of them are kind of fat. I bet the grey one is going to have kittens. Look how big its belly is'" said the more innocent child.

"I think they're both pregnant," said the beauty expert, switching his role now to that of a gynaecological authority.

"Do you think your mother would let you keep one of them?" quizzed the first child.

"She wouldn't have to know. We could trap them by putting the lid over the can and then we could take them to my basement and watch them have babies," said the expert voice of a kidnapper.

In my imagination I began to envision horns growing out of the heads of these angelic creatures.

"But how are we going to feed them?" said the naive voice, "If we have to sneak down to your basement every day won't your mother become suspicious?"

"That's easy. We can let them out of the can every few days and let them hunt rats. My teacher says that cats like rats. We can also put a big saucer of milk in with them. We always have lots of milk bottles in the house and my mother won't notice if one is missing."

That did it! Two humans plotting to rob us of our freedom! Cage us in! Destroy the sanctuary of our garbage can! And wanting to treat us like common alley cats without a discriminating palate. To think that a teacher was spreading such propaganda that rat meat was substantial food was scandalous. No wonder the quality of education moulded such biased minds. Let their teacher feast upon this choice delicacy she touts. Let her find out that rat meat is no competitor for the more succulent taste of fish. But most notorious of all was the idea that these creatures wanted to encourage Alexander's milk addiction. This was too much! No, no, little children. You'll not get us without a fight.

I started hissing in a low, menacing tone. Maybe that would keep them at bay. Alexander came awake. Over our special frequency channel I told him to play possum with full seriousness, unlike the dress rehearsal we had humorously undergone at The Fur Fair.

"Hey," said the more timorous child, "it doesn't sound very friendly."

"It's probably scared. My mother told me you have to pet them very gently and then they won't be frightened any more. Go on, pet it!"

No hand appeared on the horizon of the garbage can. Evidently my hisses were clamouring the language of battle.

"Scaredy cat, scaredy cat, you're afraid to touch the cat," taunted the boy whose list of credentials in gynaecology and beauty contest judging was growing to include cat psychology. What a blasphemer! Slandering my species – affixing "scaredy" to cat.

A pudgy hand crept over the rim of the can and began to creep toward me with the speed of a dead limb. I raised the pitch of my angry hissing, a last warning to rectify the misunderstanding that my hissing came from fear. The child did not take heed. I knew I was going to have to teach him a lesson about respecting the privacy of others. So I extended my claws and just as his hand was about to reach me I lashed out and scratched it, careful not to puncture the skin. It hurt me more than it did him, though to hear his shriek you would have thought he was in mortal pain. Fortunately I was wise to the counterfeit cries of children and felt no guilt. That'll teach you not to fool around with strange cats, I thought. Let that scratch be a lesson to you, a legacy, I mused. Maybe you'll think twice the next time you want to domesticate me and lock me up. How would you like it if I put you in a cage and took away your freedom without giving you a choice? Maybe I don't speak the same language as you do but you still ought to be able to read my vibes, respect my needs.

"You're just a big baby," bullied the other child, unmoved by the tears of his companion. "Watch me grab it by the scruff of its neck."

Playtime was over. Alexander armoured my body with his so that the bold hand which reached in grabbed him instead of me. Alexander hissed out a hideous screech, closely resembling the cry of a vulture attacking its prey. He latched on to the raising arm of the child and ejected his claws like torpedos shot out from a submarine. The child wildly shook his shirt-covered-arm free from the clasping claws, catapulting Alexander back on to me. He landed with the weight of an assassin. I gulped in air quickly, listening to the receding, bulleting footsteps of the children. I was sure that upon their return home they would malign us with vicious gossip, proclaiming us as escaped lion cubs from the zoo who ought to be hunted down. Well, at least we had our peace restored to us.

"Alexander, I think you should lose some weight. You almost suffocated me."

"Don't complain," he said, grinning. "The weight makes me stronger."

The brief skirmish had raised his solar smile. He had evidently relished a practice session where he could test the sharpness of his claws in the service of protecting me. The smile altered the contours of his face. You could glimpse the rough and tumble experiences of his kittyhood now smoothening away the wrinkles of middle age. Alexander's face unfolded how he must have looked as a young kitty. Mischief twinkled in his eyes. The effect was an irresistible combination of a winsome kitty and a seductive cat. It was an alluring moment in which I felt ensnared by a sensual power over which I had no control, this same power whose force to reduce thinking creatures to that state of passion which has charted the course of all creatures since the recorded history of heartbeats began. This eternal power of bondage to sexual mating.

At such moments, Alexander's smile was a potent contender with Claude's intimacy.

Was it possible to fall in love with a smile?

After making love, Alexander My Knight In Shining Armour pounced upon slumber once more.

Wine The Warrior had surrendered herself to the upheaval of orgasm and now Wine The Femininely Feline Cat cuddled up next to my hero, swarming in softness, my loving feelings toward Alexander renewed by his gesture of protection, an act upholding a tradition to which Claude had accustomed me. Only Claude? My mistrust had edged into a temporary oblivion. How lovely to be able to disrobe the costume of aggressiveness when you know there is a custodian of your safety nearby! I seldom felt so soft and pliable because I did not often move in safety zones of softness where physical or emotional war between beings did not run rampant.

I suddenly saw a motley parade of caring cats, faceless males with forgotten names who had clung to the umbrella of my strength, a strength which had been foreign to my awareness. I saw myself carrying a survivor's kit containing enough spare supplies to protect and bandage those males who had been felled by a rain of emotional wounds. Males needing females to heal them. Males forgetting that females also need healing. All of us wanting to crawl back into a womb of protection. I saw the tragic mythology of strength ascribed only to males and softness ascribed only to females, an unnatural schism fostering discomfort, confusion and guilt when males and females stepped over into the other's camp, only to be greeted by jeering shouts and cat-calls of derision because no-one openly avowed they belonged to both worlds.

In a current listing of a book of warriors, my name appeared at the top of one page. But nowhere was there inscribed the Wine of Softness, the Wine of Femininity. This Wine became rancid, imperceptible after the vapourization of Claude and I entered a long season of emotional hardness. Finally a solar smile promoted a come-back, a smile warming up my tenderness. Alexander had not sought me to lick his wounds, unlike those before him. Nor had Claude. This self-sufficiency, however adequate and variable in its strength, was the bridge linking Alexander to Claude. Neither needed me to do their living for them.

I suddenly saw a further extension of this bridge. I saw Alexander related to the black cat. I saw the black cat related to my professor of love. I saw all of them as competent, independent beings, with dried-up tears of sorrow and joy staining their souls, all of them sharing the same genealogy of male and female emotions. . .

Alexander's body flinched itself awake, his victorious siesta interrupted by a dream, a one-act pantomine which had executed with exquisiteness the love and hate he bore toward the one who had sired him.

"I dreamed I kissed a swine. It was my father! Wine, this is the first time I have dreamed in a long while."

"That's good, Alexander. Some part of you is loosening up, making you feel."

Zing! My comment hit the bull's-eye of his discomfort. His body tensed up, trying to repel the notion of emotionally letting go. The same old message came on from the sound track of our unspoken communication, the recording scratchy, stale: I don't want to feel. I don't want to feel. It stopped. Alexander continued to curl up into a ball. The recording came on again and in the replay the lyrics almost matched except one key word was missing: *I want to feel. I want to feel.* How could I ferret out the puzzle to these contradictory feelings which kept on throwing our attachment into a quagmire every time the tendrils of our souls intertwined? Was it only his father who stood as a solitary ghost between us, this father who had programmed Alexander to enamel himself against tender emotions which might make him vulnerable to the caprices of other cats? Was Alexander seeking the impossible, still hoping that the father of reality would coincide with the father of his dream, a father whose cheek is warm to the touch instead of giving off frost, a father who might someday tenderly kiss Alexander, admitting his emotional paternity? Or was Alexander's dream initiating a peace treaty, signing it with a kiss, bestowing upon his father a kiss of beginning acceptance, a kiss neutralizing once and for all the opposing forces of love and hate, a kiss of liberation acknowledging the swine for what he is, knowing he can never return the kiss with the same ardour?

Would a kiss of liberation splash on to me an overflow of positive emotion from Alexander and make him less erratic toward me?

Alexander escaped back into sleep. I decided to take a long walk with the sun. I left the garbage can, leaving my solar smile in the arms of whatever dream might hold him.

It had been an intense night and day for visiting the world of dreams for both us. Maybe our radar had been tuned into the same frequency, and the message from my nocturnal meanderings beaming the words "come, go, come, go" had been delivered to Alexander's sleeping world where he had decoded the words as reading "love, hate, love, hate" . . .

How remarkable the dream world is, that stage for the strip-teasing of illusion, that murky world where truths sometimes emerge so unblemished, so naked; that world where a daylight censor is blinded by the libertine quality of sleep; the world of dreams so much a collective world for all living beings. In it is gathered all of the dreams of love, hope, despair and conflict, the harmony and disharmony through which we snail our way in lifetime after lifetime.

* * * * *

Which of us has escaped from the desire of wanting to depart from the rigours of life? – of feeling ourselves falling into a void, and no matter what we grab on to, the usual props sustaining our existence suddenly elude our grasp. We become anxious and despairing by believing that life can become so bleak. And just when we most need hope we discover that our souls are not circulating this vital oxygen. Ironically, the reasons precipitating such a crisis are not always bathed in the limelight of comprehension. These things often sneak up on us like menopausal changes. Sometimes the feeling is simply due to fatigue, our energies severely dehydrated by the demands of living. Then we begin to flirt with death, half in jest, half in seriousness, muttering softly to ourselves: no more life, no more life. It's not that we really seek physical death but that we can't find a temporary retirement from life, a refuge where we might put ourselves into a deep freeze, icing whatever it is which is driving us into a hopeless cul-de-sac.

Such a situation seemed to ferment in Alexander.

After missing his presence in The Milk Bar I had a hunch I would find him in his palatial kitchen. I was right. He presented a very slovenly appearance – tufts of gooey hair, evidence of a drought of self-care. You know that when a cat goes on strike against licking himself clean that he is in bad shape. Alexander's eyes were those of a catatonic cat, unblinking, staring fixedly at five naked saucers of cream. The air in the kitchen had a rancid smell, the sweat of depression. I could feel my larynx constrict from the heavy atmosphere and I kept swallowing in order to keep the aperture to my throat open.

I respected the silence that his autistic mood mandated. Finally he spoke as though the sentences were almost too heavy to lift up from his soul.

"Look at all these riches I possess, Wine. I have everything a cat could want. Why am I so unhappy?" His voice dotted the question with a period. Indeed, who can ever answer a question like this posed by a depressed cat in the space of a few minutes? Was he digging for answers to the most fundamental matters always stirring at the roots of our being? What have I done with myself? What am I doing? Where am I going? What is the point of fighting one battle if all it does is prepare you for the next one?

Nevertheless, with that eternal image of his consoling me once upon a time, I ventured forth to break through the barrier of his gloom. I would have preferred to embrace him, but his unspoken vibrations were not soliciting gestures of affection. So Wine The Detector of Gold In Lost Souls blurted out an explanation which was maybe nothing more than a novice's clumsy attempt to unravel, the spool of a riddle.

"Alexander, I don't think you love yourself . . . and you are such a loveable cat when you want to be. How can you love yourself? You fight so hard against your feelings, all of your energies are directed toward snuffing out your wanting to feel. And of course you don't succeed because you really haven't convinced yourself you want to stop feeling. You want to be able to measure out the dosage of your emotions. You want to be able to turn your emotions on and off at will, like a machine. An impossible task. And then you get angry and disgusted with yourself because you can't function like some sort of programmed robot. Every time your heart seems to get the upper hand you panic over your loss of control and then you run to your milk or cream and with each gulp you partially regain control but the milk or cream also replenishes your self-hate because you know the drinking doesn't solve any-thing. You're caught in a trap of your own creation. Why are you so afraid to feel?"

"I don't know," he said with a defeated sigh.

How defenceless and helpless he looked at that moment, a lost kitty in search of a home, in search of himself. With that feeling always arising in me whenever I spied a stray kitty, I had to restrain myself from enveloping him with my paws and applying those tiny bandages of cheer that are the monopolistic property of mothers petting their forlorn offspring – don't fret, little kitty, mama is here, everything is going to be all right. The words may be valueless but the presence of mama is that of a saviour. But Alexander didn't need a mother. He needed to possess some fragments of himself.

Alexander peered out from his recessed world, regarding me as though his opaque vision had lifted and he was making the acquaintance of Wine The Cat for the first time.

"You love me, don't you?" he stated like a dispassionate investi-gator of a crime, trying to round up the facts.

His directness caught me by surprise and disarmed me. This sudden switch over into my presence was too hasty for me to round up all the words which might have better conveyed what I really felt, though I wasn't sure myself. And after I murmured a hushed "yes" I wanted to retract it because the expression on his face unfurled displeasure.

"Don't love me, Wine. I only bring destruction to those who have had the misfortune to feel this for me." Then he slipped back into his obscure contemplations, without further elaborating why he was a noxious element, dangerous to the health of others. Maybe the spirits of those two dead kitties had just whipped by, spraying lethal fumes of an old guilt.

Alexander's vexation rustled up all of my former shyness, my former muteness – symptoms evoked by a mild ailment of being spurned? I hadn't appraised yet just how sacrosanct this one single word was to him, this magical word – love – always shaped by each of us in so many different forms, this one word forever in the vortex of emotional storms and bliss. If Alexander had phrased the question – do you care about me? – I would have expressed an unqualified "yes!" A confession of love may sometimes sound like a holy prayer, its incantation summoning up either joy or repulsion depending on how much the feelings of the beloved overlap those of the lover. When a beloved does not reciprocate the emotion of love he quietly rages, sensing he is obligated to conjure up an impossible love. The only feeling left to him is that of remorse. Did my confession to Alexander stir up his nerve ends of guilt? Did he cast himself as dangerous in a desperate attempt to avoid furthering his expertise in remorse? Was it simply easier for him to colour his soul black instead of blurting out the words "I don't love you, Wine"? Some cats can't openly reject confessions of love. They are too embarrassed to do so, afraid that the impact of their rejection will strike long-suffering daggers through the heart of the lover. But surely honesty is a better policy, a time-saver for both, because unrequited love usually dies when an adequate substitute willingly gives what his predecessor couldn't. In many instances it isn't who we love but just having someone to love who also reciprocates this love.

And where is the line dividing loving from liking? Aren't the words rather arbitrary and relative, delineated by our experience? If I qualified love as intimacy, it was because I had been exposed to a quality of love, breathtaking in its magnitude, with Claude. Alexander didn't know this. Compared to Claude his relationship with me bordered on the realm of adolescence. Alexander liked me, in a distant way. He always seemed to regard me like a spectator scanning a piece of art work, concluding the overall effect is agreeable. But this was not love, either in his book of definitions or mine.

A megalomaniacal idea ran across the field of my thoughts. If only Alexander would chisel deeper into my soul his heart would ultimately write a signature of satisfaction, resolving our somersaulting togetherness. It wouldn't be the romance of the century but within the confines of its limitations it would be more gratifying than what it was proving to be. However, if Alexander was ever going to care more about me, or anyone else, he was going to have to begin caring about himself. Self-love is the first stepping stone to intimacy.

That night Alexander dispatched a verdict qualifying just how far he was from sampling a taste of the sweetness of self-love. After fifteen minutes more of what smelled like a maturing obsession, he outlined his next course of action.

"I'm going on a trip. There is a good possibility I may not come back. I'm going to climb every high building I can find, walk along every dangerous ledge and maybe, just maybe, knowing the rotten physical condition I'm in, my unsteadiness will plummet me down to earth and I'll be out of this misery."

"Alexander, what are you saying? That's flirting with suicide, quitting before this cat life has run its course. Please come with me to the garbage can and rest in my arms. Maybe in the morning you'll feel better. I know that thorough sense of fatigue, of being fed up with too many bumps and bruises from life. I know that suicidal feelings come and go. Please give yourself a chance, be patient with yourself. Don't give up!"

I suddenly jumped into Mack's skin, knowing the panic he had felt when his mother threatened to jump off a bridge. Somewhere, deep within the pit of my stomach, there was a rumbling, a stirring of some small eruption which had long been dormant and forgotten.

"Go home, Wine. I don't want to talk. I want to be alone," he commanded me in a calm, insistent way, without any hidden appeals to my life-saving urges.

I obeyed with that numbed state of mind, that species of disbelief which is usually the first reaction to any piece of shocking news. Only as I padded along the street with the wind slapping my face to revive me did I come to my senses with an anguished wish to cry out: somebody, something, please help me, give me a magic potion, a formula for hope which I can present to Alexander. Make me a God for one night so I can rescue him. I cannot remain as a silent witness to a being who may erase his existence. That would make me an accessory to a premeditated murder. Then the voice of Wine The Rational Cat chimed in with a cruel irony. "Aren't you always the ringleader waving the banner of free choice, the crusader preaching the inalienable right of every cat to direct his own destiny?" Another voice in me angrily remonstrated. "Surely, there must be a counter-argument, proving that suicide goes beyond the frontiers of free choice?" This voice then floundered, becoming stymied because no opposing argument came sallying forth to contest the airtight logic of the first voice. The debate had degenerated to a deadlock.

I felt myself being swamped by an attack of shudders, the eruption starting to cascade all over me, pulsating a truth which has brought many a cat life to an end. And then the truth burst out with the brilliance of a fiery magnesium ribbon: I might never see

81

Alexander again! Over and over the sentence looped around itself until the germ of the message rang out. *I might lose Alexander*! The old leitmotif of loss nailing itself to me once again. Loss, the starting point to stretched-out sorrow. Loss, the overture to a long composition of mourning.

Disremembered sensations of mourning spilled over me with a quickening velocity as though they were rehearsing me with the practised skill they had engineered in bygone times. I began superimposing past grief on to a potential one should Alexander die. I became like a widowed cat, draped in a sable piece of cloth to announce my mourning, to broadcast my entry into a death-in-life existence imposed by this loss. I turned into a zombie, impaled upon a knife of unrelenting pain which was slashing away at my psychic innards and all sensations of joy, laughter, humour and pleasure were being squashed out of my soul. I saw the hands of a clock verify that time is a relative thing – every minute seemed like an hour. I saw the hands of a clock moving forward and backward, as directionless as myself. I heard my voice stuck in a groove of monotony, asking why bother to live in such a state of emptiness, for I had become the next victim of mortality, dying with the departed loved one. I saw myself venturing forth into the street, into the world of the living and the creatures I encountered had no impact upon me for they belonged to a world of the living, beating a heartbeat different from my own, a reminder of how isolated grief makes you feel. I became immune to the exquisite filigree design of nature – trees, stars, sun, moon – hollow words decaying on my lips the moment they were uttered, an obituary to the dissolution of my spirit. And then I observed a vision of painful loveliness – two creatures embracing; and the beauty of this living contact only enticed past memories to erupt, reminding me of what I no longer had and my only recourse was to escape from this open-air tragedy to a dark basement retreat where a colorless jail might seal off the memories for a little while and I vowed I would never want to want love again, just as Alexander had once said to me.

Then I recalled the gracious welcome marking the finale to mourning, the waking up one morning without any pinpricks of pain, my apprenticeship to mourning terminated. My body and my mind were at rest, mother nature having bestowed the final benediction to grief – peace – that rejuvenative kick in the soul she gives to all of her offspring, refusing to let them mourn for an infinite time. Yes, I was now restored, in balance with myself, the old order of things relegated to history, a new order to life creeping out slowly, out of the ashes of the old.

My dress rehearsal for mourning ran aground. I was anticipating only a possibility, not a fact.

But weren't all of these melancholy souvenirs related to something more basic? Do we really respond to losing someone or does the pain of loss uncover our ever-present, private condition of loneliness? Didn't I preoccupy myself that night with only the narcissistic contemplation of what Alexander's death would mean to *me*? Didn't I swiftly abdicate trying to imagine further ways to save his life? Is love then some mythological fable, a *diversion* from this solitude of our own oneness? And intimacy merely the adequacy by which another being covers our loneliness? At face-value this reads like a chilling proposition, unless there is still more to be gleaned. My sixth sense impels me to keep spading away for more understanding. There must be a light beaming some place, where all of these questions fuse into a positive harmony. Maybe this slight note of pessimism lingers on after having raked up the consequences of loss that funereal night.

The culmination to that depressing evening carried with it a post-mortem autopsy, held for all of the V.I.P.s in the procession of my life. I saw my dead mother, last glimpsed in kittyhood. I saw my dead father, last glimpsed in adolescence. I saw blurred faces of adolescent loves and friends whose lives had briefly intersected with mine. I saw my professor of love and the black cat. I saw Claude. Some still had heartbeats, others did not. I saw that death was not the only inventor of loss. Loss had a thousand and one perpetrators. It could come from separation, betrayal, lies, disillusionment, mistakes, accidents, different beliefs, evolutionary imbalance between two beings. *Loss came from change, from the ephemeral face of life*, this inevitable reality against which I had been battling when Alexander first found me in the garbage can.

The only variable you could say about loss was the degree of its impact. And this seemed determined only by one's personal investment with another being. In retrospect, those losses in kittyhood and adolescence, while painful, were mini-losses, a time of under-developed love, when giving and sharing were only in the crawling stage. The loss of my father hurt more than my mother because he wasn't the mysterious stranger to me that early death had made her. The loss of my professor of love hurt only in tiny doses, for our relationship gradually eroded away over a long stretch of time. I could not share him with another. The loss of the black cat deepened the roots of pain because he and I had lived together on a part-time basis of emotional matrimony. But the most devastating lesson in loss occurred after the full-time bonds of intimacy were severed with Claude. Then I lived the definition of grief, when grief ransacked my life and cleaned me out of hope and vitality.

So I should have known that grief would not have been the bitter dessert if Alexander had converted himself to a ghost. Our connection was not strong enough. But past experience is often so influencial in conditioning us to expect the future will lay out the same blueprint unless we stand back and realize that no two situations are ever the same.

I realize that no clear, succinct reason has yet been given to explain Alexander's frame of mind that night. Whatever it was, it got buried with time. But the echo of my troubled voice, mandating I translate the hieroglyphics of suicide, still resonates, and only now, as I sit here on my haunches contemplating everything, does a voice come through, answering one more unanswered question.

Alexander, let me introduce you to my dear friend, Cleopatra, a cat of my generation famous for her ravishing beauty, a pure-bred Siamese, unlike myself, with pedigree papers denoting a long lineage of aristocratic blood. Every male cat becomes bewitched by her feline exquisiteness and her regal charm. You can usually find her at a nightly haunt similar to The Milk Bar. If you enter this locale you will see her in a circle of admiration, her tongue constantly dipping into a cup of milk. You won't notice her overindulgence but only the dainty way she imbibes. She has that special talent for converting her actions into artistic creations, inspiring an aesthetic pleasure in all who observe her. But not long ago the milk turned sour in her mouth when I was with her. She spewed out the story of her addiction, of how her cat mate of many years had taken his life after a series of false alarms. Instead of responding to his desire that she stay with him one night or else he would kill himself, she discarded his threat as pure play-acting. He upheld his promise, scratching the myth that one false alarm is a threat never to be taken seriously. His death willed her a fund of guilt of such staggering proportions that only milk-drinking made life tolerable. While friends claimed he had always been mentally unbalanced, no explanation could erase the image of herself as an assassin. Her life became dedicated to duelling guilt. She was condemned to live in an emotional hell.

Here then, Alexander, is the answer I couldn't supply that night. To have killed yourself would have been to transfer the hell you couldn't live with on to those linked with you. If, as you once professed, you feel a keen sense of responsibility to others, then you must not leave the legacy of guilt which suicide always underwrites. Inevitably those who survive you become convinced that some action of theirs, however insignificant, must have helped pull the trigger of a self-inflicted death. My walking away from you that night would have placed me on trial and sentenced me to guilt for the rest of my lives. And if you had killed yourself there would have been an additional charge of first-degree robbery – robbing your son of a parental heritage. Maybe you never had a father in any emotional sense, but were you willing to subject your own flesh and blood to the same sad fate?

∗ ∗ ∗ ∗ ∗

Alexander, my vibrations are picking up some heckling from some humans in the audience. They don't approve of my brand of story-telling, my meandering off from the story line on to tangent after tangent. They are thinking, let her keep her catharsis in the garbage can, after all, her insights are purely personal, valid only for herself. They are accusing me of being a renegade, of breaking the guidelines for traditional story telling. "Just stick to the facts. Forget the metaphysics and the psychology. Give us action, give us some blood and guts, give us some good raw sex." Well, Mr and Mrs Human, if it's more action you want, shall I splice together a moving reel of every word uttered by Alexander and myself? Shall I do a nice padding job of inserting extra clips of how we sat, what we ate and where we defecated? Be a good reporter of surface details like the photographer at The Fur Fair? Sure, this would be action, action at the surface of the human soul, a dead end for those trying to glimpse more than artifice. I still maintain that the real action is to be found in the subterranean layers of a being, those places where we walk so nakedly in an atmosphere of contradictory emotions and thoughts.

Maybe your real complaint is that I have robbed you of an authorship, I have made interpretations, usurping the pleasure that all voyeurs like to indulge in. I have robbed you of the pleasure of doing your own detective work of Alexander and myself, whereby your conclusions might not coincide with mine. *But remember, my words are not the gospel and my truths are always subject to revision.*

Alexander, another complaint has just been filed. I'm using too many styles, too much imagery. Keep everything simple, in nice, down-to-earth language. That's an insult. That's like asking me to exist at the most mediocre level of existence, paint everything in one dull shade of grey. I can't do this. I'd fall asleep from boredom.

Besides, I'm only a tool, an instrument for expressing things that are fed to me by a layer of consciousness over which I have no control. Anyhow, images or pictures are nice. Most humans relate more easily to pictures than to big, fancy words that live twenty-four hours a day in a dictionary and never come out for an airing. And another thing! Which of you ever feels the same mood, day in and day out! Today you are one thing, tomorrow another. Today your language borders on the realm of the mundane, tomorrow it is inspired, converted into a rich bouquet of words. So how can the style we use to express ourselves remain static? Nothing in life ever stays the same!

But maybe some of you who are still sending out complaining vibrations ought to quit now and get out of the audience. I won't feel insulted if you tune me out. Maybe you need more time before you are ready to appreciate what I am doing. Maybe you haven't been touched yet by loss or despair. Maybe you are one of those humans born with a golden spoon in your mouth and you haven't bumped against the rocks of human existence. You are still lying in some protected womb, waiting for tragedy to strike you down and only then will you be born unto yourself and at the same time unto humanity. Then you will discover that the greatest story ever told is when we try to tell the story of our unadmitted truths to ourselves. And the story will inevitably contain some variation of loss, of *change*: a lost dream, a lost love, a lost pet, a lost job, a lost country or even something so simple as a shattered, antique goblet whose value was measured by its having been handed down from a loved one. Sooner or later we all weep over something we no longer have, something that no longer exists.

Now I must resume my story. Maybe this pause has been good for all of us, a respite from a rather sobering segment of the story of Alexander and Wine. Notice I said "story", not tragedy. The only tragedy I can perceive is in running away from reflections of ourselves.

* * * * *

Alexander disappeared, without stamping a clue on his where-abouts. Was he alive, or dead? Was his suicide threat purely a bluff, a disguised call for help? Or, was he really in earnest about his intended course of action? I must have replayed his words "Go home, Wine" a thousand times in my head, trying to detect some innuendo I might have missed. Had the words summarized the eternal score of polarity marking the theme of his life – I want to live, I want to die, I want to feel, I don't want to feel? Had he then brought out his check list of treasonous cats, adding my name to it because I hadn't cared enough to stick around in his kitchen, over-ruling his order to move out? Each morning these obsessional questions unshuttered my eyelids.

I had taken to sleeping nightly in the garbage can. It was the one place where Alexander's scent most pungently lingered. To smell his aroma was to adhere to hope that he would resurface in my life. I dawdled away hour after hour, swarming myself in a tally of sporadic memories of our togetherness. I resuscitated those sexual excursions of ecstasy, fantasizing love-making with him many times a day and the scenes of passion were easy to recreate upon recalling the first time our bodies took communion; and I went on to invent scintillating variations of positions and techniques already known to devotees of the Kama Sutra. I glorified Alexander and myself as the world's greatest lovers. Such preoccupations promoted much masturbatory activity. Imagine then, the miserable let-down feeling of having to accept the tingling body sensations dangling on after orgasm as being the residue of the magic of my own paw, using fantasy as a phantom lover. But sex, even self-induced, is often a powerful visor, screening us from visions we do not want to see.

One day I concentrated very hard in sending a message to Alexander via our telepathic brain waves:

Alexander. Exotic fur looking for her dispossessed friend. Please come back. I want you. If you are in search of burial ground, come bury yourself in me. I will not disappoint you. Signing off. Oops, one more thing, Alexander. Give yourself a kiss. You may find you are more than what you think you are . . .

I didn't know if he would receive the words unless his radar was operating, but it was worth the effort.

My nocturnal dream life derailed from the track of my erotic daytime plays. Nightmares of dangling flesh gyrated like spaghetti blowing in the wind. I would awaken with an overwhelming nausea and vomit up the scanty meals ingested the previous day. On one of the rare occasions when I appeared in my mistress's kitchen for a meal, she became alarmed when the fine tuna fish she served me refused to stay down in my stomach. She rushed me to a local vet who immediately asked her before examining me if I had been fooling around with any neighbourhood "tom cats." His insinuation that I might have been some sort of promiscuous cat rankled me. My sex life was none of his business! Nor did he find any favour in my eyes by his assumption that I had to be pregnant just because I was regurgitating my food. He should have known that grief and pregnancy often induce the same symptoms! He then began to sermonize to my mistress about his disgust with the excessive freedom most female cats have. If it were left up to him, he might have installed every one of us in the confines of a fishbowl. My mistress listened to him with half an ear, knowing well the futility of arguing with those who believe they are evangelists with the power to deliver the world from its ills. Finally, as though it were an afterthought, he returned to the purpose of the visit and examined me. "At least she isn't pregnant," he surmised. "It's probably nothing more than a mild tummyache. But if I were you, I'd get her fixed, avoid problems before they occur." Here then was the inception of thought, planted in the mind of my mistress, to eliminate the possibility of future motherhood.

Just before leaving his surgery, my eyes scanned the front door. Affixed to it was a tiny cross bearing a crucified Jesus. Here was further confirmation of the doctor's hypocritical oath: I shall save life but destroy its potential.

I felt mildly jilted by my empty womb. That old, inveigling silhouette of motherhood was once again sirening forth, deflecting me from the anxiety about Alexander's dangling suicide threat. What if Alexander had impregnated me before he disappeared? Would that have been so undesirable? The years were marching by, cat lives born and extinguished and thus far, I had contrived in every way possible to abstain from procreation. Was an accidental pregnancy the only answer to my perpetual ambivalence toward motherhood?

Suddenly it seemed that the solution was sliding more toward one side of this ambivalence, judging by the bitter-sweet reaction, the slight disappointment at not being pregnant. I would not have chastised Alexander's seed if it had embraced and fertilized my egg of future life. Sentimentally speaking, if he never returned, an offspring would fill the space of his disappearance, the heartbeat of his memory preserved forever. A romantic vision to be sure! But fully as comprehensible as most other reasons for creating life. Think of all the kitties conceived in hate, revenge, disgust, mamas and papas fornicating because it is the thing to do, a recreational pastime, often the only shared experience between some males and females. Maybe Alexander and I weren't passionately in love but we did like one another. Loathing and other negative feelings did not form a single part in the mosaic of our feelings.

Assuming I was pregnant and assuming Alexander returned, what would happen? Would he regard the young one as a malicious trap, wedding him to a situation not of his choice? I would advise him immediately that my intentions were honourable, I didn't expect him to play the role of a full-time father, because he had an obligation to his other offspring. If he wanted to take any responsibility for our kitty I would be grateful because I trusted his paternal competency, his views on kitty-raising coinciding with mine. Of course my plan did not include our living together full-time because Alexander's ambivalence made me too uncomfortable. Anyhow, I didn't think a part-time father was the robbery some cats proclaim. One solid source of love from one being was worth more than the minute, erratic dribblings of warmth from a dozen beings. Look at Alexander, the offspring of the following combination: his father an emotional cripple, his mother the nourishing force whose love had bolstered Alexander's personality erect enough so that he could become an adequate father. If Alexander wavered so much back and forth in his affection toward me it seemed like the by-product of growing up in a house of conflict. He would have been better off with just his mother, without the everyday impact of cruelty indoctrinating him into assuming that the relationships between a male and a female is a continual siege of war . . .

Maybe it wouldn't have mattered whose seed had entered me then. Maybe Alexander happened to be in the spotlight of my life at just the right time when an alteration in my character was chartering me toward a season of emotional readiness to handle the responsibility of an offspring without a live-in father. Maybe external circumstances favoured this development. The arrangement with my mistress felt solid and stable, a less topsy-turvy environment than what I had been accustomed to for many years. Bouncing around from one home to another was no way to raise a kitty in my anthology of thought, though some cats might argue that the sooner a kitty learns about the transitory nature of life, the better prepared he or she is in coping with it. I didn't dispute the validity of this lesson but I adhered to the prudence of stability. Lay the groundwork in the architecture of personality first. Make sure a kitty has this bulwark against the future flux of time and change.

Speculations, speculations, speculations. The motif of motherhood was only an abstraction, not an impending reality and yet how vehemently I continued to latch on to it as a subsidiary topic by which I could sidetrack my percolating anxiety in those days. And maybe, just maybe, the underlying truth of all these suppositions was simply my reaching a saturation point with freedom. No obligations or responsibilities was beginning to pall on me. Get rid of the freedom, exchange the burden of freedom for the burden of an offspring. Think about someone else other than yourself. Get away from yourself. But could I? Do you ever escape from yourself when confronted by your own progeny, that little face gazing at you day in and day out, often a portrait of your own face in miniature? And don't you want to recreate the little one in your own image, brainwashing him or her in the gospel of your being, knowing something of yourself continues long after you cease to walk the face of this earth? How can you deceive yourself, thinking you want to get away from your own skin? You don't! You want to have a little Wine or a little Alexander hovering around you, a fresh existence to be moulded by your dictates because you are vain enough to want to populate the world with more Wines of your ilk. Yes, you're tired of freedom now. Let a little Wine come forth to inherit and perpetrate the freedom you want to abdicate. Let her bear the burden of rendering you eternal . . . .

There came a moment early one morning which unnerved me, a species of activity often misinterpreted as the onslaught of mental illness. I found myself pressing my forehead against the outer side of the garbage can. The coolness of the metal aroused in me the sensation of being alive, proof that I existed. Then I felt a forceful yearning for some other external tactile contact, a wish to be touched by another being. The disease bore the earmark of an acute state of loneliness. My life had been feeding on a daily diet of vicarious living with only the ghostly remains of Alexander. This wasn't enough.

Fate chose to intercede on my behalf with a somewhat burlesque flair. Later that morning while snailing down the street with that notable pace of a depressed mood, I renewed my acquaintanceship with Albert The Cat. Albert was a rather scrawny, underfed creature of sizeable intelligence, the latter his entrée into the hearts of many of his paramours. What really impressed everyone who met him was the special collar he wore around his neck. Attached to this collar was a profusion of circular discs, faces of watches old and new, each indicating a different hour to prove that time was a relative thing. It was quite a conversation piece, an amusing pastime to spend your time talking about time, though under certain circumstances it could be annoying as I was about to find out. Albert belonged to my marginal past, predating Alexander. Our contacts, though spartan, had merely circumscribed a sprightly intellectual zone, mostly commentaries on how slavishly devoted human beings were to clocks, how absurd they were to make a religion out of time which didn't even exist.

Albert's face suggested the fatigue of a cat who had been kept awake by a rampaging cuckoo-clock that forgot to shut down. Or else the night had been an orgy of joy.

"It was an orgy, Wine, a round-the-clock orgy of arguing with my girl-friend. She accused me of being a sexual pervert, interested only in her body and not in her mind. She says I'm too old to have these constant sexual urges, I should stop acting like some young kitty in heat. But what really makes me angry is that in the beginning she said I was too intellectual, always paying more attention to the hows and whys of things, of not being passionate enough with her. So I finally unleashed my passion and now she wants to castrate it. I tell you I'm fed up with the irrational ticking of females. They are contrary, arbitrary, illogical and impossible to predict."

"You mean they are just as insubstantial and relative as time? Maybe she's got her period and feels cranky."

"Well I get my periods of crankiness too, except I don't bleed where you can see it."

Suddenly a sopranic, shrill note trilled out from one of the watches.

"That's a reminder that it's time to lick myself clean," explained Albert.

I was amused. Albert had found a use for time after all.

After swishing his tongue up and down one paw he was preparing to carry on with this routine when his movements became arrested. Coming down the street were two humans, each carrying a long hose.

"Quick, Wine, we have to get away from those characters. They're street cleaners, real sadists. Everytime they see me they turn their hoses on me, aiming for the collar. They're two lazy bums who work as though time stood still and they think I'm trying to make them feel guilty."

I invited Albert to the garbage can, which was a mistake, for its close quarters exuded an intimacy to which we were both vulnerable, or so I thought. After finishing his cleaning chore he decided to move his washing-up headquarters over to my body. His tongue began a rinsing campaign in the area of my belly where it kept irrigating great quantities of saliva which drooled in little rivulets. It felt like a bucket of water had overturned and I thought it would be nice at that moment to have a towel and mop up my sopping wet fur. Albert needed a course in dry cleaning and a reminder that a female body is not a public bath-house. Meanwhile, he was getting quite excited by all of this. His little cock hardened, positioning itself as though it were the hand of a clock, indicating the hour to be either noon or midnight. Naturally the sound of the plinking metal of the watches serenaded us with the background music of a brass band. Thus far, my body remained inert. If Albert was attempting to ignite the sparks of passion he was not using the right chemistry, if indeed any could be found. How do you tell a cat that you don't like the sloppy way he uses his tongue! That would be like trying to make a major personality change in five minutes, all the more difficult in this case because Albert had bedded down with many a cat. If no one had complained, he could only assume they all enjoyed his brand of drool. Maybe his girl-friend didn't either. Maybe she was really trying to castrate his tongue.

Could I be the slayer of his sexual self-esteem? Today I would answer an unqualified "yes." Why perpetrate rotten love-making! Telling a male his technique is no good is doing a good deed for the next recipient of his maleness, in a gentle way, of course. You may be left with an empty cunt but it's often better than the hard labour it takes to rouse the flutter of an orgasm with a cat of amateur sexual talent. I hadn't yet reached the stage where I wanted to train someone in the wiles of seduction. Perhaps that would come later,in a future cat life when advancing age sometimes sends females in search of lusty, young males.

Without bothering to ask if I were ready or not, Albert straddled me. He began issuing professorial instructions as to the body beat of my movements. Within a few seconds, his little cock shot forth a probable stream of loneliness, giving to me what he hadn't given to his girl-friend. Well, at least time stood still for one of us – him. Then the grand climax of the encounter occurred. Another alarm sounded. The absent-minded professor declared this to be the dinner-hour gong.

I pinched his cock out of my cunt with one tiny squeeze, my silent declaration of displeasure. I didn't know if I was on the verge of an orgasm of laughter or one of tears. Why couldn't he have been Alexander! What was I doing with him? I was beginning to feel even more lonely than earlier in the day, that same kind of loneliness which is more exaggerated in crowds than when you are alone. All I wanted was for Albert to leave me in peace. I preferred to bang my head on the garbage can rather than submit to another sexual charade.

Albert took his time in departing. He chose to conduct a discourse on how the watches wasted his time. The idea was witty and original but all I could think of was how I had wasted my body. Go home, Albert. Go home. Sure, time is relative and illusory but cats are not. You can't easily interchange one cat for another like

92

you can with watches. Where was my solar smile? I was still as fixated upon Alexander while Albert was in the garbage can, as he was with his time pieces. Maybe I should have said to Albert, "Fuck time."

The nightmares of dangling flesh ceased. Another kind of dream heralded the last punctuation to the epoch of mourning. I was in Alexander's kitchen. The barman who had catered to the wishes of the discerning clientéle at The Fur Fair, was removing the bottles of milk and cream stacked on the wine racks and placing them in crating cases. As soon as one case was filled he carried it out to a waiting refrigerated truck. After several trips back and forth, he returned for one last bottle of milk which hadn't fitted into the last case. Alexander was sitting on his haunches in the middle of the room. There was a pathetic look of submissive defeat on his face. As the barman moved to exit, with the solitary milk bottle tucked under his arm, he turned to Alexander and said, "You are now a bankrupt cat. Everything that ever belonged to you has now been removed. A seal will be placed upon the entrance to this room and you will no longer be permitted to enter it. You have five minutes in which to leave." Alexander could no longer contain his tears. His big body heaved great waves of sobs and intermittently I heard him moan, "I'm bankrupt, I'm bankrupt . . ."

Alexander is bankrupt, I said to myself upon waking. He hasn't lost his milk supply. He has lost something far more precious. He is bankrupt in his soul. He is a cat, empty of a vital wish to live, a cat without dreams or desires. He is a cat living in a terrible void where nothing in this world furnishes him with joy. I cannot join him in such a place for it would be a return to a vacuous existence.

This was the antidote I used to counter my depression. Alexander had been gone for a full month. Most of my energies which had been consumed by the malaise of worry and dourness were now clamouring for reinforcements, a source of joy and laughter. One of the many voices of Wine spoke out harshly. "Pick yourself up and get back out on the street. If Alexander returns, he must not find a lifeless creature who has no vitality to offer him."

* * * * *

My mistress greeted my rebounded enthusiasm for eating by heaping extra portions of fish upon a daily fare of packaged cat food

93

which tasted like crunchy bits of bran cereal, the latter a specialty item thought up by human mentors of vegetarianism. Perhaps my mistress was going to wean me from tuna fish one day and switch me to her mode of dining on food not slaughtered by a human hand. She was ever so solicitous, intuiting that I had had some tumultuous times. Whenever I padded near the desk where she sat playing the keys of her typewriter, she would halt her work and stroke my fur very tenderly.

She, of all the owners I had ever had, was the most understanding of my subjugation to freedom. She maintained an open-door policy in the house. I could come and go at will, knowing that with just a slight nudge of my nose, I could open the back door which was constructed of a very light material.

We had first met at the animal shelter where I had been deposited by a kindly old lady who had rescued me from the street, observing my bloated, undernourished belly. This angel of mercy had remarked that while she wanted to take me home with her, she had no place she could rightfully call her own. She lived on the charitable crumbs of her daughter and son-in-law and they did not belong to any breed of animal lovers. However, she thought I should have the right to three square meals a day, so she convinced her daughter to take me to the nearest salvation shelter for animals where I was immediately fed and then placed in a large room housing about fifty cats. The only privacy each of us had was an individual square shelf jutting out at various levels from the wall. The room simulated a jungle environment where everyone staked out his own territory. I was grateful for the food and warmth provided by the keepers but I felt manacled and hemmed in, owing to my loss of freedom.

One fine day a woman entered this room. She looked like a semi-retired Bohemian with her long red stringy hair and faded blue jeans. Her eyes were owl-like, framed by a pair of enormous glasses. A big, black cape covered her from shoulders to knees in the style of Count Dracula. She was not exactly a femme fatale but she was with an extraordinarily handsome man whose eyes must have x-rayed an internal beauty within her.

As the door closed behind them, her face tightened up in a tableau of fear. Poor lady, I thought. She obviously had a cat phobia. None of the other cats took much notice of her. Most of them were snoozing, for we had just been fed.

"Which one would you like?" asked the man with her.

"I don't know. I'm terribly nervous standing here like this. I feel like I'm in a lion's cage at a zoo and any minute one of them is going to pounce on me."

"Don't be afraid. They won't hurt you."

"I know but I've never got over my fear of cats ever since I got clawed by one when I was a child."

Ah, I said to myself. So that was the problem. In teaching her a lesson, some cat had left her a legacy of cat fear. I wondered if any of my former victims was going to end up like her. With a sense of guilt, I recalled those emergent situations when I had been obliged to use my razor-sharp talons. Here was a chance to redeem my sense of shame. Maybe I could convince her that not all cats were alike. Most of us were really very gentle creatures, albeit a little finicky at times.

I leaped down from my perch and went toward her at a caterpillar's pace. I turned on my purr of contentment. She made no move to pet me when I arrived at her feet. The man, however, reached down and tickled me behind the ears, giving the impression that he had once been a dog owner.

"You see," he said, "it doesn't scratch."

I took no offence at his indiscriminate use of "it" because his voice had a lilting cadence of gentleness.

The woman stiffly bent down and stroked my back with a trembling hand. Right away I knew we were going to get along splendidly. She treated my fur with the satiny touch of a lover eager to please a beloved.

"Yes," she murmured, "let's take this one."

"What would you like to call it?" asked the man.

"What sex is it?"

"It's a female."

"Let's call her Wine."

Well, I had been dubbed quite a few different names in my life – Harriet, Judy, Priscilla – but this alias was by far the most unusual one. Why not Brandy, Kahlua or Martini? Did my mistress have some sort of fetish with intoxicants?

The honeymoon with her was marred by only one crisis. Shortly after I was brought to her house, I jumped up on her lap, wishing to display my affectionate nature. Not all cats are stand-offish, I wanted to decree. She was discombobulated by my gesture and vaulted up hastily from her rocking chair, flinging me mercilessly to the floor.

"Shall we take her back to the shelter?" asked the man sitting nearby.

The woman eyed me for a moment and then answered, "No, I'm determined to surmount my fear."

Good for you, I applauded. A woman after my own heart.

From then on our relationship continued with honeymoon sweetness. It's no wonder my depression so alarmed her. She had become very attached to me and did not want to lose me, a comforting feeling. How unlike Alexander she was in her emotional consistency!

I decided to devote all of my time to my mistress today by staying indoors, something I hadn't done since Alexander had vanished. However, I was careful not to intrude while she was typing away because the intense look on her face told me she was working for posterity. Like the models at The Fur Fair eager to be eternalized in a photo, my mistress was revenging death via a scrapbook of words. And, instead of leaving a legacy to children she didn't have, she was nourishing a creation to be bound and disseminated to a world of unknown people, a charitable donation as she titled it because she was a dismal failure as a writer. No-one ever bought anything she wrote. The rejection slips she had pasted on the wall cited her writing as too erotic for intellectuals and too intellectual for readers of eros. This used to frustrate her because she staunchly argued that humans were comprised of so many different personality facets and faces; they were more like a rainbow of selves. To try to slot a person into any one category was impossible and absurd. "Why can't you make love with great gusto and then seal your lover's lips with metaphysical propositions and wanderings?" she often remarked to the man with whom she lived. But she had learned to accept her status as a renegade from the literary world. She had learned to laugh at the stuffed-shirt criticism of her work.

Whether she had yet renounced her desire to be rendered eternal was a fuzzy issue. Probably she belonged to the vast network of humans striving to leave an indelible imprint for future generations, humans erecting pyramids of creation – musicians, sculptors, painters, writers, businessmen, even countries – all of them madly scurrying through the course of each day, sacrificing the here and now in order to build for the sum of tomorrows. Did any of them ever step off the treadmill of life to consider that futurity can only be mastered by a mastery of the present? Did any of them suspect the colossal challenge of just creating an art of living? Were these humans nothing more than a conglomerate of egos, each seeking to glorify some private vision by inserting it into the headlines of tomorrow's world?

Claude's words come back to me. "It is the doing of a thing, not the end result which counts." Is vanity really the backbone of this human mania for everlasting creations? Maybe building, designing, inventing and all related activities represent something more subtle, something apart from narcissism. Maybe humans must engage in this self-expression in order to take the chaotic reputation of life and shape it, to take the infinite and give it finite form, to affix themselves to something concrete and solid. Shaping chaos may be the human answer to nature's rule that all life seeks a sense of balance, that humans must have this balance to sustain their psychic integrity. Maybe this was the obsession which drove my mistress to her typewriter day after day . . .

Curiosity nudged me. What was my mistress writing? All of the historical weight of the world's philosophers pressed down heavily upon her this day, judging by the solemnity of her face. Had she unlocked the key to the evolution of the universe? Had she discovered how to transpose Einstein's theory of $e = mc^2$ into the realm of how mental energy is telepathically transmitted from one brain to another? Had she discovered a new insight into man's behaviour? Had she discovered a new religion? A new way to understand nocturnal dreams?

Today's confessional with her typewriter was not exonerating her from chaos. Lucidity was eclipsed by some obstacle blocking her vision. She would stall every so often, light a cigarette and sit back in her chair, staring into the space of her imagination. Or, was it her reality? She would then eke out about ten beats or two sentences and stop. At that rate, I supposed she would require years before completing whatever it was she was doing. How unlike other days when great gusts of laughter would echo through the room, her spirit puffing out from the yeast of humour. At such times, whatever melody she was singing through her typewriter was like a musical comedy, her fingers doing a snappy tap dance on the keys, her eyes rounding out into great big childish saucers. At least she did not always take herself too seriously.

Maybe if I patiently lay on the couch, today's intensity swathing her visage would be lifted. I feared she was going to weave a tapestry of wrinkles if she kept plodding along the route of too much heavy thinking. The tiny furrowed line crossing her forehead would soon have a twin and before long, her forehead would be pleated. Then people would stop saying to her, "You can't be as old as you are." She was, like myself, well preserved for her age. All of her wrinkles joined with the inner convolutions of her brain like interior stretch marks from the perpetual pregnancy of creation. I had often heard her say, "I don't understand why I have this youthful face. You'd think that with all the living I've done, my wrinkled soul would have its counterpart on my face. Wrinkles aren't so bad," or so she justified to herself. "They map character, they flaw a face and make it so human looking, so much more interesting than the polished, vapid look of youth. Anyhow, I don't want to be young again. I don't want to re-live the labyrinth of my confused youth when ignorance could not match the wits of maturity. To be ignorant is to be enslaved, to live without freedom of choice, to live not knowing what the choices are. If there is anything enviable about youth it can only be its boundless energy and robust health, two qualities which diminish with time. Aging inevitably brings more problems and unfortunately there is less and less energy to cope with them. But while my body is slowly becoming arthritic, my mind is not."

My mistress depended on her brain as the compensating force for her diminished physical vitality. She was quite discriminating as to what was and wasn't important. She had realized that there was very little in life which mattered outside of health, love, food and a warm place to live. She channelled most of her energies toward exploration, always seeking to learn something new about herself and the cosmos she called home. In this regard, she had the curiosity of a child. However, as time went on, she realized that each new discovery proved impossible to patent. Each had already been thought up long ago by ancient sages. So she concluded there was no such thing as creation, nothing was unique. All new knowledge was only a re-arrangement, a different perception, a juggling act of what already existed. But if she had managed without a tutor or a guide to stumble upon thoughts long ago invented by people who were thought to be geniuses, she then asked herself; what is a genius? And eventually she decided that a genius was merely someone who took the time to stretch and stretch the artificial limits of freedom to think and to act, someone who was not afraid to walk straight into the eye of chaos without the brass band of time-pieces marking the hour when knowledge was supposed to be harvested.

Being in her presence had a certain inspiring effect on me. She made me feel hopeful, less anxious about what was happening to Alexander. Now my worries were being transferred from him unto her. Often she had become physically ill after a serious bout with her typewriter. She would abruptly have to halt her mental excursions and lay down on the sofa next to the desk, putting her hand on her heart, and then commence certain breathing exercises. If these didn't calm down what I can only presume to be an erratic heartbeat, she would take a tranquillizer to relieve her distress. Within half an hour the deathlike pallor of her face would become restored to its normal hue and the attack forgotten. I wondered how she could devote so much of her time to doing something so injurious to her health. Maybe this was a small price to pay for immortality, for copyrighting herself in perpetuity.

My mistress stopped writing. She yanked out the piece of paper from her typewriter, tore it up and threw it into the waste-paper basket. I wish I could have said, "Don't get frustrated. Remember, Rome wasn't built in a day." She went out of the room and then came back with a glass of red wine, her ritualistic punctuation to a morning's work. It was the only alcohol she ever imbibed. The ruby red liquid sparkling in the crystal glass always enchanted her vision, her sense of aesthetics. You can see now why she named me Wine.

Without the infernal clacking of her typewriter I could take a nap on her purple velvet couch. Just watching her had tired me out. I still wanted to know what sort of project she was working on but I figured I would sneak a look when she was not in the room. Unfortunately my siesta lasted only long enough for me to close my eyes.

There was a crash! My mistress had accidentally brushed off her lovely crystal wine glass from its perch on her desk. It had shattered into a profusion of sparkling shards. She muttered an oath of complaint and after capturing a broom, swept the glittering crystals of what had been a family heirloom on to a dust pan. She brusquely transported the remains to burial ground. They were laid to rest in a satiny plastic cloth.

She then made a telephone call, asking a godly voice if it were possible to duplicate the demolished treasure. She insisted she wanted a *perfect reproduction*! Apparently she was offered the hope of a replacement, for she quickly left the house.

There was something significant to all of this, something more to be gleaned than the simple fact of a broken glass. But I thought I would save my contemplations for a rainy day activity.

The poetry of silence nestled me back into the arms of dreams.

* * * * *

That evening I rejoined the world of living cats. My anxiety about Alexander's condition had turned mouldy. Time was stealthily stealing my emotions, storing them in a place just beyond the reach of my nervous zone, converting Alexander's existence to a myopic memory. I might have mistakenly concluded that my attachment to him was only an over-dramatized feeling had it not been for a vignette recounted by my friend, Helena. It was she who reminded me how cleverly time acts like an emotional decoy during prolonged separation from those we care about. She had become separated from her beloved after her masters moved to a faraway locale. A year sang away from the lives of the lovers. Then her beloved sniffed her scent and caught up with her. Initially their reunion bore the strangeness of culture shock, Helena feeling herself in the presence of an alien. She almost concluded an obituary to their love when suddenly the old familiarity between them came back. Her emotions came out of the deep freeze where nature had stored them while forcing her to step forward to the pulsebeat of each living moment . . .

I elected The Milk Bar as the temple of my renewal . . . Maybe I would locate a fountainhead of joy and catch a whiff of news about Alexander !

It was saturated with cats on that very sultry evening, the heat so intense I wanted to shed my coat of fur down to my bare bones. Parched mouths huddled around various milk saucers, chilled by floating ice cubes – compliments of our compassionate donor. Alexander's pragmatic friends reigned over one of them.

"Well, well, well, if it isn't Wine! Come closer and let me lick your puss," slurred Randy who was swaying on his paws like a boat rocking in rough water. His tongue glided back and forth across his upper lip, emphasizing his lasciviousness. He had the appeal of a reptile, nothing subtle, only an epileptic expression of lewdness. Wine The Arrogant Cat surfaced and dismissed him with the hauteur of a patrician air. I never understood this crassness as an entrée to sexuality. Maybe Randy confused it with honesty.

Next to him was Herbert, another marginal friend of Alexander's. Instead of swaying from milk pollution he kept nipping away at his body, claiming a case of microscopic bugs giving him a ferocious itch. He vowed an end to picking up any more stray female cats unless they wore a medical collar around their neck certifying them free from all communicable diseases. "Don't get too close to me," he warned. There was little danger of this until, after I had expressed concern about Alexander's well-being.

"Alexander a suicide victim? Never!" exclaimed Herbert. "If there's one cat who will always survive, it's Alexander. He's too selfish to do himself in. Why, I remember years ago when we fought over a ball of yarn we had found in the street. I triumphed and Alexander pouted like a spoiled kitty even though he lived in the richest household in town. Listen, Wine, he's a nice enough cat but he's destroying himself, drinking himself to death. Can't you see he's finished, he's a loser?"

"A toast to Alexander! The only wake he'll ever know is waking up after a night of drinking," interjected Arthur. Such was his testimonial toast to his friendship with Alexander.

I felt like clawing all of them. They were slandering Alexander's reputation in a cowardly way, behind his back. Yes, Alexander was selfish. Yes, he drank too much. But what equation did this add up to? Perpetual repetition as a loser? Since when does a soul have a mathematical formula! None of Alexander's friends recognized his acting talent in public. None of them saw the foetal faces of finer qualities in Alexander struggling to be born. And if my dream had screened my solar smile as bankrupt, emotionally floundering, I could not forecast he would always be bankrupt. Sometimes you have to sustain your faith in other beings even when external appearances seem to contradict your hunches. I trusted my instincts. Their assessment of the raw materials in Alexander's soul foretold of a cat who would eventually blossom into a finer, better being.

This was how Wine The Cat had developed her reputation as a detector of gold in the souls of other creatures.

But Herbert scored one important point when he nominated Alexander for survivorship. If anyone could recoup his strengths and come back fighting, it was surely my solar smile. While survivors may undergo the most malicious maulings in life they do not go down in defeat. So my attitude toward the pessimism spawned by Alexander's friends was that of renewed faith. It was easier to place a bet on Alexander's winning abilities than on those who stampeded upon his reputation.

A peculiar thing then happened. A still-life painting exhibited itself like a reflex action within my interior vision. Alexander was lying on his belly under a willow tree. His face was barely recognizable. The grooming of confusion had been scrubbed off, revealing a face of lucidity! Then the exposure blurred into nothingness. My sixth sense said Alexander was alive and well. Scanty evidence if one is to be rational and logical. Was this a vision, an hallucination, or merely a desire to guide Alexander into some novel realm of existence? Yet I felt no inspired impulse working away. My senses were becalmed. It was as though an eye had blinked open, like a curtain momentarily parting just long enough to show something without time for reflection.

Was I becoming a clairvoyant cat with the onus of piling the future upon an already troublesome present and an overweight past? I hoped not!

I slanted my vision to its peripheral range, away from Alexander's crowd of seditious friends. At the far edge of The Milk Bar was Joshua, the cat who had been Alexander's understudy during our first separation. I had latched on to him that night after he had said, "Life is my best friend, just like a mate. Some days we get on wonderfully together and other days we bite off each other's head. But I wouldn't swap it for anything." Joshua was a lame cat who had been maimed by an accident in kittyhood when one of his paws had been broken. Without proper medical attention the paw healed like a gnarled tree limb, conferring a limp. Instead of cursing his handicap, Joshua joked about it. "I'm like a tricycle, a three-wheeled cat."

Tiny diamonds glittered in Joshua's eyes as I penetrated the threshold of his presence. To receive such an endearing reception made me wonder why I had forgotten him, why I had cancelled out a night which had hinted at more than just a remedial act of loneliness. But I had only wanted to drape his body with Alexander's spirit, to reverse who was the ghost and who was the body. I had wanted to keep something pure, to avoid desiring the spirit of another which might become an intrusion between Alexander and myself.

I had wanted to avoid emotional polygamy.

I had wanted to avoid duplicating my past!

As long as I hadn't looked for gold in Joshua's soul that night I was safe from being attracted to two different cats, safe from the agonies of a love triangle. Yet, appealing vibrations had come from Joshua. I resisted them by repudiating what experience had taught me long ago: that two cats could occupy different chambers of my heart at the same time; two different cats could offer separate parts of some magnificent superstar of love, possessing every fine quality I would ever need, a superstar bigger than life who only appeared in my imagination!

It still troubled me to accept what others vigorously denied – that while one cat may occupy the starring role of my love, this does not exclude the appearance of other beings who have a talent for upstaging the star of my love by offering a different interpretation of love, by giving me something which seems beyond the capacity of my beloved mate. Suddenly there are two cats who collectively complete the image of my fantasized superstar. Now there are two beings, two bodies I adore and I ask myself: how do I, one being with one body respond to this split affection in my heart?

This was the unanswerable dilemma, the coronation of the end of Claude and Wine, the result of an emotional entanglement with

102

our best friend. He was a cat temperamentally the polar opposite of Claude, a cat whose placidness calmed my skittery nature which was so easily stirred up by Claude's pulsating presence, a quality both appealing and debilitating, for the molecules around Claude never ceased to dance. His energy vibrated everything, including myself. On days when his powerful presence was like a big noise I had no retreat of my own where I could tranquilize myself. Then our best friend introduced me to a world called peace, an atmosphere foreign to Claude. In theory, I had the best of two worlds. But the gift contained an enormous cargo of guilt! Why couldn't I have both cats? I asked myself. Why indeed! Claude's teachings had underlined fidelity. "If you truly love me you cannot love another," he had said. But that was Claude's resumé of his experience. What about mine? If our best friend could wedge himself into my emotional life then I had to question Claude's definition of love. I had to define my own.

But where do you start when you are buffeted by guilt, when there is no precedent to guide you other than a mythology of love accusing you of betrayal? Where is the sage who can remedy the confusion? Claude The Teacher could not be asked to instruct me. To expose the truth might have destroyed his chaste image of love, a thankless gift to the one being who had taught me the art of loving. But if our bond of intimacy was so deep, why didn't I run the risk of putting it to the test? Did I think Claude would claw me to death in a jealous rage? Not really. Wine The Cat still believed that "truth" was the sole killer lurking next to the heart of every cat. If Wine spoke the truth she would be guilty of hurting another being, of destroying someone else's illusions. This proved to be a very costly error. Wine discovered that not speaking the truth cost her her own life!

I never deceived Claude when I vented my need to hunt for myself, to have a temporary separation while I sniffed around for wisdom without assistance. However, I didn't explain about the guilt which sparked my departure, my readiness to banish myself into an emotional exile while I atoned for my betrayal. I still believed then in guilt, in this self-punishing force, this invisible jailer conceived from a book of rules designed to keep cats in their place, keep them tame, obedient, resistant to deviancy or any self-styled liberation which might unshackle the chains of guilt. Imagine Alexander, this punishment I doled out to myself only because of an excessive fund of love, as though love could be criminal if it were given to more than one being at a time!

So Alexander, it was *synthetic guilt* which betrayed Claude and

103

Wine, not our best friend, guilt which authored the loss of Claude, guilt nourished by my ignorance about the complexity of love and my ignorance that silence was as poisonous as truth!

Now, Alexander, you understand why I began this long chronicle when I said I was fed up with the counterfeit quality of silence. I realize I was referring to my silence, not yours, my fear of the effect of truth upon other beings and myself. But don't think I'm becoming a rabid crusader for truth – no, not at all. I simply wish to be wise enough to discern when I should exhale truth and when I should cloister it. I want to rewrite the scene of our first reunion for future use – when I admitted that Joshua had been your understudy – because the truth illuminated nothing. You had my heart. I had yours. That was the only truth worthy of recognition. And when I do utter truth, I want to employ it beyond a simple cat's meow. The language of animals is marvellous – direct and uncomplicated. But occasionally I envy the potential of expression available to humans, their tools of discourse that no animal enjoys. And I wonder if mastering the human language would enhance my expression of feeling and thinking. Would I find a language for truth, giving myself time to know what truth is . . .?

"Wine," said Joshua as I went up to him, "I hear you're Alexander's girl-friend."

"Friend is maybe a better word, Josh. Do I detect a slight note of sadness in your voice?"

"Yes, I was disappointed to learn about the two of you. I wanted to see more of you after that night. I felt a little hurt."

"I'm sorry.

"Don't apologize. It just surprised me that a cat like you would be interested in Alexander. I've had a few of his cast-off girl-friends and they claim he hissed at them a lot. I don't want to see you get bad treatment."

The concern in his voice spaced him apart from Alexander's mutinous friends.

"Josh, he is a rough cat at times but he can also be sweet. However, I haven't seen him in weeks so I don't know what shape he's in . . . Would you do me a favour? Would you help me make life my best friend tonight? I've been depressed lately. Seeing you makes me feel very good."

"I'd be delighted."

Joshua and I slowly slinked our way along steamy streets, freshly hosed down by Albert's enemies. The moonlight cast shadows of streams of vapour, spiralling toward the neon lights of the moon. Every so often our paws splashed water from virgin puddles, showering our bodies with a cooling reprieve from the blistering heat. The Saturday night fever of fun and games had scattered humans in search of places humming with air conditioners. The street belonged only to those willing to forgive nature's torridness.

Joshua's coat of black fur glistened with sweat every time a moonbeam funnelled across his body. While he was older than Alexander, his body evidenced no sign of a paunch. His leanness bespoke of a rumbunctious cat preferring physical activity to the bulges created by a sedentary life. His locomotion was not hampered by his lame paw. He had perfected an exotic gait, like that of a dancer sure of the next step. He held his head erect in an unassuming dignity, not waiting for the applause of others to confirm his security.

We passed by a collection of garbage cans overflowing with rubbish. The sidewalk was garnished with granite pieces of bread. I could remember those antique days when an array like this would glitter my existence with wild joy at seeing a few crumbs of food to stick into my belly. With hunger as the dominate force then, Wine The Thinker could not afford the luxury of thought. Thought could only be served as a dessert to a well-fed body.

Like myself, Joshua could not abide this anarchistic waste of food.

"Wine, let's find some hungry cats and feed them."

We soon spotted two needy recipients, two furless cats who looked like sheared sheep, balded by malnutrition. Like two mad lions tearing apart their prey, they wolfed down the bread despite Joshua's warning to eat slowly. The food settled in their bellies without being regurgitated. Their backs began to arch a little dignity, a slight unstiffening from the humility of hunger. Joshua could not abandon these two homeless creatures to recede into an indifferent anonymity. He offered them the hospitality of a vacant garage attached to the home where he lived. He would doctor their bellies until they lost their swollen look. The cats bowed their heads in thanks and then scampered off to Joshua's house with the speed of fear that he might yank away his generosity.

"Joshua, you're a born helper."

"Maybe. But don't spread the word. I often get taken advantage of. Everyone smells my soft heart. But what can I do? I'm not going to change. Besides, we've got to help one another, Wine. It makes us feel useful. Anyhow, it's so easy if you don't start worrying about what it's going to cost you. I figure it costs you one way or another if you don't help others."

"Joshua, you're a beautiful cat."

Wine The Detective of Gold added another jewel to my strand of valuable cats. If I could be seduced by a solar smile I could also be seduced by Joshua's compassion.

We came upon a children's playground illuminated by constellations of glowing cat eyes, cats inheriting the daytime amusement park willed to them by youthful humans safely tucked away in their beds. There were cats gliding down miniature metal slides and cats vaulting from bar to bar on a Junglegym, similar to a diminutive steel skeleton of a high-rise building. There were cats tusselling about in a gigantic sandbox, flecks of sand rising like showering geysers roused by their sexual shenanigans.

The air misted an aroma of musk, of bodies responding to the sensuality of a hot night when heat fires up such a sharp outline of sex, unlike the desires of flesh dampened by cold. I knew we would eventually join the ritual of copulating couples in the sandbox. But first it was necessary to dilate desire.

Joshua swan-leaped on to the bottom rung of the Junglegym, the opening movement to a concerto of pleasure. He dared me to catch him but I wavered, coyly arching myself while his eyes blessed the mysteries of my anatomy. The space between us crackled with teasing wantonness, my body undulating like a rising, falling wave, straining to meet the profusion of kisses emanating from Joshua's eyes. His stare possessed the hypnotic power finally to levitate me to his side. Embracing me fervently, white heat oozed from his body into me and around me, cocooning me in a flush of ardour. I too, spun a web of warmth around him, woven by all of the sultry emotions which had been hibernating for weeks – emotions of giving which needed to be set free, to be put into contact with another passionate soul. It was Joshua's warmth which sparked alive my reservoir of feeling, intermingling now with his sprays of lust – all this cajoling us on a course of spontaneous combustion.

Through his eyes flowed two streams of warmth, two newly discovered channels through which I could float into his body, as though the female me had at last detected a way of entering the male body. Then he short-circuited the current between us. He leaped up onto the next, higher bar and I ravenously tailed him. Now his tongue licked an enchanted route of seduction, skipping randomly from nerve end to nerve end until my body felt itself being kindled by a succession of tiny fires of pleasure. My artful dodger now leaped earthbound and I followed behind, trembling with erotic vibrations, clamouring for more body titillation.

Now ardour sought a counterpoint to tenderness, a desire for little nips and bites, the difference between pleasure and pain indistinguishable. We inaugurated the final preparation for body communion, each playing with the other's tongue – nipping it, kissing it, ingesting it, expelling it, the vision of fusion between male and female.

"Joshua, I want to pull your body into mine, I want to pull you into my belly."

We raced to the sandbox and found a private space. Finally the exquisite movement of his stealthily entering me sent shivers of pleasure rippling everywhere in my body as he slid in to kiss my womb, my empty womb, momentarily begging to be impregnated by him, by his warmth. His thrusting became more bold and he implored me to swallow him up, pushing more violently against my womb to emphasize the sincerity of his wish. My control started to falter, the first twinges of orgasm pulsating and then beginning to swell and when he cried, "Wine, let yourself go," I surrendered to the quiver which crested into a violent shaking and then I was thrown into the bliss of non-existence. That was the moment when upon feeling me clamped all around his maleness, Joshua poured into me all the waters of his passion, accompanied by a low moan of pleasure.

We lay there, two limp bodies, exhausted and peaceful, huddling together in an aura of warmth, a long, lingering embrace which carried us together throughout the night . . .

I often replayed that scene of passion with Joshua without the residual taste of guilt which had marred our first liaison. The same props of loneliness and Alexander's absence were available as they had been the first time. But something had altered. Alexander had not fogged the visibility of my interlude with Joshua nor had Joshua stirred up any emotional divisions in my heart. It was Joshua with whom I had made love, Joshua the sexual artist who knew the secret of shared pleasure between male and female, Joshua who had created an irresistible sea of warmth, an atmosphere of sexual liberation because his soul was not entwined with inhibitions.

To compare the savoury meal offered by Joshua with the impoverished one served by Albert was to recognize the extremes between sexual feast and famine. I would never again settle for anything less than the very best of sex!

But could I claim that my rendezvous with Joshua was only a carnival of the senses, a purely carnal encounter?

My attention wanders toward a plant on a table near the window of my mistress's study. Instead of drooping, the stems are defying gravity, arching toward the sunlight like hungry refugees begging for food. My mistress has forgotten to water the soil. The sunlight is now the only source of nourishment for this parched plant. Nor does the plant judge my mistress's actions be they wilful or negligent. The plant doesn't care. It instinctively does what it must in order to survive. Just like all living creatures.

So, Alexander, I must make another entry in my bible for survival: We all have the inherent right to survive, to live, to preserve ourselves emotionally as well as physically. If we are separated from someone we love either by necessity or by callous neglect and we are shoved into a dessicated existence we can either wither to death or find something which revives and nourishes us. If sex is like the esperanto of emotional nutrition then let us revel in it, let us praise it and be grateful for its restorative powers, its infusion of hope and energy. Let us deal a death blow once and for all to infidelity as a source of guilt. Let us now call infidelity the life-saving device that it can truly be at times.

* * * * *

And now Alexander, I come to the most significant event whose outcome took all of this time to absorb. I gave no hint of it after our paths criss-crossed again though it marked another turning point in my evolutionary itinerary. Nor am I recounting this so that you will rescind any judgement about the possible shoddiness of my intellectual equipment as you once implied. I'm not looking for a grade of excellence. I don't need it. There is only one being who can assess all of my performances. That being is myself.

Alexander, there is a story about a human who went to sleep one night and awakened the following morning metamorphosed into a cockroach! Imagine the shock of discovering you are different from what you thought you were the previous day! I, too, fell into a deep slumber one evening, shortly after my spiritual and sexual loosening up exercises with Joshua and upon glimpsing the morning light I felt a strange sensation that a different Wine surveyed the landscape of familiar, external details. My mistress's study was unchanged.

But I? ... Which I? ...

Mysteriously, a psychological skin had completely peeled off during the night, a shedding process that must have begun during an age of ignorance in my unconscious world. Here in this inner sanctum dwelled another unknown colour of my rainbow of selves – a Wine who now divined the time was ripe for moving into the sunlight of my awareness.

I suspected this Wine was bringing me a message.

I scampered to the mirror wanting to read the face of this new Wine. Had a few wrinkles spread over my face during the night? No! No new physical details could be detected. But the face! Its demeanour was of a maternity I had never witnessed, the serene smile of a mother proudly bidding farewell to an offspring who is about to venture forth, alone, into the world for the first time, a mother saying, "Go fly little one, go fly."

Such a peaceful smile! Such a smile of acceptance!

This Wine who gazed back at me from two deep wells of compassion foretold of a peacemaker, a newly elected moderator for all of my contradictory selves living under the one roof of my soul, a Wine who inspired confidence that she could balance my emotional oscillations between dying of laughter and dying of despair.

Here in the mirror was the face of Wine The Mature Cat in full bloom!

Was this Wine such a novelty? Hand't I fought over the years to grow up, to surmount my insecurities, to become a more worthy creature? Hadn't I often envisioned that one morning I might awaken freed from my negative foibles, freed from behaving like a part-time monster, freed from hating those creatures who thwarted my wishes, freed from my fear of being alone, unable to cope with life, freed from my fear of death?

This new Wine whispered something in my ear.

"Your thoughts and fears are the eternal chorus of all beings. These things come and go. Accept them. Learn to live with them. And welcome me as a new friend. I promise you a soft shoulder to lean on when the rough seas of life require special navigation . . . no, not a shoulder . . . an anchor! An anchor on to which all your inner inhabitants can grasp."

How persistently and frantically I had searched for this anchor outside of myself. A natural tendency, goaded on by kittyhood ignorance when all of us see adult cats as seers, experts and sages in the magic of life because someone had once patented the brilliant idea that adults should automatically inherit wisdom as their just reward for having lived a requisite number of calendar years. (The idea had only one flaw as I learned later – wisdom couldn't be measured by a calendar.) Anyhow, I was a good little kitty and worshipped my elders. Especially renown for fantastic powers of knowledge were those who had sired me and when they no longer existed I found surrogate cats delighted to exhibit their funds of knowledge – even though many of them operated in the red. I absorbed every word I heard, both the spurious and the profound without a sense of discrimination. After all, they were older, they were wiser!

This faulty assumption of wisdom arising from age was bolstered too by the relationship with my professor of love whose expertise in matters of the heart and exercising freedom protected me from pessimism of any kind. However, when I felt inclined to move my body and soul into his, he thwarted my urge. Instead of understanding his honourable intentions to help me lean more on myself, I chastised his domestic situation as the evil hindrance against his becoming my full-time, worldly guide. So I continued to haul around a mixed bag of dependency – emotional, mental and metaphysical.

Now I have sketched myself as a very strong-willed, independent cat, which was true in part. But I always wanted to have an escape route, someone to catch me and hold me when life became unmanageable. Two different colours or characters of my rainbow of selves began a fierce boxing match. The two contenders were Wine The Independent Cat and Wine The Dependent Kitty. At first, my dependency showed itself to be of superior strength. I learned this after I fell in love with the black cat, when he became the barometer of my emotional existence. When he was happy, I was happy. When he was melancholy so was I. His whole being became the centre of my existence until that shocking day when there was a gravitational split-up between us. I was blown up into a thousand fragments because I had no orbit of my own to hold me together. My dependency proved to be as potent as an activated bomb.

It was Claude The Saviour who found and mended me. And while he was doctoring my emotional wounds he discovered I had an inquisitive mind which could be trained for mental gymnastics. With his penchant for teaching and mine for learning, we laced together a tight bond. He became the trustee of my existence until I asserted my readiness (fed mostly by my guilt about involvement with our best friend) to take on the world without his arch support. And once again surviving alone caused my interior house to collapse. Had I learned nothing from my experience with the black cat? With Claude? Yes, some of Claude's techniques for physical survival gave me first aid. Eating rancid rat meat was not the awful meal others thought it to be.

But physical survival is one thing. Emotional survival is another issue. Alone in this world, I continued looking for guardian angels to whom I could entrust a large portion of my spirit, creatures who would answer my every call of emotional distress. All of them failed this test! *They had to*! Who in this world can respond to your every need? NOBODY!

Now I come to the work begun in this secret underground lab of mine. After each disappointment with another cat who sooner or later had to abdicate his assigned role as saviour, Wine The Mature Cat started undergoing the incubation stage known as *self-help*. I was being forced, against my will, to rely more and more upon myself, or selves, in all matters of the heart and mind! What a burden! What work! And to show you my resistance to all of this I refer back to that day in the garbage can when Alexander's solar smile resurrected me from a deadly depression. I was still determined to christen him a saviour, determined to enshrine him in an impossible role. I still believed in saviours outside of myself. I still believed that if only one other being would let me share the planet of his existence that this act alone made the difference between living in life and dying in life. Or, so I thought until this day when the sun rose with revelation, when other truths became unveiled.

Wine The Mature Cat awarded me two new degrees, two synonymous titles, after a brief speech.

"The sign of maturity in any being is when you can recognize the potential for your own wisdom rather than worshipping the wisdom of others. Today you have become your own teacher. Today you have become your own saviour."

It was like hearing a loud speaker announcing an unexpected stop during an interminably long, perilous trip with many stops and starts, a voyage begun at the moment of birth, a voyage whose only destination was an expanded awareness of existence, a voyage without a final destination. This was not the reality of life envisioned in my previous existences. In those days I always had the feeling of waiting for something outside myself, of dreamily walking along a street, assuming that at some intersection of my life I would turn a corner and meet up with my *real* reality. Then it dawned on me one day that this real reality was facing me every minute, it wasn't something lying in wait for some non-existent future!

In one split second my perception of life had altered, just as it was doing now!

Yet all new awareness, all new truth is double edged – exciting and frightening. It was challenging to think I had become my own teacher. But it was also disturbing. Was I excommunicated forever from encountering a sage? Could I ever trust the wisdom of another being again?

111

Then a new question popped up. What was wisdom?

Was it like a supermarket exercise in which each of five experts promotes a different brand of tuna fish as the most healthy one for your cat? Which brand do you choose? Which expert do you listen to? What determines your choice? The colour or the shape of a can? The eloquence or persuasiveness of one expert over the others? . . . One thing is for sure. Whatever factor determines the outcome, I still am the one who makes the choice, the final decision. And I may even decide the next time I go to the supermarket that another brand of tuna may be more palatable, so, my choice is always subject to being repealed.

Suddenly wisdom seemed as arbitrary and relative as Albert's fiddling with his watches and setting them to different hours. Wisdom was just as capricious as a summer breeze – variable and undefinable. Basically, wisdom represented my changing perceptions in each successive stage of life.

I then wrote in my anthology of life: Wisdom is growth, a greater awareness of life, a greater awareness of myself, a move toward an inner harmony, a move toward finding my mature face which helps me renounce impossible demands on the world. Wisdom is the ability to accept life as it is, without trying to make it what it isn't.

Many was the time I would have to refer back to these words because frequently my wisdom took an unexpected holiday.

That day of revelation was like a pilgrimage to the four corners of the earth. And I discovered a fifth corner – myself, my core – like discovering the eighth wonder of the world. Or said in another way, I felt like a cat who had finally caught her tail after countless, futile attempts.

An inspired hope germinated in me for all catkind. If I, a simple nobody without pedigree papers could find the saviour in myself, why couldn't others meet the same fate? What hurdles blockaded this discovery other than the tendency for all of us to lie in the arms of a best friend called *blame*. How much easier to fault others for what we are denied, beginning with those who sire us. But surely we have to pardon our genetic creators. (Recall Alexander's dream, when he gives a kiss of forgiveness to his swine of a father). We have to excuse their frailties, their imperfections. They never intentionally plot to lay the bricks of conflicts at the base of our being. Nor can they claim to be the sole architects for all our strife. Each of us has enough talent to design our own difficulties. This then suggests that we must admit another truth: all mamas and papas are offspring of other mamas and papas.

If blame lies anywhere it rests in the inherent condition of just being alive!

Suddenly I grasp why Wine The Saviour was born. Alexander had become the catalyst whose contribution of conflicts had set off a search in me for further comprehension. Because he owned a greater share of emotional disequilibrium than other cats I had known concerning love, dependency and independence, it was impossible to escape a close scrutiny of these dynamic corner-stones of my life, my soul. Every time I x-rayed Alexander's being I found some remnant of myself, some conflict which I inevitably brought home for further inspection. Wine The Mature Cat then subtly began stitching together the scattered pieces of confusion into an orderly, tailor-made design for herself. When her work was finished she made her modelling début to the admiring glances of the other Wines. But she cautioned all of them to mute their applause. "After all, I'm just doing the job my birthright hired me to do."

Dear Alexander. Aren't you proud of the legacy your smile accidentally bequeathed me? After all, it was the first ray of your solar smile which helped dawn the slow rising up of my own sunlight, my awareness. You didn't offer me the safety of a saviour though your smile seduced me in that direction. By default, I had to stiffen up my back with independence. I couldn't duplicate with you the dependency I had enjoyed and later hated with Claude.
You threw me out into the sea of my own foul wisdom.

It is a propitious moment to amend a section in my anthology of life called Transitions From One Cat Life To Another. Tragedy, loss or misfortune are not the only agents terminating one stage of life. The end of an epoch doesn't have to ring out a note of sorrow. We may also end one life and start the next by discarding one form for another, by replacing ignorance with epiphany, similar to the conversion of a butterfly from a wingless creature to one that can fly.

It would seem then that the phoenix is not the only relative between you humans and we cats as I suggested at the beginning of this story. Now I must add the butterfly and of course the cockroach who was once a man. And who knows how many more relatives we have in common? Now I have to devise a list next to my anthology of life and jot down what characteristics I find in common between the family of man and the family of animals. My gosh! A whole new area of study and I haven't even finished the one about Alexander, myself and love! It certainly is true that life is never finished.

Despite the miracle of that day of revelation, I felt a peculiar feeling of dispossession, a loss of the last vestige of ignorance. So I garnered my troupe of selves, led by Wine The Saviour, and padded along the streets, listening to the pulse-beats of other creatures, looking for kindred spirits.

I saw a parade of strangers to life, using life as an alibi for not living.

I saw faces pinched by resignation. I saw faces quivering from fear. I saw faces contorted by idiocy. I saw faces envious of the velvet visage of youth and horror in those faces glimpsing wrinkles. I saw cats crowding together in rings of security. I saw couples in clinging embraces, rescuing one another from empty selves. I saw faces of regret over unpollinated dreams. I saw faces of arrogance made up by material comfort.

I flashbacked to The Fur Fair and saw people grasping at every pound of fur, their synthetic anchors.

The design for spiritual anchors was still a great mystery.

I saw only a few faces made up by peace. Those creatures so blessed stood at the edges of the masses, alone but not lonely.

I heard a loud, dissonant orchestra of heartbeats – moaning, groaning, creaking, weeping – comrades of fear, all facing the same wailing wall of life.

The world as I perceived it at that moment was reduced to a global nursery school, populated by children and kitties unsuccessfully masquerading as mature representatives of their lineage.

More isolation doused me, a growing sense of remoteness from other beings. How easy it was to identify with that man exiled to a cockroach shell. But in lieu of admiring it as a miraculous change, I now translated his metamorphosis as a hideous form of separation, as though truth were a disease which quarantines your existence from others. Once again, I felt a disassociated reaction similar to the one of my kittyhood when the awareness of my own mortality struck a truth nerve.

Was this isolation the grand Croix de Guerre, the magnificent award for heroically locating my own saviour? If so, I wanted no medal, no enlightenment. Wine The Saviour could look elsewhere for housing! Give me a flesh and blood saviour, I thought, someone who puts his paws on me, something solid, not some phantom who seduces me to enter a well-illuminated inner-sanctum and then, without warning, turns out the lights! No thank you.

After I mulled over these thoughts, I was seized by an uncontrollable compulsion to make a public announcement:

Hey, all you fear-ridden creatures. Start clinging to yourself. Give yourself a kiss. You *are* more than what you think you are. When you become your own saviour you achieve real intimacy with yourself. And it is this which makes intimacy with others possible and meaningful.

I expected the cats I passed by to regard me as a freak! But no one noticed me!

No one heard me!

The words were microphoned only in my mind, the broadcast authored by Wine The Saviour.

"There is no public address system which can carry this message to anyone other than to yourself. Epiphany, awareness, is a silent experience," she said. "I just wanted to remind you of what you already know in order to ease your loneliness. You must conquer this tendency to walk off the face of the earth. Find the linkage between yourself and others!" she ordered.

I obeyed her like a hypnotized subject.

I continued strolling and strolling, listening with my auditory stethoscope to a welter of heartbeats and every so often a pulsation of sorrow and joy synchronized with my own. The canvas backdropping this activity was composed of living elements – grass, trees, flowers, sun – each pulsating other rhythmic heartbeats. In a flash I felt an awareness of a cosmic anatomy obeying a splendid blue-print of harmony set up by Nature. And I was part of all this, a microscopic part, but still a part. My heartbeat resonated the heartbeat of the multitude. My home was no longer just my flesh and bones. My home was expanding into the universe. What did it matter if everyone perceived life in a different form? This was but a movie set façade behind which lay a veritable oneness, a communal home uniting all of us!

If I discovered a universal heartbeat that day it was because I discovered a unity in myself, thanks to the birth of Wine The Saviour. At last I saw myself as a miniature replica of the cosmos. I realized that all creation mirrors itself in all other creation. I was no different from other creatures!

Here was the link I needed to dissolve my isolation.

Yes, I lost my ignorance that day. Evolution always demands you leave something behind. And, instead of dubbing the universe as a disorderly array of chaos, I saw it as a thing of perfection, patiently waiting for me to discover it.

Chaos had only one address – within me, not elsewhere.

Don't think, Alexander, that my lucidity came all at once. Wine The Saviour and Teacher held many conferences with the other Wines from that day on because it took much time to absorb all the insights that rippled forth. Nor was the absorption of these thoughts a cerebral affair. The insights entered the mainstream of my "being." Unfortunately, isolation did not go into the total exile that I hoped it would. It still haunted me. And Wine The Saviour still disappeared at critical moments though I was usually ninety-nine percent sure of her return.

Then there were the lectures about things dear to my heart such as freedom. "You can have all the freedom you want," said Wine The Saviour, "assuming you are willing to work twenty-four hours a day. And if you fall asleep on the job you'll have to tolerate the consequences of someone else's dictates, be enslaved by their de-cisions. And if you're too lazy to make a decision, that too counts as a choice. Just so you know that flexing freedom is an awesome responsibility." (As if I hadn't already known that!) "Now you understand why it's so delightful when others tell you what to do. This is the secret to an easy, lazy life. Are you sure you still want to guard your freedom with such a gluttonous urge?"

Another topic which also caused a ruckus was pain.

"Don't think that because your vision is more encompassing and wiser that this will exonerate you from pain. You still must accept the hurts, the disappointments which plague you as inevitable collisions with life. But I predict that the bleeding time for all wounds is going to shorten. And now that you have me, you don't have to worry about future blackouts of your soul. No one will annihilate you or render you a helpless creature. That some cats will yank at the roots of your being? Yes. But once the essence of your saviour is perceived, robbery of it becomes impossible."

Yes, Wine The Saviour certainly had a way of spotlighting things precious to me until they were reduced to searing truths.

* * * * *

Saviourhood accompanied me to sleep after that fateful day. The dream it engendered featured Alexander as a prisoner strapped to a white marble surgeon's table. A veterinarian presided over the scene, with an electric shaver poised in his hand. When he switched

116

on the benign-looking tool, a sadistic smile neonlighted his face. Two tiers of rat-like incisors fenced the inside of his mouth. Verbal torture came lashing forth from this potential "cutter" whose savage scheme for Alexander was a threat to all catkind.

"You are going to become a bald cat. I will shave off all your fur and design it as the first cat wig available to the public, a superb display sample for an advertising campaign to lure prospective clients who want a keepsake of their beloved pets after I put them to eternal rest. My method will soften the human sorrow of losing a pet. Imagine the fame and riches I will collect!"

I wondered if this humanitarian had been one of the clients at The Fur Fair who had been inspired to devise something new for the human who had everything?

I witnessed this plot in a spectral form while sitting on top of a glass cabinet containing a brutal array of surgical instruments far more menacing than the razor being brandished by this publicity hound. Since he couldn't see me I commenced to jiggle the cabinet with a few bumps and grinds. The evil grin on the surgeon's face sutured up. His reaction became typical of humans unfamiliar with ghosts. His hands started to tremble. My next bit of hocus pocus was to inhale a deep breath and send out a torrent of air toward him. His white gown billowed out and his hair stood up on end – a rather poor imitation of a cat because his hair wasn't bushy enough. Unlike Alexander he was already partially bald. The surgeon's earthquaking hands dropped the razor which hop-scotched on the floor. The moment had come for me to adopt an earthly guise. So I transformed myself into an enchanting Cinderella. The astonished veterinarian quickly regained his poise and while he sought to throw off his operating gown for something more comfortable, I hastily made for the razor, yelling to Alexander, "Don't worry, there's enough time to save you."

And then I awakened, frustrated that the dream had terminated without a conclusion, though part of it could be fathomed. Evidently, the previous day's epiphany must have inspired in me a new career – S.O.S. . . Save Other Souls.

Wine The Saviour reminded me I could not save anyone other than myself.

This was followed by several days of repose on an island of peace – my head emptied of questions.

Then came the collision! At The Milk Bar! With Alexander!

There had been no warning, no telepathic message. Only an accidental arrival at The Milk Bar because I had nothing else to do. And there he was! Alexander, plumply alive, no longer a ghost! In record time the ice around my heart alchemized into adrenelin being wildly shot through my nervous heart. Helena's rule of needing timely transitions to recuperate feelings had just found an exception.

There was also something else which jarred my heart. Alexander's head was a hairline away from a lovely female whose lush fur would have excited the surgeon of my dream.

I became paralyzed! What should I do? Pad over to Alexander as though nothing were out of whack or keep my distance and observe his reaction?

The controls to our common frequency station were not turned on so I held my position. He must have seen my approach from the grove of trees which fringed the area of the milk saucers. If so, he was snubbing me. Was this really the same cat I had sought to save in my dream? Or an impostor of Alexander The Caring Cat? Maybe the compassionate Alexander had committed suicide and all that remained was the skin of a cruel cat!

I captured the nearest cat I could find with whom I began an agitated prattle, a warming-up exercise for regaining control. Through my peripheral vision I noted Alexander periscoping his view toward me. At last I gave him my stereoscopic face.

He fired off one round of a sentence. "I got your message but I decided not to answer it." He paused. Then he illuminated his face with a triumphant smile. "I WON," he declared.

My vibrations deciphered his shorthand code. It read he had successfully distanced me from his heart. He did not want an exotic fur looking for her dispossessed friend.

Alexander, what do you win if you cut the emotional tie to another being? Besides, isn't this a charade, a blatant lie, an illusion of the mind when you claim the power to eliminate feelings? You may as well say you can amputate space with a magical pair of scissors. How can we cut away emotions which we can't possibly draw or know where they live! Only their shadows reside in our minds. But their essences? Feelings can't be rounded up and controlled as though they were a pack of wild horses. They aren't part of the material world. They are ghostly presences, dancing within us and around us. But more to the point. *Alexander, we ARE our emotions.* We are not separate from them as many thinkers erroneously believe. The only time bonds are truly broken between two beings is when there is a change in attitude or perception and then it is this altered attitude which clips the emotional tether, not an artificial act of will. No, Alexander, you didn't win anything except first prize in the art of self-deception. Your mind tricked you into believing it was something more than it was. You failed to recognize it as an inadept translator for some realities which have no fixed form or address . . .

I was tempted that night in The Milk Bar to confer upon Alexander the gravest insult I could think of – Alexander is a scaredy cat. He's lost his balls. I was also dismayed by the waves in his voice, agitated by too much milk. My vision of a reconstituted Alexander bathing in lucidity had only been a parlour game, a poorly executed wish, dreamed up by my optimistic self.

The garbage can, my peaceful retreat, started shimmering a seductive lure. "Run to its soothing tranquillity," ordered Wine The Conscientious Objector To Emotional War. "You don't have to stay here."

I swivelled my face away from Alexander and then walked in the direction of peace. However after a short distance I froze my motion, scolding myself – you are surrendering, undertaking a cowardly act for which you have just admonished Alexander. Is he really rejecting you or jousting – challenging Wine The Cat to skillful manoeuvers in a delicate situation? Is Wine The Cat afraid to face the truth, afraid to admit that the sour taste in her mouth is . . . jealousy?

Ouch! The truth is pinching me. Yes. I'm jealous. It's been eons since I've coped with it. I'm out of practice. I don't know whether to display it or burn it. I want to hide it from Wine The Saviour so she won't be disappointed in my regression back to tomfoolery. Suddenly the face of epiphany is now only a dream. A few days ago I had become wise and now, once again, I'm an ignorant alley cat with the predatory urge to hiss and scratch out someone's eyes. Well, that's ironically reassuring. If I thought I was gliding off the crust of the earth the other day I have just been magnetized back to the throng of beings who share the communal pool of jealousy.

"Jealousy, thy name is symptomatic of forgetting your sense of worth." Wine The Saviour was back coaching me. "Retrace your steps back to Alexander. Trace reality, not the fictionalized version you are concocting in your mind! Already you assume carnal knowledge unites Alexander with that lush creature. How do you know?"

I arched my back and lumbered toward the unknown, back to The Milk Bar, resuming my stance next to the former victim of my verbosity, only now I switched to silence. It was his turn for an unsolicited soliloquy while I sneakily peeped at Alexander, occasionally crashing into him with a head-on stare. The drama was becoming comical.

Impulsively I belted out to Alexander, "Still five hundred or five hundred and one?" Alexander could have filed a complaint – betrayal and indecent exposure of jealousy. I had just publicly broadcast the secret tally of cats that he had slept with during his various lifetimes. We had once treated this as a private joke when it was first mentioned. Had he added to his body count?

He grinned an inscrutable smile and turned away his head.

The game between us was warming up.

Minutes of boredom ticked away. The ticker-tape conversationalist by my side rattled off a lot of noise which funnelled in one ear and out the other.

Alexander and my competitor finished their rendezvous.

The lush cat shifted her residence from my solar smile to the crashing bore beside me.

"Darling," she said, "let's go home. I'm tired. Alexander doesn't know the difference between cat boxes lined with rayon or silk. He says it's all the same to him!"

What a relief! Alexander wasn't interested in her fur!

Mr and Mrs Cat exited.

I paid my condolences to Wine The Paranoid Cat. May you rot in hell!

Then I apologized to Wine The Saviour for my premature judgement of Alexander's adultery. And how many other times in my past lives had I lit the fuse to paranoia because of faulty perception? I shuddered when I multiplied the effects of this tiny event. If all cats behaved as rashly as I nearly had then life was surely the greatest tale ever told – total, sinful fiction, cats squandering their lives, sniffing false scents leading nowhere.

My next chore was to test out the temperature of Alexander's feelings; tropical, temperate or polar cold? This meant a direct confrontation. I had to initiate an action which still wasn't my forte: grab the bull by the horns as humans say or in this case grab Alexander's tail. I would have preferred the intimidation of a snarling dog. I was going to take a chance, give Alexander the right to breach my security, wound me if he liked. So I snailed toward him in a swarm of nervousness which he certainly smelled. Whether this provoked him to capriciousness or seriousness I'll never know. He quickly retrieved his tail and tucked it under his body after I made a clumsy attempt to swat it! And this being what I feared the most made me commit the supreme blunder; I opened the door to a gust of rejection which ruled me like a despotic leader, mandating me to flee The Milk Bar.

I forgot that everything was supposed to be a test!

I was the one who failed, not Alexander. I crowned vanity as the ruler of the situation instead of curiosity. If only I had stayed I could have culled more about Alexander's feelings. But no. Wine The Paranoid Cat rushed me home to the garbage can, though not without backward glances to see if Alexander was following me. And of course he wasn't, which infuriated me even more. Now my paranoia was stewing with anger and tears. Alexander is abandoning me . . . not, I am abandoning Alexander . . . and my rage boiled and percolated . . . go ahead and drown in your milk you rotten son-of-a-bitch, son-of-a-cat or whoever . . . . . You are nothing but a coward, scared to death of intimacy with me . . . Go ahead and withdraw if I've gotten too close to your heart. What do I need you for? All you do is throw my life into a revolving door – love entering and leaving. You're nothing but a mess of conflicts. You aren't worth my efforts. I don't even know what I love about you. I don't even know *if* I love you. Maybe I love what I think you can be, not what you are.

Maybe I have created Alexander in an image of my own making!

I fell asleep that night pondering the wonders of the sun of my revelation. I recalculated the sum of my conclusions. I was now a wise fool instead of an ignorant one. But the common denominator was still a fool!

* * * * *

Wine The Fool wept that next morning under a quilt of depression, sobbing, "Alexander, you aren't what I want you to be!"

I wanted to plead an illness unwritten in any medical textbook: love as a source of durable sorrow. There was no healer to whom I could meow, "Help me, help me, my soul is haemorrhaging from the despair of thinking that what started out as a promising beginning with another cat is now entering the terminal stages of disillusionment. I'm not even lamenting the apparent impossibility of Alexander loving me. I'm bemoaning something more devastating. *Alexander has filched me of hope*, the hope of achieving an intimate relationship. Without this hope I feel the hole of my loneliness deepen. Without this hope I don't have the life-supporting oxygen I need."

"But *life is hope*," said Wine The Saviour.

"And *life is love*," I retorted.

"Yes," replied Wine The Saviour. "Life is hope and love and many more adjectives and experiences. Life is a series of blank spaces we fill in and erase, a thing of fluctuating, relative definitions. Be grateful, Wine, that you have life, that you can wake up each day to ponder its mysteries and even lament its miseries as you're doing this morning."

"Now you're making me feel ashamed when I complain about Alexander."

"That's not my intention. My role is not to be the villain of guilt but to help you shift the line of your vision when you fruitlessly try to chase your tail, when you try to impose what you think should be on to what is. Sorrow is an inherent part of love if you want to view it that way. But can't you recall something you already know, that the adhesion between two beings is intrinsically slippery because the fluctuating quality of love reflects the fluctuating quality of life, of yourself. As long as living creatures prowl the earth there is movement, flow, change; so love too has to be a kinetic, vibrating experience that frequently tilts you off balance."

"But can't love be peaceful?"

"Sometimes. But if you're looking for constant peace you'll have to renounce love – renounce life – and withdraw into a monastic existence where you won't risk collisions with other beings. Besides, if it's peace you want, I can promise that someday you will meet death, the deft master which punishes sorrow eternally."

An electric silence generated for a time while I murmured prayers to the powers within me which had impregnated and given birth to Wine The Saviour. She was proving to be the best friend I would ever have.

I asked her one more question.

"Where can I find a supply of hope?"

"Be patient, Wine. You haven't exhausted the supply you have. Hope doesn't become extinct unless you wish it to be. If you want to find hope you can. Just open up your eyes. As long as there is life there is hope. You and you alone are capable of sparkling it alive. Now, what other lamentations do you have?"

Unexpectedly a feeling of mirth menaced my depression. Wine The Saviour was daring me to laugh at myself. If Wine The Cat could brazenly challenge mangy dogs, surely I could bite and hiss at this feudal fiend entitled "gloom."

I began to tongue myself clean in preparation for leaving the garbage can. Further solitary confinement would only fertilize negative thoughts. I would visit my mistress for a few hours, get out of my skin, forget myself.

As I made my way to her house I envied those cats I knew caring for their young. Yes, having to think about the needs of others certainly allows for an intermission from your own despair.

How expensive it is to own and maintain freedom . . .

No sooner had I purred my presence to my mistress when something lassoed my body back out into the street. My sixth sense named the Houdini invisibly tugging at me. After quickly scooting along several scorching blocks I met my magician lying on his belly in the middle of the street laughing at hosts of moving vehicles braking to a halt so they wouldn't flatten this plump cat to a slim pancake. What a spectacle! Alexander improvising a street version of Russian roulette. Hadn't he exhausted his suicidal wishes during his long absence? His effrontery was too brazen to be cited as self-destruction. It was more symptomatic of an unruly kitty looking for mischief.

I was infuriated that this parade of hicupping autos, directed by Alexander's whim, should make him so irresistibly appealing when only the night before I had monsterized him. Alexander could certainly reaffirm his claim to being indestructible.

"Wine, what took you so long?"

"You didn't pull me here fast enough. What the hell are you doing?"

"I'm conducting a safety check."

"On the cars or yourself?"

"Both! So far no one has dared to run me down. Must be a good day for humans. No homicidal drivers. Maybe no one has turned on his TV and got fuelled up with violence."

"What do you conclude then?"

"There's still hope for humans, they aren't round-the-clock-murderers."

"You are optimistic!" And so was I. His escapade had squashed my earlier unhappiness about him. As usual his facility to swivel his moods awed me.

Alexander quit his game and joined me on the pavement. He wanted to go to the garbage can. Then his voice moved into another gear – bittersweet.

"Why did you have to send me that message: exotic fur looking for her dispossessed friend! Why didn't you leave me in peace?"

"I wanted you to know I care. And I still care about you."

He wrapped up my sentiments and tucked them away in his brain to be examined later in his own solitude.

A short distance away from our sanctuary we were nearly accosted by a Doberman pinscher. He was on a metal leash, reined by a human who believed a big animal, like a big car, was a good trustee for one's personal safety. The dog impressed me as a furious

123

animal eager to do more than pinch. His ungracious reception terrified me. My fur shot out perpendicularly from my body. Fortunately I didn't have to pray for a saviour. Alexander The Public Defender of Scaredy Cats was on call.

"Wine, don't go to the garbage can yet, there's something I want to do."

He watched the dog's owner tie him to a telephone pole and then disappear into a store. Alone at last, Alexander and the Doberman faced one another as though readying for a showdown between a grisly bear and a mouse. While the dog made a lot of noise, Alexander didn't utter so much as a squeal. He affixed his stare on to the dog like a potential hypnotist. The next phase began with Alexander slinking toward the dog with an indifferent air. The tempo of the dog's barking accelerated to that of orgasmic joy as he struggled to free itself from the prison around his neck. Alexander answered the dog's leaping shenanigans by beaming his solar smile. Then my hero took a different tack. He started to emit soft sounds of enticing meows. Such coquetry surprised the dog who had expected the hisses of a clawing enemy. The dog's ears perked up and he stopped jumping. Soon the lovely cadence of meows silenced his barking and then the dog sank down on its belly, copying a circus lion obeying his master. A fully confident Alexander went up to the animal and licked its neck. The sensual pleasure of touch completed the pacification of the beast. Alexander had cast the same spell over the dog as he had occasionally done with me.

Was there anything he couldn't tame? Perhaps only himself.

Alexander's solar smile flashed on again with the sureness of a cocky kitty, victorious after unpunished mischief.

Without warning another solar smile superimposed itself upon Alexander's!

The smile of BILLY THE KITTY, resurrected from my kittyhood. Billy The Kitty, a smiling prodigy. My first playmate. The neighbourhood dare-devil whose fearless antics were the forerunner to those of Alexander. Billy The Novice Trapeze Artist practising his balance on fluttering clothes lines in full frivolousness of youth. Billy The Kitty, sportsman and lover of games who used to roll himself up in circles of yarn until he was mummified and then he would bid me to unravel him because he was tied up in knots. Billy The Kitty playing doctor to Wine's body, fully innocent of sensual pleasure, his solar smile seducing Wine's soul. Billy The Laughing Kitty full of zest and joy, too young to be introduced to sorrow.

Alexander had inherited Billy's smile!

Were there others also willed the same legacy? . . .

Alexander's taste for mischief abated. He shucked off the image of a kitty and donned his wardrobe of malehood.

"Come make love with me, Wine."

The simple relief of feeling his body next to mine after such a long absence banished any wish for spectacular sexual exploits. I'm home, I'm home, I thought . . . this bulging body of yours, my favourite resting place where I feel safe, soft, pliable and yielding, so wonderfully female and I love myself more like this and my self-love spills out of me into you . . . but if you feel this you don't respond, for there is still no direct communication to your heart . . . yes, Alexander we go through the motions of love making but I am unable to fully devote myself to you because my brain is zig-zagging around on an itinerary of one-way love and no matter how many intimate postures we engage in the most import-ant engagement is missing. Is this why you are unable to let go sexually? I am using every trick I know in the art of sexual seduction but I've not yet mastered the art of breaking open a heart closed to love . . .

"Why can't you come, Wine?" asked Alexander.

"I'm too tired," I lied.

When you hear the grunts of your sexual partner straining too hard to touch joy your lust evaporates. Truth was now creeping into the arena of sex for both of us.

After an intermission of sleep we treated the symptoms of our sexual failure with success, though not the cause. We fornicated without making love and afterwards we lay in our separate silences. Small crystals of tears walked down my cheeks. Alexander pre-tended blindness. There was a timebomb set to go off in my head but so far it only clicked a nervous beat. It still needed to decode a slushy message from my heart before it could explode into an acceptable truth.

Alexander continued to ignore the crisis between us.

"Wine, let me tell you about a cat who seduced me last week."

News of an understudy speared my heart!

"She pursued me so persistently that the only way to get rid of her was to submit!"

My face marbled. A sense of decorum stilled his tongue. The announced score of understudies was now even – one to one. I could have upped the body count and heralded my second en-counter with Joshua but in taking the lead I would have gained in spite and forfeited the residue of feeling for me in Alexander's heart. I still believed he *cared* for me even if he didn't love me.

Alexander returned to his role as a petulant kitty, complaining about his mistress's rationing his cream to only three cupfuls a day. She intended to slenderize his flabby pouch. What a homecoming! To be asked to streamline himself after living such a destitute existence in the woods for more than a month on a diet of berries. A lot of berries I judged because his belly had not shrunk. Alexander plotted his revenge. He would metamorphose into a glowering, snooty cat, witholding his affectionate favours whenever his mistress brushed her leg against him. He might even scratch her. Or worse yet, abandon her and go back to the woods. There were some very clever beings there who knew the mystery of shedding your skin on a regular basis. Alexander had spoken to these miracle workers about the art they had perfected. They had expressed reluctance at giving away their secret, fearful that such a talent would be commercially violated and give the world a false impression that shedding your skin could be done by whim. To the contrary, these wizards emphasized that not until the season was "right" could any creature be ready to shed his skin. Alexander wasn't quite sure what they meant by the "right" season. Nor could Wine The Cat reveal it to him as the full bloom of saviourhood from the seed of oneself.

Alexander's verbal meanderings skidded into depression. He needed to lap up some milk or cream. Approaching night promised an abundant supply of his joyous gold so he left me in the blackening interior of the garbage can and padded toward the alabaster tranquillizer lying in saucers at The Milk Bar.

Later I joined him when he radared his desire for my presence. Shortly thereafter there were strange thumps in my heart. My radar caught signals of an emotional storm heading directly on course toward Alexander. The storm would pass from him to me. The first sign of the storm became visible when Alexander's body tilted from one side to the other. An attack of nerves? An overdose of milk?

"Alexander, what's the matter?"

The question had to move many light years from me to him.

"Wine . . . I'm . . . in . . . love."

It took the same number of light years for his answer to reach me. And then it only had the same impact as an uneventful weather forecast.

"Anyone I know, Alexander?"

"No." His solar smile mused at something in his interior, shaded world. He began looking through me with the blank stare of an animal used to living alone in the woods without ever having seen

126

other forms of life. He might have seemed retarded or mad.

"What's her name?" I asked in my finest nursing tone of compassion.

"Antoinette . . . dear . . . dear . . . Antoinette."

"Where did you meet her?"

"Not far from here."

"How long have you known her?"

He paused to measure a special relationship with time. "Years . . . I've known her all my life . . . all my lives . . . since we were kitties together."

"Have you seen her recently?" My questions were rattling off with the methodical logic of a private detective hired by Wine The Cat to snoop around.

"No." He closed his eyes and voyaged backward in time. "Do you know that Antoinette and I never made love . . . except with words!"

"Where is she now?"

"She lives with a cat and has his kittens. She's been with him a long time."

And then I knew. *Alexander was chasing a phantom.*

Antoinette was the unknown celebrity, the star always shining at the apex of the triangle involving Alexander and Wine. Finally, knowledge of her existence was ironing out the confusion of former innuendos uttered by Alexander; witness the scorn in his voice at The Fur Fair when he had said that no one needs a word for soul-mate, it's an experience, not a word. And another time when he had advised me not to love him, implying that a heart opened to him was a risky venture. His warning had stood upon valid grounds after all.

I prompted Alexander to unveil the whole truth.

It was a lovely story of love from which unhappy fairy tales are founded.

Antoinette and he had been playmates from the moment they could stand on their paws. She was the pet of a family living next door to the sadistic fur seller. They spent all their time together. On those occasions when blood was spilled in his master's house Alexander would run to her, run to his peace place as he regarded her and she would receive the secret rivers of his being – his tears and fears. And if she did not understand something she would seek some way out of confusion or at least try. She possessed a wisdom far beyond her years for reasons no one could comprehend. Thus, she was Alexander's companion and platonic lover – his best friend. They used to devise marvellous adventures of future explorations together after leaving their masters' homes. They intended to visit every lovely creation bred by nature. But she was content to sit and dream and wait until she got older before going off with Alexander. Contrary to her, he was constantly restless, eager to roam the world. Antoinette's serenity and peace anchored these tendencies. But there was another Alexander, a facet of him that could not tame all the pressures of sexuality which tormented him at times. Then he was prey to kittens who knew how to tempt and seduce him. These wild orgies of pleasure would alleviate his sexual appetites, restoring him to a more tranquil state so he could return to Antoinette and continue making love to her with his soul. She was deeply wounded by his escapades, bewildered by this need of his which was so foreign to her ethereal world. Alexander would gauze her wounds but once he healed her he reverted back to sexual betrayal.

The compilation of intolerable hurts eventually superceded what was acceptable. One day Antoinette felt her soul shrivelling up, her body taking on the odour of charred flesh – symtoms of the end of a cat life. A desperate Alexander hoped that the promise of no more promiscuity would save his soulmate. But he also knew he couldn't lie and promise the impossible. What a dilemma! Honesty was going to kill Antoinette's kittyhood. Yet, in that special soft, tender way of hers she bore him no rancour. She thanked him for not pledging a sham.

This fond farewell without anger doomed Alexander to love her forever.

Reproduction of this same fond farewell threaded the bond I still felt toward Claude.

Antoinette left behind the perfume of love in its most pure, chaste state without a whiff of disillusionment. This same perfume swirled around Alexander through each of his lives. He was a cat still mourning a lost love, or maybe only an illusion . . . .

My solar smile dropped off to sleep next to a milk saucer, a public spectacle giving rise to chitchat for the local habitués. I paid them no attention. I felt as exhausted as Alexander. Envisioning my mistress's velvet couch tempted me to scoot home to an easy, restful night. But I was unable to abandon Alexander or disturb his siesta. I wanted to protect him, a feeling new to me, partly maternal and something else. A sleeping Alexander could not blockade or frustrate this nascent need to feel useful. Nor could he run from my warmth.

I suspected I was about to inherit Claude's legacy – the pleasure of giving to someone without demanding or expecting something in return. Wine The Cat did not want a good Samaritan reward for her vigil. The valuable prize came from Wine The Saviour who said, "Congratulations, you have just confirmed your talent for loving." One more golden epiphany, one less doubt about my worth.

Alexander regained wakefulness hours later without a hangover.

"What a wonderful rest I had, so peaceful." He glanced around at the few stragglers remaining at this late hour. "Did anyone talk about me while I was asleep? I've never done this in public before."

"Why should it matter? If you're tired you have the right to sleep where and when you want. How strange you should worry about social decorum! Do you want to come with me to the garbage can?"

"No, I feel like prowling around."

"In that case I'll leave you. I'm tired. Take care, Alexander."

"I always take care," said my solar smile.

Our leave taking contained some new element. Alexander did not engender any paranoid plot that he wanted to hurt me or run from me. Hopefully he might run toward himself instead of playing hide and seek with the ghost of his past. If only he could shift his energies from repression to squeezing out the pus from this festering sore, go through mourning once and for all so he could liberate himself from his past. Just as I had to do and was still doing with Claude.

Was it pure coincidence that the rising up of my forgotten Billy should be the stimulus conjuring up the appearance of Antoinette, suggesting some strong psychic correspondence still moved between Alexander and myself? Was there some subtle replay of our past in which I became Antoinette and he was Billy The Kitty? Yet the tie between Billy and myself had naturally dissolved with time, each of us having flowed into different paths away from kittyhood. Sorrowful good-byes had been unnecessary. But I had forgotten one obvious fact. We often seek to duplicate our joy. Later, we learn we can't.

Truth must have accounted for the helium lightness of my soul as I headed home that night. The unknown had become known, a real form, albeit the ghostly one of Antoinette had replaced the question mark in my imagination.

The relationship between Alexander and myself was moving closer to a bas-relief clarity. Only one more chiselled stroke was necessary. That had to be done by Alexander.

129

* * * * *

A serene silence spaced Alexander and me apart for some days. My flirtatious morbidity did not taunt me with the silhouette of Antoinette. Instead, it went into hibernation. I celebrated this unexpected achievement by pursuing my favourite, solo pastime – wandering the streets.

The streets! The streets! The two-ring circus of the real and the surreal billed together as Siamese twins! The greatest show on earth, always inviting you to participate in its dramas and comedies or observe them as a non-paying spectator whose only price for admission is the presentation of your native, sensory endowment. Where else but on the streets can you witness life pulsating, tickling, saddening, enlightening, so firey, so intense? Where else can you stroll through a thousand books of knowledge, of life, block after block, where your senses are so energetically exercised?

Unhappily, in some countries of the world this electrifying carnival does not reign. The greatest show on earth has gone bankrupt, cluttering the streets with death and blight. Life has moved indoors where humans huddle in cells of sameness, their voices muffled low enough so that lonely, spying neighbors can't even catch a crumb of one warm word. What a scourge! What a disease! Mankind castrating its lifelines between people who have become too fearful to greet one another, publicly or privately.

Why not kick everybody back out into the streets! Let humans get used to sniffing other humans again so they can settle back into a minimum grudging acceptance of one another. Isn't this the way animals become acquainted? No one really wants the streets as a battle ground. Neither man nor beast is professionally cut out for full-time war, contrary to sensational myths created by journalistic Gods. Living beings prefer peace to war because life is easier this way. Peace doesn't tax human resources in the same manner as battle.

I praised whatever unknown forces had stationed me in a country where hate and fear did not demolish the vibrant spirit of the thoroughfares.

Upon leaving my mistress's house, I anticipated an endless array of open-air surprises. I was not disappointed.

The first carnival act was offered by a small band of gypsy children decked out in flashy yellow and orange taffeta dresses, swishing in the breeze. They stood together, jiggling tambourines, a modest orchestra accompanying an animal act. The two stars were a saddled, scrawny goat with a monkey on its back. The goat was glaring at a step ladder with three rungs on either side, resistant to scaling this Olympian height. It preferred the more sensible stance of all four legs on the ground. The monkey grew bored, dismounted and found more interesting business. It swiped a bunch of bananas from a spectator's straw bag. Everyone applauded this robbery, convinced it was part of the script. Had this been the work of a hungry human, the audience would have fled or demanded the police remove the bandit.

After the last banana was tucked away in the monkey's stomach it took up the reins once more. It whispered something to its lower class cousin. The social division between the two remained unrecognized by the goat. So the monkey using the wits it was born with, dismounted again and plucked some grass from a nearby lawn. Then it resumed its role as a cowboy, only this time it dangled the grass in front of the goat like a windshield wiper. The goat bolted up the ladder in hot pursuit. Only when the ungainly pair pressed back upon earth did the monkey give its poor relative its due reward. Now the children hushed their tambourines and quickly over turned them into begging church plates, their sphinx eyes cajoling the onlookers to lessen the weight of their pocketbooks.

If only Alexander had been present for this harmonious contact between humans and animals! Or would he have charged the audience with corrupting the morals of innocent animals?

The humans sprinkled themselves in various directions looking for more action.

I followed the sun's plume into a diminutive plaza, ringed on four sides by sun-sunburned buildings. In the centre was a large piece of sculpture crudely hewn out of stone. It depicted a seated female dressed in a flowing robe. Across her lap sprawled the body of a deceased male. Her arms were clasping his torso with an air of quiet submission. The lack of refined lines or carefully chiselled details did not dull any of the poignancy, beauty or strength of the two figures. If anything, the spirits of both escaped confinement by either stone or death. Maybe it was the roughness, the naturalness of this incompleted mass which gave out such raw power, as though there still lived within this stone a tremendous reserve of human energy.

A plaque at the base of the statue bore the title – "The Unfinished Pieta." The rest of the inscription stated that this was the fourth attempt made by a famous sculptor to carve this historically notable duo. Four times he had tried to match an idea with an outcome. Four times he had failed in his estimation. Maybe he finally accepted the futility of matching the conception of something with the final result – so similar to the no-win games that humans play when they try to impose the past on to the present or envision the future as a replica of the present. Whatever. Maybe the sculptor adopted a new attitude and put away his carving tools once he understood that he could not chisel anything to an imperfect perfection, that the artwork of creators, of life, is never finished.

Thinking that nothing has an end dialled an optimistic mood in me about Alexander, despite the echoing of his dreamy description of Antoinette. This optimism was being nourished by a renewed appreciation of myself and a remembered aphorism heard from Wine The Saviour that it is not life which loses its hope but only my lost vision of it.

I continued my exploration of the street circus. An ermine breeze glided through a bouquet of windchimes, blowing a trail of metal delicately kissing metal. The sound recalled a lover's whisper buried in hazy sleep long after bliss has been quieted. What a day! What a day! What pearls of life rolling all around me!

Suddenly something tickled the underside of my paw. I looked down and noticed I had stepped on a moving piece of yarn that looked like an infinitely long train. I decided to follow one end. Either I was going to locate the locomotive or the caboose. I located the pulling power – a cat with the longest, fuzziest fur I had ever seen.

"What are you doing?" I asked.

He stopped his locomotion and spat out the beginning of the spool of yarn from his mouth.

"I'm carrying one end of a skein of yarn and a friend of mine, who you can't see, has the other. We're going round the world in opposite directions. We plan to meet at the halfway point. We'll probably set a record for long distance yarn. Between us we'll explore the seven wonders of the world."

"Maybe you'll discover an eighth," I said.

"What's that?" he asked.

"Yourself," I replied. I thought Wine the Saviour would be proud of this answer. It followed along the track she had already laid down even if it wasn't marked by yarn.

After giving me a long, queer stare, the cat invited me to accompany him.

"No thank you, my wanderlust is getting tamed. I have other

journeys to make. Good luck to you."

He moved on, his yarn snaking after him.

Was it true that Wine The Nomad, pitching questions wherever she went, had refused an interesting trip? My, my, changes were certainly being made in my character.

The dry heat of the day began crowding my mouth with dust. Before I could search for some liquid refreshment my hearing antenna picked up the sombre sound of cat meows wailing a dirge. Curiosity compelled me to scout around. I ended up on top of a stone wall enclosing a luscious garden foliated with lemon and orange trees atomizing the air with an intoxicating aroma. It made me slightly tipsy.

From my vantage point I spied a parcel of cats in the centre of the garden. They looked like professional mourners beseeching the heavens to welcome their laments. Every so often more cats joined the scene by coming into the garden through various holes at the bottom of the wall. These late-comers first headed over to a bucket of paint near the crowd into which they dipped a paw before moving toward the swelling numbers of bereaved cats. No wonder the ground was covered with black polka dots.

The focal point of attention was a child's shoe box lined in purple satin. It contained the tiny body of a stillborn kitty. The mother of this corpse could easily be detected. She was the only cat not looking skyward, the only one for whom loss had no public or private consolation. Her face retained the becalmed movement of shock, her spirit linked by an invisible umbilical cord to the dead body which she still expected to be born. Next to the mother were six kittens of various ages, clinging to her familiar body midst this confusing spectacle. For them, death was an intrusive playmate in their lovely playground.

I felt choked up with tears. Here I was, alive, swollen with joy and there before me lay a dead kitty who would never know the embrace of life, one more kitty prematurely slated to become a servant to eternity. Curse the capriciousness of death, I thought! It's not fair to snuff out a young life.

Whoever said that cats have nine lives? What a preposterous lie! We're just as vulnerable to physical death as any other living creature.

"Hold on," retorted Wine The Saviour. "Nine lives, nine lies is defamation of character. You know better than to rampage against death. You know that nine lives is only an arbitrary number representing the *rhythm* of life, the ebb, the flow, the light, the dark, the joy, the sorrow, the beginning, the end. Nine lives is our random itinerary for walking through time which is the same as walking through growth, walking toward awareness. For some, the flow of life is curtailed, for others it travels along an extensive route. You must accept this." And then in a more soothing voice, "Try to make your peace with death, dear Wine. It's the most important thing you can do for yourself."

Wine The Saviour corked my rage, though not my sorrow.

Death was still not the friendly enemy I wanted it to be.

It became easy to identify with the mother's grief. How do you forget that your body has housed, nourished and protected a future life? Isn't this truth the unsevered umbilical cord made to last a mother's lifetime?

While the cat chorus carried on lamenting, the mother snapped out of her trance, scanning the crowd for something. She abruptly moved from the side of the shoe box to the side of a small, delicate white cat among the mourners. The mother then sank her teeth into the neck of this surprised wailer and dragged her prey back to her progeny. Perplexed glances flew among the crowd. Had grief slipped into madness? The kidnapped cat, sensing something that the others hadn't, offered no resistance to the mother's fondling and lavish licking of her body. The mother was determined that someone was going to be a substitute for her dead kitty.

This scene swept me back to Wine The Melancholy Cat retapping Alexander's recording: "I'm in love with Antoinette. I'm in love with Antoinette." Tiny daggers of hurt, earlier secluded, now began to thrust home the reality of Antoinette's existence. Ghostly or otherwise it made no difference. Antoinette still dwelled in the sacred chambers of Alexander's heart.

I felt the old, condemned sensation of eternal solitude.

Would I always move alone, the rest of my lives?

My memory backtracked into my past and there was my lost Claude, standing in a golden aura of desire.

Soon I would lose Alexander even though I never really had him.

This was the message which my head had sent out but it still hadn't settled in my heart. I pleaded for more time. Alexander, wait a little longer before you bump me off the surface of your soul. Let me have the illusion that I mean something to you because once this illusion is gone I have to pick up the ashes of lost hope and begin the search again for the soul-mate who can offer more than just the paring away of loneliness. Wine The Saviour cannot fulfill this need for mating, this coupling, this joining together. She cannot cure me of being an intimacy addict looking for a fix!

I was so immersed in thoughts of mourning that I stumbled off the wall and aeroplaned to the ground where a nasty blow to my head set me sailing along another stream of consciousness while my body lay deathly immobile. A strange and fantastic scene debuted. It began with some humorous words spoken by an old cat who magically appeared before my eyes.

"If you stopped weeping over what you have lost, mourning would go out of business. Don't you know that laughter is the greatest exorcist against seriousness?"

The cat's voice sang the words like a lullaby, not as a reprimand. A paternal smile dawned on his face until the heat of it reached a scalding temperature. What warmth! What compassion gushed forth from this stranger! Could he be the one I had secretly awaited all of my lives? The perfect job applicant answering my unspoken psychic advertisement which had long read:

WANTED: SAVIOUR, SAGE, MESSIAH, SPIRITUAL HEALER. QUALIFICATIONS: WISDOM. (ONLY THOSE CATS WITH WISDOM NEED APPLY. IF YOU HAVE TO TALK ABOUT YOUR WISDOM YOU DON'T HAVE IT.)
MUST BE A CAT WITH WARM VIBRATIONS WHICH CAN BE EMIT-TED EVERYWHERE AT ANY TIME.

I wondered if Wine The Saviour would resent some outside competition? She shouldn't. Weren't two heads better than one?

The sound of cars careening on either side of us startled me, though no drivers took notice of our presence in spite of our sitting in the bullseye of a traffic intersection. I suggested we adjourn to a less hazardous place, but the old cat dismissed the danger. "We're safe from those humans in their killing machines because they're moving in a different time zone. They're driving toward the future so they ignore those of us living in the present. It's really remarkable watching their rush hour escape from the only reality we can ever claim – the here and now. But since much of life is founded on illusion and mythology I suppose they're entitled to believe in the future. You and I can't assume exclusive rights to fairy tales."

With all due respect for the cat's age I resisted challenging his denial of the future as unreal. Perhaps he lived in a different time zone from me and his wisdom needed a bit of stretching. I was becoming convinced that time was more and more of a chimera where divinations of the future could suddenly overlap the present and reincarnation might be the past usurping the present. I could conceive of a situation where the past, the present and the future

135

might all try to occupy the same space at the same moment, an unnatural physical law some might say. But I saw these three time zones as a vertical tic-tac-toe or a sort of overcrowding of too many cats jammed into one cat box – uncomfortable but possible. But to play around with the meaning of time produced only one result – another question, hence another game for a rainy day. I was more interested in what was happening *now*. I wanted to thoroughly interview this cat and determine how skilfully he could fulfil my job announcement.

I began with an innocuous question, so he wouldn't catch on to what I wanted.

"Where are we?" I asked.

"We're right in the middle of where the real and the surreal converge, where the real is just as surreal as the surreal is real."

"You mean I'm not dreaming what's happening to us?"

"I'm afraid I don't have the wisdom to answer your question. If this feels real to you then it is."

He scored several points on my achievement test for saviours.

"May I ask who you are?"

"My name is Solomon. I am an ancient resident of this neighborhood. I live midst an open city of ruins where the most lovely buildings once graced this section of the city before hungry bulldozers gobbled them up. I was fortunate to escape their appetite."

"Don't you have a home?"

"Oh yes, I even carry it with me everywhere I go. *I am my home*, a mobile home," he punned.

I fell silent. Solomon had just expressed something which sounded so simple and so profound, as though he had solved the riddle to a long, complicated problem which had ceased to be complex. I listened to his vibrations to see if I could decipher them accurately.

"Do you mean you are a liberated cat at peace with yourself, that you have stopped asking questions for which there are no fixed answers, that you have come to accept the mobility of life, its ephemeralness and that of your existence? Is this the home you inhabit?"

A worshipping look sprang into his eyes. "Yes it is. Those were very perceptive comments you made . . . the comprehension of a healer, a saviour!"

Something was jumbled up. I wasn't applying for anyone's job as a saviour. Who was interviewing whom?

The glint left his eye in response to my discomfort. "Yes," he added, "I accept the appetizers, the entrées, the rich and bitter sauces and the desserts served by life. I ask for nothing. I strive for nothing. I desire nothing."

"Ah, you lucky cat, wanting nothing. How did you accomplish this?"

"By frustrating experience and mistakes. Whenever I wanted or anticipated something I inevitably met with disappointment. The best pleasures I ever had were the unrehearsed, spontaneous ones which happened of their own accord, without any controlling effort on my part. Slowly I became more adept at appreciating the joy of each moment, milking the potential of each day, spying and capturing the jewels of life whose sparkles were often faint. The pinnacle of success, if you want to use that deformed word, came when I could sit on my haunches doing nothing, without feeling any guilt. Now some cats would say, 'You're wasting your time, throwing away your life.' And I would respond. 'Nothing is a waste unless you wish to see it that way.' But I don't have to explain this to you. Unless my vibes are mistaken you understood everything I just said – remarkable considering you didn't have to reach my age in order to attain some of this wisdom."

"It's true a lot of nagging questions of mine have been shot down by a modest fund of wisdom. But wisdom in whatever supply doesn't fill an empty heart. Wisdom is not the goal of life!"

"Of course it isn't. There is no goal. All you can do is live and black out the illusion that anything has a goal. Recognize that the end of one thing seeds the beginning of something new. I wish my former mistress could have understood this. She was a famous actress who won a most coveted award for her fine acting. Yet instead of feeling thrilled she sat in front of her trophy day after day, muttering to herself, 'Now what!' She didn't comprehend that in realizing her dream she had lost its quest because it is the quest or the doing of a thing which brings its own reward. That's why I say that sitting on my haunches is fulfilling. I'm realizing 'my doing' . . . . Your vibrations are registering accord on this but there is a tailing resonance of discord within you. What's missing from your life?"

I flashbacked to Alexander's first compassionate gesture and etched out on the ground the spelling to what often seemed to be the basis for my emotional survival: L O V E. Maybe I was also spelling out a universal, biological need.

"Solomon, I want to share my life with someone who can be my best friend."

"Ah, so you know that all deep love ends in friendship."

"Yes, but I had to lose that love in order to know its worth."

"We must usually lose something precious as the only way to

appraise its value. It's too bad it's so easy to fall in love. We assume that once we are loved we are safely and forever emotionally bankrolled. All we have to do is collect the interest love pays out. But unfortunately the contrary is true. It is we, each one of us, who must sustain love, nourish it, refresh it, augment it with our efforts, remembering that what isn't cared for dies. Nothing lives without sustenance, without a contribution of effort from ourselves. How often in my younger years I saw the demise of love. How I suffered at the end of each love affair vowing I would never love again, at least not until the next opportunity presented itself. I became so confused about this four letter dictator of life that I made a drastic alteration in my living mode. I renounced cat boxes, special meals and the security of being someone's mascot in favor of retreating to the woods where I would be free of conflict. I hoped to meditate upon all serious matters of life, to seek the truth of things and to discover myself. The experience was a vain effort. After a long, solitary vigil I was no further along in my goal – you'll pardon this artificial word – of self-awareness. I concluded that you can't seek awareness or truth. Instead it awaits you when you're ready to perceive it. Nor can you cordon off your existence from other cats because your awareness of what you are comes from contact with other beings. They mirror what you are. If you run from them you run from yourself. So I had to go back to the very training ground which had proven so painful, back to involvement with other cats. Fortunately upon my return from exile I met a wise cat who consoled me after I had voiced my fear about losing future loves. He said the following: 'You should feel grateful that another cat is capable of spiking you alive when love is offered to you. Love comes, love goes just as the rhythm of life. Remember, it's how you view life that determines how you cope with lost love. Knowing that within a split second life disappears how can we expect to possess something forever when we are so fragile, so mortal. So we must praise whatever loveliness comes to us instead of adopting a tragic or cynical view that love is excrement. Love is never disgusting and those beings who love and are well loved never lose anything. If you have the gift for loving, someone will extract it from you again and maybe both of you will be mature enough – assuming each of you has met your personal saviour – to treat the gift of love with tender care.'"

Solomon paused a moment.

"Please don't stop talking. You're helping me," I said.

"Well, that speech I just quoted not only helped me but it changed my life, or rather my attitude. From then on I became a

relaxed cat, dismissing my fear that love provokes disastrous consequences. It was soon after that when I noticed my talent for
perceiving the psychic currents coming from the inner sanctums
of other cats. I could detect the real sentiments often hiding
behind their silences and dismiss false purrs of contentment. Most
cats I met quickly smelled my talent. But what was I to do with this
facility? One day I heard a cat meowing in despair. 'Why, oh why,
do I have to be a cat?' The poor thing had just been separated from
her mate because her mistress had given him to another family. I
tried to comfort her and said, 'Even though your mate has been
taken from you doesn't mean you're destitute. You still have
yourself, you still have the qualities which make you so attractive
to humans. Count your blessings. If you don't want to be a cat,
what do you want to be? A human? A human who doesn't have
your feline appeal? Would you rather have a human mind, the one
mind in all of nature's creatures which is so successful at fighting its
own evolution, arresting its own growth, stagnating, fossilizing
itself? Is there any animal which fights against its own nature more
viciously than humans, any animal which so arrogantly presumes it
lies beyond the control of Nature? No, of course not! Only
humans tie themselves to a wheel of frustration merely because
they suffer from delusions of grandeur, believing they can become
Gods of the universe. Only humans with their endless theorizing
can use life as the greatest alibi for not living . . .' Well, once this
poor cat was reminded of her advantages she thought her life
wasn't so bad. At the end of my oratory she even smiled. It was her
thankful smile which set me on the course to help other cats, or
rather, help other cats help themselves. So I entered the most
active, gratifying part of my life – consultant to cats unable to
cope. With each one I stipulated one condition from the outset:
that answers or truths which didn't come from themselves would
be like injections of placebos – false truths that wear off sooner or
later. Everyone had to cleanse his or her mind of all formal
teachings and ideas. Sometimes I was a little rough with some cats
who were feigning deafness, dumbness or blindness. I would shout
certain blasphemies at them:

IMPEACH FEAR, COWARDICE, IGNORANCE AND STUPIDITY.
SCUTTLE CIVILIZATION. PULL OUT THE PLUG. LET THE WASTE
SINK.
THROW OUT THE SANCTIMONIOUS BALLAST.
DEFOLIATE THE INTELLECTUAL SHRUBBERY AND WEEDS
PLANTED BY MENTAL MIDGETS.

THINK FOR YOURSELF . . . OR SINK.
And when someone began to call me Saviour I would harshly retort:

STOP LOOKING FOR SAVIOURS TO VACCINATE YOU FROM PAIN, FROM LIFE.
PETITION THE GOD WITHIN YOU TO RUN FOR SAVIOUR OF YOUR SOUL.

With cats too delicate for such rough language I spoke more tenderly because I saw the paucity of tenderness in this world. But no matter what my approach was I insisted that all cats disown judgement and let life seep into their pores, recognizing that one cat's folly is another cat's salvation. Also as a critical part of my treatment I fostered a sense of humour in everyone so there would be no drowning casualties from tears. Then I gave each cat a pat on the head and sent him or her out on the open road of life, promising that the journey would be a miraculous, exciting safari, provided no-one tried to hunt for anything special. Some cats were never seen again. Others returned, their bodies battered by burrs and barnacles. But their spirits were unscarred. They all reported a similar finding – they hadn't lost the license I had given them to be themselves. You can imagine the joy that filled me. I felt like a father capable of raising a brood of cats who could tackle the world without parental guidance chasing them around."

"Solomon, weren't you sorry to see them go after putting so much investment into each of them?" I asked.

"Yes, but remember, while I lost my followers there were always new ones to replace the lost ones."

"Do you still practise helping other cats?"

"Yes, in my spare time. But I also have another career now."

"What's that?"

"Love in old age! Not long ago I encountered a wonderful companion with whom I share a large portion of my time. Like myself, she has known many seasons of sorrow and joy, loss and laughter. You might say we perceive life through the same shaft of vision, an important ingredient for togetherness. We treat one another with the empathy and compassion taught to us by sorrow and we don't take ourselves too seriously, a lesson learned from laughter. We find loving to be very easy now. If there are moments of anger, we devise a one-act play in which I assume her personality and she simulates mine. It's called 'getting into one another's skin.' We become so engrossed in imagining the lines the other would express that we forget about our individual anger. This has

140

proven to be a wonderful way to alchemize negative feelings into something beneficial and creative. So we sleep well at night on a pillow of peace, not trapped in a web of anger. Of course old age has one minor compensation. It keeps everything simple because the only real issue facing the aged is death. This is why love is the uncomplicated thing in old age that it isn't in youth . . . I feel deeply for the young. How difficult it is to be a neophyte to life, knowing so little about yourself and the world in which you live. It's no wonder that when two young things mate you can usually expect they will tarnish the image of everlasting love. And for good reason! Mating the young with the young has about the same degree of success as mating two clouds – there just isn't enough substance to form a solid bond. But as you get wiser you are more able to draw closer to rich, meaningful love because you draw closer to meeting the saviour in yourself which you need for establishing intimacy with another being. This is what I call the secret to the trinity of love: the 'you,' the 'me,' and the 'we.' This is when the saviour of the female meets the saviour of the male. This is when the female becomes the true femme fatale and the male becomes the irresistible Don Juan. What a powerfully linked couple is formed! Two beings united together at the same water-mark of development, two beings, in harmony, in balance with one another. Without this balance the depth of love doesn't reach beyond shallow water."

Solomon was paraphrasing thoughts of mine.

Suddenly I had the answer to an old, nagging question: Is love a mythological fable, purely a diversion from our personal solitude?

At last I could claim an unequivocal "NO!" Love exists. We simply have to grow up, find it and live it!

I was ready to award Solomon a position as my saviour.

I asked him one more question.

"Solomon, why does it have to be so difficult to achieve balance between two beings?"

"Wine, how can you ask a question whose answer you already know?"

"Maybe I need to be reminded of what I know from time to time . . . Say, how do you know my name? And how do you know what I know?"

A sly, familiar glint came into his eyes. However, he ignored my queries.

"Wine, the question is really why is it so difficult to get a sense of balance, of equilibrium, of peace within oneself? Remember that every event, every change outside our daily routine disrupts our

141

balance. A new mistress, a new catbox, a new brand of cat food, a new love or a lost love, all these tilt us off balance."

"You mean then that love isn't the stabilizer or anchor of life we think it is?"

"Right. To be sure, love can help us achieve a sense of balance. Certainly it's more than just an agent covering the hole of our loneliness. But just think how frequently love goes awry, think of the upheaval it can cause when there is a disagreement, a clash between two beings. What happens in such cases? Clumsy or sophisticated attempts are made at some point to erase hostilities. Why? Because living creatures cannot go for too long a time without needing to regain a sense of peace. If they continue to live within emotional fluctuations they will experience bizarre behaviour unless something remedies their turbulence. So while love plays a starring role in our lives, the hidden director of our existence or the staple of life is really balance or peace, or harmony, or equilibrium or whatever epithet of the same family you want to use. Now if two beings are to attain a communal balance each of the two has to already have mastered the art of calming personal storms. This is why I postulate that the wise and tattered combatants of life who have met their saviours with a sense of humour and disrespect for the absurdities of immature behaviour have the best odds for forming a couple living in harmonious balance."

"You mean that if Alexander and I were two older cats with creaky bones we'd stand a better chance of knitting an intimacy between us?"

In a voice slipping into a nearly recognizable tone he exclaimed, "In this case, no. Alexander is still emotionally under-developed. He is scampering away from reflections of himself. You are not. This has been the basis for the incompatible, emotional imbalance between the two of you."

At long last, the truth clearly stated about Alexander and Wine.

"Solomon, you're a wise cat. It's a pleasure to meet you. Funny, but you portrait the spiritual outline of someone I know except you're an older, more mature version of this cat."

Solomon could have been Wine The Saviour shot forth into a future time capsule. It was a propitious moment to award him the job for which I had just finished researching his references. I had found a duplicate for my best friend! Imagine! Two saviours to help me instead of only one!

Suddenly the old cat tore off a mask from his face and unzipped a body suit, impeccably tailor-made to imitate an old, wrinkled cat.

142

The impostor was none other than Wine The Saviour, bursting with laughter.

"So you thought you'd found another saviour outside of yourself? Shame on you, Wine The Cat, for trying to replace me with someone else. My feelings are hurt. When are you going to put 100% trust in your own wisdom? Or at least give me the sole concession to sell you wisdom!"

"But I wasn't trying to reject you . . . I don't think . . . How is it that you seem older and wiser than when I first met you?"

"Elementary my dear Wine. It is *you*, Wine The Cat who has matured. All I've done is organize the scattered experiences of your life into something comprehensive. I've done good work with your help, don't you think so? I'd say we have formed a very compatible relationship, a balanced one in which I soothe your self-doubts and you put into action our joint thinking. Now, do you still need to advertise for another saviour . . . ?"

And then I awakened, lying next to the stone wall of the garden of mourning. Even though I'd been knocked unconscious from my fall, Wine The Saviour didn't suffer the same fate. She had cleverly engineered a distinct tier of consciousness – the fantastic dream world where I couldn't rebel against her. Under her spell pieces of thought were being rearranged in my head, another moving job – an altered attitude.

The long distance message telegraphed from my head to my heart was delivered. In response, preparations were begun to evict Alexander from my heart without undue strain.

* * * * *

Days crawled into nights and nights crept back into days. My emotional colorations copied the same rhythmic procession of light and dark while I awaited the final beginning of the end of my connection to Alexander. Surprisingly it came with the softness of drizzling rain.

Accidentally or fatally, one of my nocturnal hauntings situated me in front of Alexander's ostentatious manor which was resplendently lit up. Cats were landscaping the premises, slouching about in humble deference to Alexander's wealth. There was an unmistakable festive air of a celebration.

"Alexander is throwing a going-away party. He's renouncing his worldly possessions, deserting his mistress. He's going to wander on the open road, become a stray cat," explained a stranger.

Apparently Alexander was ready to wander the uncharted itinerary of his evolution said my sixth sense.

I quickly understood I was an uninvited guest whose invitation read: I hereby serve notice that Wine is being evicted from Alexander's heart. How else could I decipher my exclusion from the festivities? But I was not going to leave the scene until he had formally ruptured our bond. Without this ritual there would be the temptation to believe in the mistaken possibility of hope which silence sometimes construes. Time decreed it was ripe to hermetically seal all hope of a pairing between Alexander and Wine.

How curious to be greeted by a host with whom you are not on a first name basis. He was called Alexander The Lucid Cat, the Alexander of my visionary still life. The grease-paint of confusion did not cover his spirit; nor was there any of the habitual opaqueness in his eyes. Alexander may have fallen into a drunken stupour long ago but his present aura was that of a cat awakened by the sun of his own enlightenment, ready to shed his skin, cast off one more cat life. This was the Alexander with whom I had fallen in love, the Alexander of my third eye who was becoming more than what he was.

Yet, time had concocted a paradoxical joke. Our private roads of evolution did not have a juncture called intimacy. The best of Alexander was to be denied me. Unfair, unfair, I thought. Just as with Claude, our clocks of development were pointing to different hours. What a fiend evolution can sometimes be!

I moved to kiss Alexander but he swerved his head. A paternal smile fluttered on his face, a hasty apology for enlightenment which excluded love for Wine The Cat.

"Alexander, you have something to say to me, but it must wait until the end of the party."

His radar blipped a "yes" to mine. Then he went to hob-nob with his guests.

The party was a refined affair, uneventful. The guests took great care not to topple over the priceless antiques nor to leave unruly cat hairs on the plush upholstery. Such is life, I supposed, in a museum. The supply of cream, though abundant, was not abused. Alexander's mistress must have suffered great pangs of guilt over her regimentation of his liquid intake because prior to her unexplained absence from the mansion she had set out an army of golden saucers, the ban on drinking lifted. With Alexander's shift to dry docks he chose to share his wealth with the neighbourhood cats.

Among them were former lovers of mine – representatives of various stages of psychic encounters or cats with whom sex was the undressing of external appearances down to naked, honest spirits. This was the description of sexual romping I finally entered in my anthology of life. I greeted each of them: Albert, who was fawning over his girl-friend, his mind anesthetized for the evening to appease her whims; Mack, who was conversing with an older, Cleopatra temptress, priming himself for another sexual act in which he would try to exorcise the image of himself as an incestuous lover; and then there was Joshua, surrounded by a harem of admiring cats attracted to his vitality. Like Solomon, Joshua was the epitome of a cat comfortably living in his own skin, his own home. There were others too, vacantly familiar whose existence had been too temperate for my taste, cats who exuded no vibrations, cats whose paw-prints would never be detected near the garbage can.

There too was Alexander, tranquilly purring his way from guest to guest. You might have thought he was edging toward dullness because the air waves around him were not pulsating their typical, fluctuating rhythm.

My mind snapped an indelible photo of Alexander The Lucid Cat, this mature side of him so that he could never trick me into believing he was a loser, no matter what indignities he might inflict upon himself.

And then I ensconced myself upon a thickly cushioned couch, the incessant spectator at all public gatherings, waiting for the affair to be finalized, waiting like a patient being wheeled to an operating room with a jittery stomach, my heart convulsing the same irregular heartbeat as my mistress. I would be emotionally numbed for a day or two after Alexander completed his oral surgery on me, even though I already knew the bad news.

Improvisationally a picture show flashed on upon my mind's inner screen, the theme contradicting the present emotional separation between Alexander and myself. There we were, teasingly rubbing our bodies against one another. Behind us was the garbage can with a fresh coat of purple paint! Such a strange colour! Only an eccentric would dream up such a decorative scheme, someone like my mistress! Was this encounter a sequel to the present? a confluence between the present and the future? the same poetics of divination which had once soldered me to the cat from the Coliseum? The dialogue on the sound track made the scenario seem too far-fetched even to be a fairy tale.

"Alexander, you've lost your paunch."

"And you've become svelte."

"Time becomes us."

"So is what we're doing. Come closer Wine, so I can lick you everywhere."

"Alexander, why couldn't we have been like this in the old days? You're so sexually free now, so relaxed."

"So are you with me. We were/both in bad shape then. Your anxiety was intolerable."

"Really? I knew I was skittery and nervous but I didn't know it was so intense."

"That's because you weren't receiving your own vibrations. I was. I caught them wherever I went. I could have had you arrested for disturbing my peace, the little I had."

"But what was driving you so crazy?"

"Claude's mother. She kept telling me to come back to her, then she'd change her mind and order me out of her sight. Come. Go. Come. Go. She had me spinning until I didn't know my head from my tail."

"You mean *she was the reason for your unpredictability*?"

"Mostly. I didn't love her any more but it still wasn't easy to separate from her. Bad habits are difficult to break."

"And all that time I had forgotten about her existence . . . the incredible explanations I invented about your behaviour then. When you cited her treacherous nature I automatically dismissed her as though it took only one nasty deed which could act like a mortal bullet and wipe out someone's existence forever. It goes to show how stupid I was to ignore the most obvious fact of your living conditions at that time. I don't know what I must have thought every time you went to visit your Claude. Obviously I didn't think. Well, my musings were good for a story, good for stretching my brain, my imagination. But tell me, Alexander, what about Antoinette? Was she real?"

"Wine, please don't mention her name. I don't want to think about her!"

"Ah, so not everything I invented had a false bottom. All right, she's forgotten . . . How do you like my vibrations now?"

"They're just the right pitch."

"Alexander, I think we have a friendship that will last a lifetime of lives. I know I can count on you if I'm ever in trouble. But promise me one thing."

"What's that?"

"You won't ever broadcast to me if you intuit I'm in an intimate posture with another cat. It would be impossible to explain our special relationship."

"I promise," laughed Alexander.

He had become my platonic lover . . . .

The movie show finished. What a jumble of realities were

swirling around me! Here I was expecting to be cast out of Alexander's life and a premonition unveiled a transformed relationship with him. I could only marvel at how the real and the surreal document the landscape of life.

The party dissolved. Alexander positioned himself next to a window, staring out at the palette of the universe speckled with stars – miracles of nature that knew their place.

His vibrations were cascading toward me like energies of guilt flowing out of an etiquette book which deemed it mandatory that he apologize for the decorum of his natural self. I could only counter these cumbersome vibrations by presenting a simple, unwrapped gift: BE YOURSELF, ALEXANDER. And then I asked him for the truth so that I would not have to charter the course of my soul through a chaotic unknown.

"Wine, dear Wine. I have been dying a slow death, murdering myself drop by drop because of disgust and remorse for past thoughtlessness I committed under the heedless influence of my selfishness."

A short time ago a hidden voice, foreign to Alexander, asserted itself, determined to answer the cry of "give me life." The self-centred voice of Alexander, sensing a strong competitor from the voice of maturity began a slow, but persistent retreat. The victor – maturity – promised to protect all beings whose life would intersect with Alexander's. Alexander The Great had become worthy of the special name given to him by his mistress.

"I regret, dear Wine, that I do not love you. You are such a lovely being, worthy of being loved . . . Will you at least be my friend?"

"That's a proposal I happily accept . . . Alexander, one more question. Do I remind you of Antoinette?"

A bitter-sweet solar smile answered affirmatively. I was almost flattered by this truth. The last piece of the jigsaw puzzle fell into place. "Perhaps she loved the image of another in him", Alexander had once said, when drawing a hypothetical reason for what bonded his mother to his father. But he had miscast his actors when he really should have hired himself and Antoinette in that star-studded sentence which all along had been the inner lining of our aborted relationship. Alexander had been chasing a phantom, pursuing every female who might have exuded the slightest aroma or characteristic similar to Antoinette. It was as though he would find pieces of her but never the whole, his comings and goings, his emotional oscillations coinciding with his clumsy artistry of trying to fit the soul of Wine into Antoinette's. Perhaps there were moments

147

when Alexander conquered the hope of a nearly perfect match, convinced he could redo the present and make it the way the past used to be. And by not asking me personal questions he lessened the risk of any verbal novelties which would skew his image of myself as Antoinette. Thus must have been telepathically transferred to me, inhibiting my free expression, confining me to mental monologues. But he always had to awaken from this charade and feel the ebbing of his hope that Antoinette had returned.

Alexander was obsessed with an antiquity. This was the heart of his guilt. He had seduced me to make a one-way journey with him back to his past. Now he was repentant, wishing to transport me back to the present by kicking me out of his life.

"Alexander, go find her, confront your ghost!"

"No, I can't reappear in her settled life. If she still loves me it would plunge her and those who depend upon her into chaos. That wouldn't be right. I would have to shoulder more guilt."

"But would the Antoinette of today match her former self?"

The question risked tampering with a probable illusion. How many beings ever stay the same!

Alexander couldn't answer me. Poor cat, torn between moral principles and the risk of disillusionment.

What if Alexander did see her again and discovered that Antoinette's love for him had faded into a sweet memory? Would this unchain him from his obsession? Or supposing his lovely soul-mate had flowered into a more splendid creature, so alluring that Alexander's love for her would surpass the heights of his youthful years. And if he couldn't have her he would be tied to a new torment. Or, what would happen if she glimpsed the dissipated hints in his face and ejected him out of her sight? Wouldn't Alexander feel betrayed by the one precious being who had sustained his faith in the value and steadiness of love throughout his lives? What if, what if, what if. These are some of the haunting questions we often carry in our baggage of memories when a first love, or any love for that matter, remains pure, without the patina of disenchantment.

I thought of Billy The Kitty.

I thought of my Professor Of Love.

I thought of Claude.

I concluded that Wine The Cat had a treasure chest of untarnished love. No wonder love knitted my life together in such a tight weave! No wonder love was my narcotic, addicting me to intimacy. I had seldom been without this nourishing life force. Even as a small kitty, wobbling on all four paws, I had been covered by the warmth ... emanating ... from a solar smile ...!

Alexander, I have seen your smile before, long before Billy The Kitty. It belonged to a blurred face, obscure in all details except for the smile, the solar smile of the cat whose paternal seed assisted in my creation – my father – he, whose life was short-lived but who lived long enough for me to feel the inner glow of contentment when he bathed me with smiles. Naturally Wine The Kitty associated love with a smile and from then on Wine became easily seduced by anyone radiating a sunny smile. I wasn't seeking to duplicate a father, only to immerse myself in an atmosphere of genuine, loving warmth.

Remember Alexander when I said that what I called a beginning with you was a connection with something that began long ago? I based this supposition more on hunch than on fact. And time, or expanded awareness, has depicted the accuracy of this. So then I ask myself why it took such a meandering voyage along so many verbal tributaries to get to the source of my solar smile? Must the rhythm of awareness, of evolution, be best suited to snails, or is it that our vision of ourselves emulates nature with its seasonal fluctuations of frost and bloom, seasons of unconsciousness followed by awareness?

The hour was late. Everything had been said within the limits of our paltry wisdom. Alexander excused himself from bedding down with me, even for old time's sake for it would have swollen his guilt about me.

Guilt! Guilt! Guilt! If only Alexander could gift himself the same compassion and tolerance that he undoubtedly gave to his offspring and pardon the hurts and irresponsible behavior he had inflicted upon others long ago. How could the young Alexander have had today's perception when his vision was still in its infancy then? What was the key phrase which might soften this ponderous cargo of remorse?

"Good-bye, Wine."

His solar smile arose, then set slightly as he dialogued in his head a silent lamentation which filtered into my auditory nerve endings: *if only I could have loved you, Wine*.

"Good-bye, Alexander."

I flashed on my solar smile to help burn up his guilt. I felt relieved and grateful. I was not exiting from a war-ravaged relationship.

149

As I streaked across the lawn of the mansion there was a hideous clanging of bottles and dishware. A lady with long red hair, profiled by the moon, was pulling a child's wagon filled with empty milk containers and saucers. She bore a striking resemblance to my mistress. What a peculiar fluke of fate, or was it? She headed toward the rear entrance of Alexander's mansion. I assumed she was his mistress and perhaps the anonymous patron saint of The Milk Bar. Alexander had always described her as a generous supporter of animals and so it made sense to think of her as a fairy godmother to those of us who frequented the local bar.

How lonely she would feel after Alexander left. Would he try to get her used to his going away by arranging several trial runs in which he disappeared for several days at a time before his final departure? I hoped so. But once gone she would no doubt take in some stray cats to fill the void Alexander's absence would create – replace her lost Alexander with another cat, just like the grief-stricken mother in the garden of mourning who had grabbed an innocent bystander from the crowd as a substitute for her dead kitty.

And isn't this the most natural thing to do? Replace someone who is lost in order to restore your sense of tranquillity, your equilibrium, your balance.

Alexander! Stop looking for the perfect reproduction! Stop resisting change, the movement of life. You can find a substitute for Antoinette, not a carbon copy! If you give yourself the chance to evolve more, perceptions of yourself will alter and so will your need to hold on to the past. I should know! I've lived the experience I just preached. I've finally been able to relinquish my obsession with Claude. I'm free of him free of that chain to my past. I have moved back into the present.

My gait away from Alexander's house was to the stacatto rhythm of epiphanies racing through my head like popcorn. An explosion blew away the last cataract of confusion. I heard the words I wanted to gift Alexander so he could carry them along the road of his enlightenment and examine them at the rate of his readiness. But I couldn't turn back and reappear at his door. Our good-byes had already been punctuated.

I spied a muddy patch of earth near the gate of the estate. Alexander was sure to pass by this spot. With my paw I entrenched the following:

A MATURE CAT LEARNS TO FORGIVE HIS IMMATURE SELF.

* * * * *

Whew, Alexander. I've been sitting so long that my haunches have jellied. But it has taken so many discarded calendar pages to sort out what belonged to you, what belonged to me and what belonged to us communally. Maybe all of my conclusions are only as substantial as puffs of smoke. But one thing is certain. I managed to clarify one of the three parts of the holy trinity of love, the part which belonged to me. That's not a bad batting average – one out of three – especially when you consider the labyrinthine quality of some questions I had to squirm through. And I've discovered something important – evolution or better said, awareness, undresses complexity and reveals the starkness of simplicity. Questions which initially seem complicated really aren't. All we need is patience – time – and a well oiled brain to untangle them. Perhaps complexity is good for unemployment. It provides us with work, like a pill against boredom or protection from mischief.

I'm reminded of something else related to simplicity. Alexander, have you noticed a change in my form of expression, a reduction in my flair for the baroque? I suspect the reason for this is a change in my attitude toward language. I used to think that words communicated something, that they were as real as people, trees or cat-boxes. Now I don't believe this. During various intervals of telling our story I eavesdropped on those humans eavesdropping on me. And you know what? I'm not convinced humans really know how to talk because what they say and what they do are often two different things. So I'm beginning to ask some new questions: Of what value are words? Do humans really talk? Or do they just make noise like cats that meow? However, cats don't need to talk! Everyone who observes us can read our character and our moods merely by the vibrations we emit. Wine The Saviour, alias Solomon, was quite right when she called our vibrations the most meaningful communication between all beings.

I now have to retract an earlier desire to learn the language of humans no matter what the dialect. Ironic. Initially I chastised myself for my brand of counterfeit silence. Then I began to talk, shout and even roar during the course of my long monologue about Alexander and Wine. And now that I have finished I find that silence can be meaningful and loud. And words can be so terribly meaningless and silent.

The implications of this make me shudder a bit. If humans don't honestly express themselves, then the world is governed by noise! Noise, king of the world, the basis of civilization, staunchly supported in its tyrannical rein by money. Humans living in a world of illusion, bowing to words which are at best untrustworthy emissaries of realities without fixed addresses. Imagine, for example, that every day people promise something to someone but in fact the only thing they really promise is . . . noise!

With this in mind I don't ever want to metamorphose into a human unless I can be like my mistress. I'm sure she doesn't make noise, or at least not very much because while she's an eccentric, she matches her words with her actions. Just like Wine The Saviour. She doesn't make noise either. She only makes sense.

Dear Wine The Saviour. I'm sorry, Alexander, you couldn't meet her. She's an unusual character with a tendency toward snobbery. She would agree to meet only a relative of yours called Alexander the Saviour but he was too young for her, she said. She likes her saviours older and as wise as herself. That way everything is kept in balance.

Let me tell you, Alexander, that Wine The Saviour continues to amaze me. I've often wondered if she could have been born from seeds other than questions but she doesn't give me time to ponder this because she's still hard at work. She keeps on recreating me, smoothing out the wrinkles of confusion from time to time. And she's drawing laugh lines around my eyes. She insists upon practice laughing sessions in front of a mirror where she often lampoons me so that I will feel humble in comparison to her – a measure designed to keep me awed by her wise powers. Maybe she still has the image of Solomon in her mind and doesn't trust me out of her sight . . .

Recently I awarded her a good housekeeping medal for her splendid job of cleaning out the clutter in my mind from some useless, mass-produced stuff that all cats get from their masters and mistresses: guilt, repression, judgement, defensive shields, obsessions – to name only a few. Wine The Saviour didn't feel these things suited the decor of my mature soul. "They only glue cats to function at the lowest level of their emotional and mental capacity," she said. So far my mind has shown no traces of this discarded rubbish. However, Wine The Saviour keeps an alert eye open because she knows that in low or weak moments I'm prone, like everyone else, to buy some of these items because they are so cheaply made and inexpensive.

One outstanding result of this mental clean up is a greater agility to move in and out of other dimensions of existence – the dimensions of dreams, clairvoyance, ESP – in short, the invisible world. Maybe what I called destiny or fate is basically the freedom to navigate from one state of consciousness to another. Just recall Alexander, the "circumstances" of our first sexual encounter. That was one of the rare times when we were both relaxed enough so that our vibrations could arrange a meeting, a time when no interference came from ghostly presences. Sound simple? I don't think the invisible world is as complicated as it seems. It is we who complicate it. We have to stop making a division between the visible and the invisible. Both are equally real. Both plot their own geography. We have to accept that there is always a bridge between them. How we cross back and forth is a matter of how we use our inherent powers of being, of seeing, of hearing, of smelling, of tasting, of touching. Surely we must be careful not to litter the byways between these two worlds with the kind of clutter that Wine The Saviour tossed out of my mind . . . .

Imagine, Alexander, when I began this story I thought love to be more mysterious than anything else. Yet when you seek to unwrap one mystery it often travels to another. With love as the starting point I journeyed to the far reaches of my soul and brought back the most incredible souvenir – I became more than what I was . . . .

Now that I'm finished recounting our story I must excuse myself, Alexander. My sixth sense is receiving a watery message. I feel compelled to visit my mistress.

* * * * *

My mistress's study shows signs of renovation. A purple guitar, stripped of its strings, now hangs on one wall. Is this the guitar she used to strum? Or, did she buy an old, battered instrument, good for being a paint receptacle? She also has had the walls newly dressed up in purple velvet to cover up the old, black chipped paint, an impressive improvement. It seems that purple has become her favorite colour. Maybe the change in colour corresponds to some change in her life. Recalling the lady with red hair playing a purple guitar in one of my dreams, I imagine my mistress grabbing hold of me one day and dyeing my fur purple. Who can tell what the limits of eccentricity are in humans!

Today my mistress is sitting on her creative throne in front of her typewriter, bordered by several thick piles of typewritten pages. Surely her ponderous project ought to be in the terminal stages if bulk is any symptom.

It's not a propitious moment to peep at her creative offspring, because she has a visitor – Isabel, a dear friend.

They graciously interrupt their conversation and smother me with affectionate caresses. Ah, this attention is wonderful. I purr my gratitude. Isabel gathers me in her arms and sets me on her lap, a splendid place for eavesdropping. Her perfume clouds about us, the scent of a famous brand called Joy. Unfortunately the aroma does not blend with the scent in Isabel's heart. She is dressed in sorrow, all black.

"You know, I can't get over it," says Isabel to my mistress. "It's only four months since my sister died and her husband, with whom I scarcely ever spoke, has begun to call me every day. He keeps asking if there is anything I would like. I tell him 'no' and then he sends me some little gift. The last thing he sent me was a ham!"

"A HAM?" exclaims my mistress. "A LEG OF HAM?" She erupts into uncontrollable, uninhibited laughter, her body trembling with such volcanic mirth that it spills over onto Isabel until her laughter temporarily buries her grief. It's difficult to see who is more amused. "Was it tamed?" asks my mistress. And their hilarity carries on, insulting death.

At last! I am privileged to witness one of the qualities which endears me to my mistress, this jovial human whose recipe for life is laughter. Like her kindred spirit, Solomon, she believes in a creed she has affixed to the wall behind her typewriter. It says:

LAUGHTER MUST BE THE MOST DIFFICULT TASK FOR HUMANS; OTHERWISE, WHY DON'T MORE PEOPLE LAUGH?

Isabel and my mistress mop up the tears of laughter on their faces with handkerchiefs.

"But why a ham?" asks my mistress.

"Because in my native country, it's a custom to give a ham as a gift. It's a sign of material well-being. Don't forget that during our civil war there was no meat and almost no bread. And while scarcity isn't a problem its memory is. Anyhow, everyone in my native village, including my mother, thinks I should return and marry my brother-in-law so his children won't be motherless. Can you imagine that? Why there's something repulsive about the whole idea. It would be . . . like committing incest!"

No, no, that's not incest, I want to say to Isabel. It's the same situation as Alexander needing me to replace Antoinette, similar to my needing Alexander to replace Claude.

"Hold on," says my mistress gently. "Let me read something to you I wrote this week. She pulls out a piece of paper from the bottom of a pile and reads: "WE SEEK TO REPLACE EVERY LOSS."

I feel relief. My mistress and I are on the same wave-length.

There is a long silence. My mistress begins to sip some wine from a glass marked by a remnant of the price tag stuck to its bottom. The goblet closely resembles the family heirloom she shattered a while back. Alexander would envy the ease with which she has replaced her lost treasure.

"Isabel," says my mistress, "your brother-in-law is in a state of prolonged shock because the physical similarity between you and your sister is retarding his acceptance of her death. You must be patient with him."

"But doesn't he realize he is offending my sensibilities? I too have my grief."

"Yes, you've opened the door to the truth of your loss. He hasn't. He still has yet to hear the overture to mourning before he takes the long promenade along the trail of grief . ."

Isabel shakes her head negatively. Frown lines crest on her face.

"I feel so empty . . . no, not feel . . . I *am* empty," she says.

"And you will be for a long time. It's how I felt when Claude ceased to be part of my life."

Oh no, not another Claude, I'm thinking.

"But he's still alive. You can see him again. It's possible. There's no finality other than death," responds Isabel.

"But there's no resurrecting a lost relationship. Nothing is ever duplicated in its original form."

Their exchange stalemates.

Mistress! Isabel! You're both right. Yes, Isabel, death kills the hope of a reunion with a loved one which separation doesn't guarantee. But death bestows one blessing – it doesn't tarnish the soul, the reputation of the deceased. The solar smile of my paternal heritage never threatens to become a frown. Nor is his memory clogged with nagging questions, requisitioning an emotional autopsy.

"Hold on," pipes in Wine The Logical Cat. "Antoinette fills the requirements of what you just said and she's very much alive."

"Yes," replies Wine The Psychological Cat. "Antoinette circulates through Alexander's life like a goddess because he never separated from her, he never altered his vision of her."

And then I think of Claude . . . Would life have been easier if he had died at the zenith of our love? Would mourning his death have sealed off our connection in a way that is foreign to separation? Our separation planted so many questions in me which sprouted up like weeds. I had to stop living in the present, risk capsizing in the past while I tried to find reasons for every nuance of our behaviour during our togetherness that had already been swallowed up by time. And after every motivation was examined I couldn't say with any certainty what went wrong. All I knew is that a change had come about and that the guilty party was called evolution. How was I going to punish evolution for robbing me of a loved one? Put it in solitary confinement? Send out a warning to the world: Beware of this unseen force, it may be lurking close by . . .

Mistress! Isabel! We've all missed the essential issue troubling us. It's so simple, so transparent. When death is responsible for loss we call death the problem. When separation is responsible for loss we call ourselves the problem, whether or not this is true. Isn't it time that evolution or change be named as the majority force inspiring loss!

There is now only one being left who hasn't fallen under the full scope of my vision – my mistress. It must be more than a coincidence that she too had a Claude in her life. I must unravel this mystery.

Isabel is departing. Good, that means my mistress will accompany her to the front door and I can sneak a look at her manuscript. I have a hunch it will clear up the enigma of who she really is.

There's a page in her typewriter, nicely cleaned and pressed without any human scribblings. My eye spots the following paragraph:

Isabel departed. She thought about her friend's final words. Every end of something seeds the beginning of something new.
The end of mourning becomes the aphrodisiac to living. She supposed that was true but it didn't offer much consolation in her hour of grief.

That's funny. Isabel just left! Or did she? I'm getting confused. A strange sensation is overtaking me as if I might be looking at myself in a mirror reflecting my looking at myself in a mirror reflecting myself looking at myself in a mirror like a visual echo.

I peer back at the page and see the following:

THE END
THE BEGINNING

What an eccentric way to end a book! Typical of my mistress.

Then a shock runs through me upon my next sneaky look. There is a simple drawing of a cat holding on to the stem of a question mark.

HEY, I KNOW THAT CAT. THAT'S ME . . . .

"Wine, what are you doing?" asks my mistress in a stern voice.

I am startled. I didn't hear her footsteps. I'll have to imitate a human voice, speak to her for the first time.

"MIS... TRESS... I WAS CUR... I... OUS... A... BOUT... YOUR... BOOK."

How incredible. I just uttered my first human words. I just made some noise.

My mistress laughs. "Oh Wine, haven't I cured you of your insatiable curiosity? What more do you want to know? I can't pull apart Alexander, Claude or Wine any more. They are a closed book – finished!"

"Finished?"

"Yes, Wine, finished! Please don't look so sad. It makes it harder for me to eliminate you from my life!"

"You mean you're going to kill me?"

"How can I kill you! You don't exist!"

"Don't I? But I think, therefore I am."

"No you think because *I* make you think."

"But Isabel just held me on her lap."

"No, that was part of your imagination, I mean *my* imagination."

"But you've convinced me I'm real... It must be true that all fictitious characters take on a life of their own."

"That's right, Wine. That's what makes it so hard for me to part from you. I've grown so attached to you that I feel as though you exist outside of myself."

"Well, mistress, if that's the case, why can't you let me go on being myself? Keep me around... like a pet!"

"That's tempting. But I have to let you go. Just like birth, all creation has to be expelled from the womb of imagination. But it hurts to lose you, to lose something I have nourished for a long time. Anyhow you will like your new existence. It is the same blissful state you experienced when you gazed upon that weeping willow tree and lost all sense of your self."

"Yes, that was bliss... Tell me mistress, before you 'discharge' me will you answer a few questions?"

"Of course."

"Why did you make me a cat? Why not a human?"

"Because I didn't want to burden you with the material clutter of human existence. I didn't want to waste words on things which bear no relation to the interior life of human development. This made it easier to move around the world of emotions and reflections – the spirit world if you like – without bumping into useless foreign objects."

"That makes sense. And what about the man at The Animal Shelter with you. Was that Claude?"

"Yes, that was."

"He seemed like a very nice man!"

"Yes, Wine, he was."

"I'm sorry you lost him."

"Don't be. My mourning for him is over."

"And what about the man I've seen around here?"

"Wine, he's none of your business."

"Excuse me, I didn't mean to be so nosey . . . Just one more question. What finally happens, I mean happened to Alexander and myself?"

"You saw the answer to that in your vision. You became . . . I mean . . . we become . . . we are . . . platonic lovers. Of course you should know that the whole story was written on hindsight. I lied when I said, 'Dear Alexander. I don't know where to begin.' However I wasn't sure of the end. Was I going to convert you into a human, do away with you as a thinly disguised metaphor and claim you were a human who had dreamed you were a cat? Or was I going to leave you in your raw state – accept you as the dream you were which inspired me to write this story? Ultimately I felt I had no choice. I had to follow my instincts and leave you as a cat – after all I'm not a missionary who wants to convert creatures to become what they aren't."

"Well mistress, it's been interesting, acting the life of a cat. I don't know how my performance will stack up with other fictional characters. Some may say I didn't emphasize cat features enough. For example, I never mentioned if Alexander's whiskers tickled me or not. But would it have mattered? Would that have altered the course of our destiny? . . . Oops, mistress I just thought of one more question and I promise this will be the last."

"Wine, you remind me of a little kid who keeps asking for water because she doesn't want to go to sleep. Are you stalling for time?"

"No, mistress. I accept my fate. I just want to know if there is anything you don't lose in this world?

"Hmmm. All I know is this. No thief has stolen my soul yet . . . So dear Wine, that about wraps things up. Do you have any final request?"

"Yes, mistress. I'd like to be transported out of this world on the stem of a question mark. That'll be my keepsake from you. That's what started our relationship."

"Your wish is granted."
"Good-bye, mistress. I guess curiosity killed the cat after all."
"Good-bye, Wine."

THE END
THE BEGINNING